LBD

it's a
girl thing

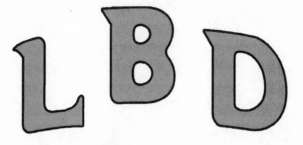

LBD
it's a
girl thing

by
grace dent

g. p. putnam's sons
new york

First American edition published in 2003 by G. P. Putnam's Sons, a division of
Penguin Young Readers Group, 345 Hudson Street, New York, NY 10014.
G. P. Putnam's Sons, Reg. U.S. Pat. & Tm. Off.
Published in Great Britain in 2003 by Puffin UK, London.

Published simultaneously in Canada. Printed in the United States of America.
Designed by Gina DiMassi. Text set in Wilke Roman.
Library of Congress Cataloging-in-Publication Data
Dent, Grace. LBD : it's a girl thing / by Grace Dent.—1st American ed. p. cm.
Summary: Barred by their overprotective parents from attending a rock music festival,
fourteen-year-olds Ronnie, Fleur, and Claude, also known as "Les Bambinos Dangereuses,"
decide to stage their own music festival at Blackwell School.
[1. Music festivals—Fiction. 2. Rock music—Fiction. 3. Schools—Fiction.
4. England—Fiction.] I. Title. PZ7.D4345Lb 2003 [Fic]—dc21 2003003984
ISBN 0-399-24187-6
1 3 5 7 9 10 8 6 4 2
First Impression

ACKNOWLEDGMENTS

A massive thank you to Sarah Hughes at Puffin UK for suggesting I write a novel, then badgering me politely again and again when I forgot. I'm so, so glad you did.

Also, big thanks to everybody at Puffin UK for absolutely "getting" the LBD from the very first word and bringing it to life so beautifully.

Eternal gratitude to Caradoc King and Vicky Longley at AP Watt for their fantastic support and belief in me.

Thanks to Sophie, and lastly, thanks to Bryok Williams for reading every single word as we went along.

You're all brilliant.

for mam—

who lived with the world's worst teenager

contents

Chapter 1

life is harsh . . .

"Nope. No way. Absolutely not. Not over my dead body, matey."

Negotiations with Dad about my summer holiday plans have hit an all-time low. In fact, unless I'm much mistaken, Dad's turned his back on me and shuffled halfway across the saloon bar in the Fantastic Voyage.

He's fiddling with beer mats and urgently rearranging slices of lemon, almost as if my fate is decided. Now, my friends, this is NOT the air of a man "carefully mulling his daughter's future." No. It's the look of a man ignoring me. Someone hoping I'll vanish. Or at least "cease being so flippin' cheeky and squeaky" in his general direction.

I, Veronica Ripperton, am, in fact, a full fourteen years and two months old, for crying out loud. Not "squeaky" at all. More "husky" and "womanly." What does he know anyway? He can't even pick his nose privately.

So here are me and Dad, hovering around each other, in a deadlock. This must be how UN negotiators feel just before bombs begin getting lobbed. Eventually, the great fun-stopping ogre speaks:

"Look, Ronnie. There is no way whatsoever you and your little posse of clowns . . ." (bit harsh, I thought) . . . "are getting tickets for Astlebury Music Festival. It's far too dangerous, what with all those hairy lads sniffing about. And different trains you'd need to catch . . . and drug dealers injecting you with acid or stealing your tent . . . and, well, trouble like that. You're just not going. No way! Nicky nacky nada way."

Dad's sandy sideburns virtually bristle at the thought of his offspring having such pure, unadulterated fun. Pah. If Dad thinks dressing up the word "no" by saying it *amusingly* will earn him forgiveness for being "the man who killed summer," he's soooo wrong.

"And while we're at it, Ronnie. Go and put a bigger T-shirt on! I can almost see your boobs." (Heaven forbid! I must be the only girl in England with a pair. Call the nipple police.)

"And I can see your belly button too! And your knickers! No wonder my profits on bar meals are down. All that flesh. It's just not right. . . ." Dad gazes at the fifteen-centimeter gap between my T-shirt and jeans with utter disdain, then slumps his shoulders woefully, as if the weight of the Western World rests upon them.

Fine, so Dad isn't *loving* the crop-top, low-slung hipsters look, I can live with that, but by this stage, I'm so seething about the whole Astlebury thing that I'm fantasizing about strangling the furry-faced loser with a beer towel.

Dad's not a happy man either; as I begin to huff and puff around the bar, slamming chairs around rather insolently, his eyes are bulging with rage . . . something is going to blow.

"It's a *thong,* actually. *Not knickers,*" I announce, yanking the offending lacy garment up even farther, out of the back of my trousers, proving my point nicely. Very bad idea.

"It's a WHAT??!" shrieks Dad, his lips thinning into two pale lavender strips.

Ooops, time for a sharp exit, I think, hotfooting toward the pub's back doors. (Okay, hotfooting as quickly as a girl can with a knickers-up-bum-crack situation going on.)

But before I can hobble out the door, making a rather undignified exit, suddenly Dad is in front of me. He places a big hand upon my shoulder, his face quite calm again.

"No. Stop, Ronnie . . . wait a minute . . . ," he says, obviously wanting to make things up.

Lawrence "Loz" Ripperton (aka "Dad" or "Keeper of the Wallet") doesn't like arguing. He's all about peace and love, is my old man. It's a good job really, as in our household: 1) I quite enjoy a good row and 2) Mum positively relishes a proper bust-up. While Dad is a bit of a mellow soul, my mother, Magda Ripperton, the female face of the Fantastic Voyage, is like a Tasmanian devil with lipstick. As the Fantastic Voyage's chef, Magda's at her happiest churning out dinner for two hundred, with a flaming griddle pan in one hand, a pan of boiling salted water in the other, holding a blazing row with the *sous-chef* at the same time. No wonder I go to Dad with all of my far-fetched requests, such as today's "being let loose at a music festival with my best mates for the weekend." Dad is far more likely to simply mishear me, get a bit mixed up and think I'm asking to go and see a band at the local town hall. Magda, on the other hand (or "that bloody woman," as she's known to the postman, the gasman, the meat suppliers, her accountant and various family members), would have sussed my game right away. She'd have hidden my shoes and put me on round-the-clock watch for even thinking about Astlebury.

Thank God my dad is a pushover.

"I'm sorry, love, if I'm spoiling your fun," he mutters with a reproachful half smile. "I'll make it up to you, eh, chooch?" He runs a hand over my hair, which makes me feel about five again. "Why don't you ask Mum about the festival? If she says yes, I'll have another think. . . ." Dad has obviously banged his head on a beam and forgotten ever meeting his wife, Magda; I'd have more chance asking if I could fritter the petty cash float on sparkly lip gloss and Belgian truffles.

This for Ronnie Ripperton is a D.I.S.A.S.T.E.R. In fact, it's a big, fat, flatulent sack of poo-flavored mess.

Game over.

My cunning-as-a-fox plan—get the green light for Astlebury from Dad, then get straight onto that premium-rate ticket hotline before word on the street reaches the basement kitchen—is scuppered. By the time Empress Venger was *supposed* to find out about Astlebury, me, Claudette and Fleur (aka Les Bambinos Dangereuses or the LBD, as we're known universally) would be well on our way to forty-eight hours of watching all our favorite bands play live, camping out under the stars . . . oh, and, like, meeting up with just about a million totally lush festival-going boys. The LBD have seen and noted the sort of lads that go to music festivals on MTV. Meow! It's like Snogfest Central, with a lot of loud music, dancing, crowd-surfing, staying up all night and eating veggie burgers chucked in. We want to go so so much, we talked about it for the whole week after seeing the ads on MTV. Astlebury Festival sounds like the natural habitation for an LBD member.

"Hang on! I've got an idea!" chirps Dad. "Why don't I take you girls to Walrus World in Penge instead!?" he says.

My heart sinks. I'd rather jam my head in the tumble dryer, then switch it on.

"You used to love those walruses, Ronnie. . . . Remember the one that juggles the balls!? . . ." Dad's voice fades to a well-meaning whisper as I trudge into the early-evening air.

In a previous life, I was obviously Vlad the Impaler.

I'm paying big time for something.

my manor

The Fantastic Voyage: The pub on the high street where we live, in reality, isn't all that "fantastic." Well, it maybe was at one point (in medieval times when most of our regulars first started drinking here, back when people were thrilled just to be inside a pub and not being mauled by wolves or ransacked by high-waymen). Nowadays, it's a bit sucky.

The Voyage punters are a lost cause: All they want is comfy sofas, cold beer, local tittle-tattle and darts. Which is just hunky-dory as that's the Fantastic Voyage in a sentence. So here I am, storming down the high street in a really bad mood. Past the funny beardie-weirdie bloke who dances for spare change out-side the bakery, almost getting flattened in my haste by a spotty geek pushing the bins out of McDonald's. What a way to die!

Squished into a big human Filet-O-Fish. I'm checking my reflection in the shop windows. (Hairs are a bit wonky, skin's a bit shiny, but overall not bad, considering my trauma. I think I'm at my best when I'm fuming, just like Mum.) It feels good battering out my aggression on the pavement, covering ground quicker than anyone else on the street. Right now, I'm on my way to Fleur's house. Fleur Swan lives just along the street here and around the corner, halfway down Disraeli Road. If I'd turned left out of the pub instead of right and walked the same distance, I'd be at Claude Cassiera's flat. That is one of the most marvelous aspects of being in the LBD; we all live so close, we can summon an emergency meeting in minutes, which comes in handy as there are a lot of emergencies. Like today for example. I love this high street; the clothes shops, the cafes, the makeup counters, the alleyways, all of these are the LBD's territory. It's a good thing this street gives me a kick, really. If my parents have their way, I'm not going anywhere for a very long time.

Blip. Blip. Bleeeeeep. Text!

MAY KILL SELF B4 U GET HERE. HATE THEM.—FLEUR 6:46 P.M.

evil paddy and the chocolate stain

In the front bedroom bay window of the Swan family residence stands the lovely yet extremely angry Fleur Swan, her dainty snub nose pressed against the glass, awaiting my arrival. On spotting me turn the corner into Disraeli Road, Fleur disappears from view, leaving a chocolaty smudge on Mrs. Saskia Swan's otherwise pristine windows. Fleur must be hopping mad if she's scoffing sweets; normally she's a highly saintly, plenty of fruit and veg, three liters of mineral water daily, glossy-haired, peachy-skinned kinda chick. Oh, and she's five foot seven too, with honey-blond highlights. If she wasn't one of my best friends, I'd definitely hate her.

"Get this!" Fleur shouts, opening the door. "Apparently the loud music will damage my eardrums. Huh!" she says with a little false laugh of disbelief. "So I'm barred from going to Astlebury Festival? Can you belieeeeve that?! God, I hate them both!" she snarls, beckoning me in. I half expect to find Mr. and Mrs. Swan chopped up into small bite-size pieces on the den floor, but thankfully they're both in full working order. Patrick "Paddy" Swan, Fleur's dad, is reclining in a deep leather La-Z-Boy chair in their lavish cream den, while Fleur's mother, Saskia, is fiddling about with a bonsai tree and some mini-clippers. Neither of them seem very concerned about their imminent murder. (Fleur's house is a bit like one in a glossy mag. Except that in magazines people are rarely photographed yelling with chocolate all over their faces. Or enjoying a large post-work gin and tonic and the *Racing Times* like Mr. Swan was at this precise moment.)

"Ah, Miss Ripperton, we've been expecting you," Fleur's dad announces. (He's a big James Bond fan.) "So you'll be in on this little fandango too, I suppose?" He sniggers. "Ha ha. If you two girls imagine that I'm letting you run riot in a field for an entire weekend, you're obviously dippier than you both look," he says, pausing briefly to tickle Larry, the Swan family's excessively smug-faced pure white Persian cat, under his chin. Larry purrs contentedly, like a furry road drill. Mr. Swan, in his navy pinstriped suit, with smirking sidekick Larry perched beside him, looks every inch the dastardly Bond villain. I'm far too scared to begin my "but it's a reeeeally good life experience" argument in case he flicks a switch on the arm on the leather chair, depositing both Fleur and me into the cellar, where we'd have to survive by eating earwigs.

do you like my dancin'?

There's a somber mood up in LBD headquarters (Fleur's bedroom, which is split-level with a walk-in wardrobe. Can you believe it? My room's like a cigarette packet compared to hers . . . sheesh).

"The air is ripe with the remnants of dashed dreams," I announce morbidly.

"Oh, flipping shut up," Fleur says. "It's not over yet. The fat lady's not sung. That's what they say, isn't it? We might make it."

I picture Magda, only a hundred pounds heavier, discovering I'd nipped off to Astlebury without permission. "Singing" would not be her first response. She'd fricassee my ass and serve it with dauphinoise potatoes.

"Hey, you wanna hear this," Fleur says, cheering up. Fleur flips on *Classic Deep Ibiza House: Volume 20* and whacks on the parent irritation button, aka the Mega Surround Blast switch that makes CDs more echoey, intense and altogether fabulouso.

Bumph! Bumph! Bumph! Bumph!

The bass line kicks in at 132 beats per minute, loud enough to make Paddy Swan's back teeth rattle downstairs in the den.

Bumph! Bumph! Bumph! Bumph!

A flurry of activity breaks out in the Swan household. Doors are slammed, footsteps race upstairs, then what sounds like:

"Turnghghhh thaaaaaaat muuuusssiccc dooooowwwnn!!! Cannn yoooou heeeeear me???!!! Dowwwwn! Noooooow!!!"

He's loud, Mr. S, but not as loud, however, as the bone-shaking cymbals, synths and the track's wicked vocal:

"Gotta move yer body
Gotta make yer mine
Gotta move yer body
In the house tonight . . ."

If this tune doesn't get you dancing, well, you're either dead or deaf. Quickly, we're both up on our feet, me and Fleur, wiggling our hips, pointing our fingers, kicking our feet, giggling like nutjobs, ignoring Mr. Swan (one of the dead/deaf contingent) and his loud door-thumping.

"Turn it down!!! Or I'm turning the electricity off at the mains!" he snarls. Fleur does a little hop and skip over to her bedroom door, throwing the bolt across, locking her dad out. Silly Paddy; he should know the LBD rule by now. If we can't SEE him shouting, then we can't HEAR him shouting, and if he can't get in to begin shaking us warmly by the throats, he'll have to wait to be heard during the gap between songs.

Brilliantly, what grumbly-mumblies like Mr. S never realize is: There are NO gaps between songs in dance music compilations! Hee hee! That's the best bit.

"If we keep this up, he'll drive us to Astlebury himself!" yells Fleur, doing a very rude uppy, downy, shake-it-all-abouty motion with her behind.

Not if he saw you doing that, I think.

From where I'm standing, Fleur looks every inch the disco queen. You could just imagine her really going for it, up on a podium at a cool London warehouse party, wowing the crowds, shaking her tushy in a furry bra and neon hot pants.

I'd probably be the one giving the DJ a hand carrying his record box.

"So, tell me the latest with Jimi," says Fleur, swapping Ibiza grooves for a more mellow *Ultimate Chilldown* compilation. We're sprawled on Fleur's double bed, scouring *Bliss* and *More!* for pics of "blond babe" haircuts for Fleur to show Dimitri at Streets Ahead (our favorite hairdresser).

"*Pggghhh* . . . nothing to tell," I say bleakly. "I'm not entirely convinced he knows that I exist." And this is true, I'm not sure Jimi Steele does know who I am.

In case you don't know Jimi Steele (which I find very very hard to believe, cos he's just about the most beautiful thing I've ever seen in my whole life), I'd better explain:

Deep breath.

Jimi Fact Number 1. He's beautiful. (Have I said that?) No, he's more than that, he's totally gorgeous with pale blue eyes, long eyelashes and lovely plump lips. If he lived in America he'd probably star in his own prime-time show called simply: *Jimi: Season One.*

Jimi Fact Number 2. He's got amazing arms which are all toned on the tops. He's also always tanned from being outdoors doing rugged laddish stuff like frittering entire days with a football or mountain biking . . . or being . . .

Jimi Fact Number 3. . . . on his skateboard! Yep, he's one of those skatey boys. And he does, like, really dangerous stunts such as skating down flights of twenty stairs and jumping off really high curbs. Sometimes Jimi even has to limp to Blackwell School on crutches with a sprained ankle and get called "a blithering idiot" and "a lesson in stupidity" in assembly by Mr. McGraw, our headmaster. But Mr. McGraw is so wrong. Jimi Steele rrrrocks.

Jimi Sort-of Fact Number 4. He once held open the door to the chemistry department for me and smiled!!! "Conclusive proof that he's hot for you," according to Fleur.

Jimi Sort-of Fact Number 4a. Other LBD members (me and Claudette) are not entirely one hundred percent sure whether Jimi smiled at me. He might have been burping or remembering a funny bit from last night's TV or something.

Jimi Fact Number 5. He's almost sixteen years old and is in Year 11. That's why he's so manly and mature, in absolute contrast with the high-pitched, football-sticker-swapping morons that make up Blackwell School's Year 9 boy zone. Thus, I've got zilcho chance of turning Jimi from "boy who is a friend" into "boyfriend." (And that's if you can count burping at me in the chemistry department as being "a friend.")

Let's face it, he probably thinks I'm a bit kiddified. He probably wants a woman in his life that can at least *mention* going to Astlebury Festival without her dad's eyes exploding, or her being forced to put on a polo shirt and a pair of big, frumpy, Victorian-era granny-knickers that cover her kneecaps and nipples.

When I'm older and require expensive therapy and rehabilitation in Arizona like all the A-List celebs do, Loz and Magda Rippertons' ears will BURN.

So, in essence, I love Jimi Steele. He just creeps into my head and messes about with it all day and sometimes during the night. He, on the other hand, doesn't really know I exist, which is sort of depressing, especially when I spend much of my free time with Fleur Swan, who needs a stick smeared with animal poo to keep boys away. Very often I feel like an insignificant speck of space dust orbiting around Planet Fleur. Fleur is just plain gorgeous, everyone can see it. She's plainly charismatic and fresh-skinned. I have a deep-rooted fear that I'm simply "plain." Being plain, to my reckoning, is far worse than being pig-ugly. Being plain means being invisible to lads like Jimi. I get depressed when I look in the mirror and think, *Well, so this is my lot. And I'm really nothing special.*

Every boy knows Fleur exists. Fleur's the sort of girl who lads honk their car horns at, or that Year 7 brats send aftershave-scented love letters to. Fleur once sashayed into the dinner hall in her tightest-fitting school blouse (the one that looks like she's smuggling M&M's under) and I watched a Year 11 lad pour orange juice into his left ear. And yes, friends, I would switch the oven on and slow-roast my own head right now, if it wasn't for the fact that Fleur is habitually just as stressed about boys as I am.

"I hate boys," says Fleur, lying back on her bed. "I've had enough of them. I'm not going to fancy them anymore," she announces. Considering Fleur is only fourteen and is in love with almost half of Year 13, I can't help doubting her word.

You'd think Fleur would be happy, but she's not. Her frantic love life causes her as many tears, sleepless nights and bitten nails as my shambolic, laughable excuse for one does me. Fleur's men, you see, usually vanish off the LBD scene just as quickly as they appear. Er . . . funnily enough, usually *just after* meeting Mr. Swan, when he greets them with one of his famous "I will strangle you and turn your corpse into a novelty lamp shade if you even touch my daughter" stares.

"And you're never going to get anywhere with Jimi if you don't start making it a bit more obvious either," Fleur tells me, shaking her head.

"I know," I mutter, changing the subject. "Anyhow, what about you and Dion? I've not heard the latest."

"Oh, yeah, well, you know he walked me home last Thursday?" Fleur says tragically. "And we had a proper snog outside the garden gate, you know, tongue in and swirly about sorta thing?" Fleur waggles her cocoa-stained tongue to illustrate. "Well, then he said he'd text me on Friday, after football," she continues. "But he, er, didn't. I don't know what happened to him."

"Vanished?"

"Vamoosh," she says.

"Have you checked the cellar?" I mutter.

"What?" says Fleur.

"Oh, nothing," I say, passing her another magazine.

Poor Dion, I think, imagining him captured, shackled and starving in Evil Paddy's cellar prison. Everybody knows there's not enough protein to survive on in an earwig.

Then something earth-shattering happens.

my life changed forever

Blip. Blip. Bleeeeeep. Another text! It's Claudette.

Oh, by the way, that's not the exciting bit. This is:

WHY IS JIMI STEELE CHATTIN TO YR DAD OUTSIDE THE VOYAGE?!!! TEXT ME BACK NOW!!!! SCREEEERM!!—CLAUDE 8:21 P.M.

Scccreeeeeeam!!

The following five heart-thumping minutes are a bit of a blur. First, me and Fleur leap up and down for a bit, waving our hands in the air and squawking. I'm opening and closing my mouth, trying to express the wonderfulness of the news, but nothing comes out. (I look like a pleased cod.) Fleur is shouting repetitively, "Ooooh my Gawd!" and "What does he want?" with the occassional "This is it, Ronnie! This is it!" sprinkled in for hysterical effect. Eventually I catch my breath.

"WHAT IS IT?" I ask Fleur. "Why would Jimi Steele possibly be chatting with my dad?" (And please, God, say Dad didn't tell Jimi to get a "proper well-fitting pair of jeans" on too? I'll implode with shame.)

"Ooh, can you not see!?" squeals Fleur. "He's come to ask your dad if it's cool to ask you out! He's SUCH a gentleman. That is soooo sweet! Oh my God, what are you going to do?"

Life rarely gets more exhilarating, joyous or utterly scrummy than the past three hundred seconds. I sit on Fleur's bed, conscious that Ronnie Ripperton, the schoolgirl, the legend, the foxy strumpet, will never be the same again.

"Er, excuse me," shouts Fleur, disturbing me from an awesome fantasy involving Jimi, myself and our twenty-bedroom Las Vegas love palace (paid for with Jimi's "World's Number-One Skateboard Champion" zillion-dollar sponsorships). "What *exactly* are you waiting for? Go home and find out what's going on NOW!" yells Fleur, throwing my left shoe just past my head.

Ahhh, I love life!! On my way out, I even give Paddy a big toothy grin and cheery wave.

"Until next time, Miss Ripperton," says Paddy eerily as I stride up the garden path. "And believe me, Veronica . . . there WILL be a next time," he shouts after me, accompanied by a booming theatrical evil laugh: "Boo hoo haa haa haa!!"

Mr. Swan really does watch far too much television.

shoot me now, it's the kindest way

One A.M.: I'm not going to school tomorrow.

I'm waiting until the coast's clear, then I'm running away with the nearest circus. (Almost any circus or traveling fair will do. Well, except for the Chinese State Circus. They don't even have any lions or tigers or dancing elephants or anything, just jugglers and acrobats—*zzzSnorezz*. Who the heck exactly WANTS to see jugglers? Grown-ups mystify me. When I rule the world, anyone caught balancing spinning plates on canes and encouraging people to applaud them will be placed under house arrest and have their crockery confiscated.)

I can't face Blackwell School, Jimi or the LBD ever again, not after tonight. I'm humiliated, utterly. In fact, it's 1:00 A.M. now and I can just about talk about it without hurling.

Deep sigh.

Right, so I scurried home, hoping to catch Dad at a quiet moment to grill him for every second of Jiminess. Every juicy word and sentence, every arch of eyebrow or hand gesture.

Okay, it's worth a shot, even if Dad is typically worse than useless at this sort of thing. Mum once left Dad for three whole days following a row over a new deep freezer; Dad only noticed she'd gone when some customers pointed out they'd waited four and a half hours for a Sunday roast.

So, I wasn't expecting Dad and Jimi to be STILL talking outside the pub. Jimi was wearing extra-baggy dark green combats with quite raggedy bottoms and a Final Warning sleeveless

T-shirt. (Jimi always knows about cool bands BEFORE everyone else in the whole school, he's so *now*.) His hair was spiked up and he was nursing Bess, his skateboard, under one arm.

(Oh my God. I know Jimi's nickname for his skateboard. I'm turning into a stalker, I'll have to buy a stained anorak and binoculars soon.)

My first mistake was that I flounced up with a "guys, I know you're talking about me" smug expression plastered across my face.

Because both Jimi and Dad completely ignored me.

Or at least didn't notice I was there. They just carried on talking.

"Ah, the Fender Stratocaster. What a guitar," Loz was droning on.

Noooo! Dad's on a "when I used to be in the music business" rant.

Run now, Jimi! I thought. *Run like the wind! Man has evolved extra fingers listening to these stories! Brush the cobwebs from your spiky hair and flee! Save yourself. It's too late for me!*

But, no. Jimi seemed fascinated.

He was even joining in with comments about amps, acoustics and guitar strings. So I stood there, grinning like a spare Barbie at a tea party, for, ooh, just under a year, until they both clicked I was with them.

"Oh, hi, er, ooh . . . Bonny?" Jimi said. (His eyes sort of glazed over for a bit while he groped around for my name. Then he got it wrong. Not a good start.)

"Ooh, hello, love!" said Dad. "This young man's just inquiring about using the pub's function room for a rehearsal space for his band."

Ouch. So, that's Las Vegas canceled, is it? I thought.

Then, just as I crashed, burned and imploded into a toxic ball of shame, Dad sealed the deal as only a dad can:

"And I was just saying, Ronnie, well, it'll give you and yer little pals something to watch, as you'll not be going to Astlebury, eh? Hee hee!"

Congratulations, Father, you've finally killed me. That's saved me a messy job. Dad could only have bettered this by escorting Jimi up to my laundry basket and showing him my period-knickers. You could have fried bacon on my cheeks, they were so hot.

But, don't worry, with a bit of quick thinking, plus a large helping of style and finesse, I turned this dire situation right around. Coolly, I licked my lips, looked straight at my father and purred:

"Mmmm, well, Daddio, we'll see about that. The fat lady hasn't sung yet."

Then I turned to Jimi and whispered firmly, but sexily:

"Babe. It's Ronnie, NOT Bonny. You better learn that name, sweetcakes, cos you'll be using it a whole lot more someday soon," before wiggling off, triumphantly, into the Fantastic Voyage.

Oh, no. Hang on. I'm getting confused, that's NOT what happened.

What ACTUALLY happened was this:

It's all true—up until the "little pals not going to Astlebury" bit—to which I then pursed my lips like a dog's bum and grunted, *"Gnnnnnn pghhhhh gblaghhh,"* before skulking off to my room.

I've edited from my memory the part where I attempted to push the pub's "Pull" door for almost a minute while Jimi watched me pitifully.

(NOTE TO SELF: As far as I know, neither *gnnnnnn, pghh-hhh* or *gblaghhh* are actual words. Well, not ones you would use in front of someone you really fancy, anyhow.)

Two A.M.: Something freaky-disco is going on. Loz and Magda are having a loud conversation in the den. I'm almost sure I heard Mum crying, which is totally illogical. Mum doesn't cry, not even when making French onion soup. But I'm pretty sure I heard Mum sniffling and Dad almost shouting, "But it's far too late for this, Magda—"

And Mum yell back, "It's never too late!"

Then some doors were slammed.

Then Dad followed into the bedroom where Mum had stormed and the bickering continued.

"Pah! You would say it's too late," shouted my mum. "That's you all over. Selfish! You only think about how *you* feel."

That's not really true, I thought, but I decided, sensibly, to stay under my duvet and not make it a three-way debate.

"But I'm thinking about you! Not just me. And all of us. It doesn't feel right, this happening so late . . . ," my dad persisted.

Blooming right it's too late. It's two in the morning. Small wonder I've got under-eye bags the size of Peru, living with Freak o' Nature and his missus. I can't put my finger on why, but that little squabble I heard has made me feel a bit weird. It's okay for me to fight with both of them—that's normal—but I don't like it when they do it.

Chapter 2

banging the drum of love

Mr. McGraw exhales one of his deep trademark sighs.

Long and deliberately mournful, like a punctured airship falling miserably to Earth, Blackwell's headmaster takes to the podium. Tapping the microphone twice with a *thdunch, thdunch,* a squeal of feedback rings around the antique Tannoy speaker system, deafening the hideously jam-packed gym. McGraw (or as he's often known, "Quickdraw," or lately by some meaner kids, "Prozac Mac") surveys his six-hundred-strong audience with a heavy heart.

Once . . . , I can almost hear him thinking, *Sweet Lord Jesus, just ONCE, can't I get a phone call to say they'd all called in sick?*

My eye lingers along the row of ten miserable-faced teaching staff required to be present for today's assembly. All of whom seem to be in another world, entertaining those special thoughts which pretty much *all* teachers do between 9:00 and 9:30 A.M. in schools far and wide.

You can just tell Mrs. Guinevere, our deputy headmistress, is wishing she could be in beddy-bo-bo's, sipping a mug of milky Earl Grey with the *Guardian* cryptic crossword. One look at the twisted face of Mr. Foxton, our new music teacher, shows the appalling hangover he's suffering. Well, what I can see of his face does. His head is practically in his hands. The fact that Mr. Foxton (according to Blackwell gossips), at the age of twenty-four, still insists on visiting local pubs with his friends midweek and staying until almost TEN-THIRTY P.M. sipping lager and laughing is fine by me. It just makes it all the more hilarious watching him sit through a whole assembly, then toddling off to a double Year 7 glockenspiel and drum workshop. The other teachers just stare ahead, seemingly in some sort of depressed trance.

McGraw's third-, fourth- and fifth-year crowd are grumpy and restless, largely due to the early hour (8:45 A.M. For the love of Moses, some of us still have pillow creases on our faces and sleep-snot in our eyes) plus the fact the hall smells of a pungent cocktail of feet, farts and cheap floor polish. Blackwell Sports Hall isn't nearly spacious enough for four hundred chairs, so while Year 10 and Year 11 get a seat, us Year 9 bods make do squatting at the front of the hall, jumbled all over each other on bare floorboards. We look like refugees waiting for a food drop.

Honestly, I cannot wait for next term when I graduate to a proper seat and can live through one assembly *without* rampant pins and needles and someone's pelvis in my face. Everybody seems to have forgotten the "mobiles on mute" rule too, thus a zillion techno bleeps and hip-hop ring tones criss-cross the airspace.

"God has dealt me some very harsh cards," mumbles McGraw under his breath, raising one hairy hand for silence.

"Good morning, children," sighs McGraw.

"Good morning, Mr. McGraw," we all reply.

And we're off! Battering through Song 42 of the *Happy Voices, Happy Lives Songbook for Children*. Ooh, it's a chirpy little number, this one, all about "banging the drum of love" and "putting your arms around the world."

"I have nothing whatsoever to hug the world about," I grumble to Claudette, who's resting her *Happy Voices* book atop her generous C-cup bosom.

"Ooh, shut up," Claude says. "I love this one. It's one of my favorites," she shrills, turning up her mouth volume to LOUD, savoring every syllable of the chorus.

So, as the rest of Blackwell drones through "Banging the Drum of Love," Claude swoops and hollers, allowing every word just the right annotation and bags of *whoomph*.

"Ban-geeeeng the drrrums of luuurve!" Claude sings. "I waaant to geeeeeeve the worrrrld a beeeeeg huuug!!"

Claude winks at me and begins waving her hands in the air and clapping, satisfied that the entire assembly hall is beginning to stare at us. I'm giggling so hard now, I almost wee. Even the super-cool Year 11 bods are starting to snigger.

Mrs. Guinevere, deputy head, looks up from her sheet music, at first overjoyed that one pupil is putting true grit into the task, until her eyes rest upon the LBD and she sees that on either side of the songbird, I'm rolling about on the varnished floors with snot flowing down each nostril and Fleur is texting Dion a long, pleading love missive on her mobile phone.

If you had to sum up Claudette Cassiera and why she's so flipping fabulous (and really one of the grooviest people in the cosmiverse too), this is a fine example. With her perfect uniform (three-quarters-length white virgin socks/proper blazer), scrubbed nails (no sneaked nail polish) and face *au naturelle* (just fresh ebony skin and rich brown hair pulled into two neat bunches, held with asymmetric hair bobbles): Claude is the epitome of extreme wickedness, masked by an air of extreme wholesome goodness.

A pretty darn useful trick that only true A-List minxes can carry off. Face it: You can't get told off for "enjoying yourself too much" singing lame nonreligious cheeseorama *Happy Voice* hymns, can you? Nope, course you can't.

That'd be like getting detention for demanding more French homework.

Or suspended for running the 100 meters too quickly.

Claude Cassiera is as clever as a brain baguette in more ways than one; acing all of her tests, always completing her homework on time, she also frequently earns us lesser Blackwell mortals a slacker half-hour break during lessons by engrossing the teachers in long intellectual debates.

"But Mr. Reeland," Claude will inquire, adjusting her reading specs with her index finger, "how exactly *did* the former Yugoslavia become so war-torn? Was it simply a boundary issue, or is it a deep-seated religious struggle?" she'll ask.

Hurrah!

Obviously, old Pa Reeland's face will flush with pure ecstasy (let's be blunt: He's spent periods one, two and three teaching kids who can't find their own bottoms with two hands and a map), so he'll begin waffling away, fiddling with slides on the overhead projector, searching in his drawer for a newspaper clipping that Claude can read at home, while the remainder of the class gossip, sleep, throw ink cartridges at each other, or draw pictures of willies and lady-front-bottoms in their *Your World Today* textbooks.

Teachers love, love, lurrrrve Claude, never quite making that link between her angelic face and the naughtiness which lies beneath.

"And every beeeeat of the drrrrrum is like our hearts beeeeating as one!" sings Claude, turning to the rest of the LBD and adding a little "All together now!" for good effect.

I can't help thinking about a little incident back one warm summer Wednesday afternoon in Year 7, when Claude Cassiera had the bright idea that the LBD should pinch a jar of Bovril from Magda's kitchen and smear the beef extract down the backs of all the lower school's door handles, covering four hundred children and teachers in spicy bovine-flavored brown stainage: a good example of Claude walking away without as much as a ten-minute detention.

"I find it VERY hard to believe you were involved in this, Claudette Cassiera," muttered McGraw, more depressed than ever at that moment. "You're a credit to Blackwell School. I was telling your mother exactly this at parents' evening . . ."

He then stuck Fleur and myself on school-pond-dredging duties for three weeks. Even when Claudette cried and told Mr. McGraw that Bovril Day was all her idea in the first place, he simply put an arm around her shoulder and said that "trying to cover up for those two was a true sign of her inherent loyalty and generosity of spirit." Obviously, we would NEVER do anything as childish and pathetic as Bovril Day now, no way, not now that we're Les Bambinos Dangereuses, with bras and boyfriends (occasionally), but it's worth noting this injustice simply to give you a taste of Claudette Cassiera's magic. Claude and her big sister, Mika, have both got this rep for being "lovely girls"; in fact Mrs. Cassiera can barely get down the high street without some grown-up stopping her to relate some act of niceness her kids have been up to. It goes without saying Magda Ripperton does not have this problem.

NB: Anyone considering a career in serial killing, kidnap or gangland terror, please remember to wear something really smart, like a proper school uniform with very white socks. As far as I can see, you'll get away with, well, quite literally murder.

"He's blocked my number," yelps Fleur. "That pig Dion has blocked my number, look!!" *CALLER DENIED ACCESS* is flashed across Fleur's phone. Ouch. Techno knock-back. That's gotta hurt.

"Thank you, Blackwell School, that was very, er, nice," says Mr. McGraw as finally we limp toward the finishing post, verse seventeen of the drum song.

"Very tunesome," he adds.

He's just fibbing now.

McGraw then commences a twelve-minute nag about "things that really depress him about Blackwell School." This gives everyone, including the teachers, a good chance for forty winks, but I tried to stay with him until I felt my eyelids closing. The bits I caught were:

1) People not bringing their ski trip payments on time. Apparently Blackwell School is "not a bank" and "can't finance school trips for children up front."

2) Children have been spotted waiting for school buses outside of the designated "waiting zone," thus creating a "potential death trap."

3) Somebody questioning the school librarian's authority to dish out detentions, thus making her cry and mess up the Dewey decimal system.

4) Somebody has been stealing bread buns from the dinner hall and eating them around the back of the sports hall. Crumbs have been detected.

(Note: Interpol were not called for any of these aforementioned heinous crimes.)

"Maybe it's a mistake?" whispers Fleur. "I'll text him again."

Claude and I both grimace, but let Fleur embark on her own self-destruction.

"Oh, and finally," McGraw mutters, "due to various reasons, there will be, ahem, no Blackwell School Summer Garden Party this June." (Cough.) "And, well, that's it for today. File out quietly, everybody," he says quickly, hooking a silver fountain pen back into the lapel of his bottle-green tweed jacket.

Nobody moves.

A growing mumble rattles around the assembly hall.

"That sucks!" one Year 10 lad says, accidentally on-purposely dead loud.

"Er . . . excuse me, Mr. McGraw," shouts Ainsley Hammond, a pale Year 11 gothic type. "Like, why are we not having a fete?" he asks.

"Yeah!!" choruses a few dozen voices.

"Why? Why not, Mr. McGraw?" people mutter.

"Now then, that is a very good question, Ainsley," says Mr. McGraw, turning his gray face toward Mrs. Guinevere, "and one that perhaps the deputy head would like to explain, as I have an urgent meeting to attend . . ."

Guinevere shoots McGraw back an expression which seems to say, "You're on your own here, mate, and I will hammer you to death with my own open-toe sandal if you get me involved."

"Very well, children, I'll say a few words . . . ," he concedes.

McGraw gazes out at the sulky crew. What on Earth can he say? Everybody knows that our headmaster loathes the annual Blackwell School Garden Party from the bottom of his sensible brogues. Making light-hearted banter with the pond-life parents? Mmm, what fun! Fending off flying buckets of water and custard pies hurled in the name of charity? Yes, please! Judging the "Guess the Weight of the Fruit Loaf/Yucca Plant/Obese Toddler" competition? Swapping glib pleasantries with the Blackwell School "Old Boys," a dismal shower of ex-pupils, all now making more money than McGraw, all of whom now have kids who attend Blackwell; which is disconcerting enough, but not as scary as the Blackwell Old Boys' inability to STOP

HAUNTING THEIR HEADMASTER FIFTEEN YEARS AFTER LEAVING Blackwell!

McGraw doesn't merely dislike the school garden party; he has to be poked and prodded by Edith, our fire-breathing school secretary, every single day of January, February, March and April before penciling a date into the school diary.

According to school folklore, this simply was not the way Samuel McGraw had envisioned his life panning out. All these headmastery shenanigans, it had all been a huge, hideous mistake.

"I should have been a poet-in-residence or an astronaut," McGraw has been overheard lamenting to Mrs. Guinevere as they trudged to their cars together after another long day. "Yet a few wrong turns on life's highway and my destiny became discussing the weight, to the nearest milligram, of Mrs. Parkin's fruited slice . . . oh, and dodging buckets of water. I have great hopes for the next life. It has to be better than this."

Now, don't get me wrong, I'm not saying that the Blackwell School inmates are such a shower of bed-wetting weirdos that we treat Garden Party Day like one of the highlights of our lives, comparable, say, to VIP passes to Euro Disney or a night at the MTV Music Awards or something dead fabulous like that. However, the Blackwell School Garden Party was a pretty good laugh and we all wanted it to happen, and for better reasons than an addiction to raffle tickets and homemade lemonade.

First of all, the garden party usually takes place on a Saturday, so you can make a fashion statement in your fancy-schmanciest clothes and stun the opposite sex by emerging like the "After" instead of the "Before" part of a "Dump that Frumpy Look" makeover. The LBD spent weeks planning what to wear to the garden party last year. Eventually Fleur wore hot pants and three-inch stiletto heels. (And punctured the bouncy castle, almost making McGraw cry.)

Secondly: You can wear makeup too. Well, the girls can (plus Ainsley Hammond and the gothic types who usually wear more lip gloss and blush than a glamour model on a night out).

Third: So the whole school's looking sexier (not difficult), the sun's shining (ideally, putting folk in the mood for summer loving), the teachers are in a chilled-down mood (largely due to the beer tent) and your parents are distracted by the Police Dog Display (as I say, Blackwell Garden Party is NOT the MTV Awards): These are all extremely cop-off-friendly conditions. This makes Blackwell fete a legendary Snogtastic event. Everyone is at it! Even I pulled once. Yes, me! Okay, it was with a Year 9 lad called Adrian—who, Fleur pointed out in the cold light of spring term, "had a forehead like a satellite dish"—but it was a very very exciting event during those nine minutes we stood with our arms draped around each other and lips scrambling about. (Our kissing technique could have done with some polishing up.)

Nevertheless, there's just something highly delicious about Blackwell Garden Party that warrants an otherwise unseen in-termingling of the year groups. In everyday life, sexy Year 11 boys use Year 9 pip-squeaks like me as footrests during assembly. However . . . as the day tumbles toward its climax and the small, very low-key disco begins (only until nine o'clock, annoyingly), not only do you get the pleasure of watching the teachers dance (ha ha! Most of them are over thirty years old! Old people should stop pretending to like modern music just so they look cool. It's really pitiful to watch), there is one helluva-lotta snogging occurring. All those hours spent flirting, batting your eyelids, complimenting each other on your chosen outfits and "ironically" enjoying the bouncy castle, they've got to lead somewhere. And if Lady Luck smiles down, well, you could end up joined at the tongue with some hottiebuns you've had your eye on for months. This year I'd had my eye on Jimi Steele. (But I'd have settled now for somebody who my father hasn't already ruined my chances with by being a prize dweeb.)

"Ah, but you're forgetting one small element, Hammond," snipes McGraw rather forcefully. "Last year's party was a shambles. In case your memory deludes you, there was an England-Germany soccer match the same day, so few of your families showed any Blackwell loyalty. Does nobody remember that fiasco?" McGraw is really warming to the subject now. "It was a shambles! In fact, the highlight of my entire fete was paying eight pounds on the raffle to win back a bottle of Vanilla Uzo that I'd donated in the first place." Several Year 7 girls titter, then notice the raised veins on McGraw's neck and swap giggles for sympathetic nods.

"But what about the charity money we raise?" argues Ainsley.

Ha! That had McGraw scuppered!

"Mmm, well, we'll have to find other ways to continue our good work. And if anyone conjures up any of these 'good ideas,' er, approach Mrs. Guinevere. She'll talk through them with you."

Mrs. Guinevere gives a withering smile. Oh, how I'd love to watch her laying into the miserable old goat once she gets him through those staff-room doors.

This morning, as I flung back my bedroom curtains and watched Mum in her slippers being sick in the backyard bin (how vile is that? It serves her right for gobbling down past-their-sell-by-date scallops—her luck was bound to run dry one day), I thought that life could not grow any more bleak.

I was wrong.

First, no Astlebury and no Astlebury snogging, then no Jimi and definitely no Jimi snogging, then no garden party and no sexy post-party disco snogging?! What have the grown-ups got up their sleeves next? No talking to boys full stop? Full Muslim burkas to be worn by all under-eighteens?

The way these last two days have panned out, I'll probably be still living, aged thirty-seven, with Loz and Magda, in a shoe-box at the Fantastic Voyage, my lips sealed together through underusage, my boobs still untouched by human hands (aside from my own).

This world certainly does not deserve a hug.

"So, who else?" I say, burying my head in Fleur's duvet.

"Mmm, let's see," says Claude, leafing through the back pages of a brand-new issue of *New Musical Express*.

"Right," she announces. "Bands newly confirmed for Astlebury Festival this week are, ahem, the Flaming Doozies—"

"Oh, I looove the Flaming Doozies! They're the ones with the lead singer who sets fireworks off onstage," I moan.

"And the Long Walk Home have confirmed too," reads Claude.

"I've just bought their CD," says Fleur mournfully, tweezing her eyebrows, with a large strip of cream bleach plastered across her top lip.

Fleur is a bit like the Forth Road Bridge in Scotland: She's under constant maintenance. There's always a bit of Fleur that needs painting, waxing, tweezing or scrubbing. Just as Fleur finishes making one area gorgeous, another zone needs urgent preening.

"And you're not going to like this . . ." Claude winces. "Spike Saunders is now the headline act on Saturday night."

Fleur and I both let out angry yelps, like stabbed pigs. Or even: like totally depressed LBD members who've just discovered that the most handsome, sexiest, unbelievably talented and all-around amazing solo male singer in the entire history of world music is playing somewhere that they've been barred from. (Sorry, Jimi, for seeming disloyal here, you *do* give Spike Saunders a good run for his money, but he *just* pips you to the post.)

"Spike, tell me it's not true. Don't do this without me," Fleur pleads toward her Wall of Spike poster area, just behind her headboard.

Spike smiles down a perfect-toothed grin at Fleur, as if to say, "Sorry, mate, you know I love the LBD, but the money for playing Astlebury is amazing. Don't worry, though, I've heard that Walrus World, Penge, is very nice this time of year."

Fleur and I sit in silence for about ten minutes, staring into space, while Claude reads quietly, cuddling Larry into her bosom.

"Prrrrrrrrrr prrrrrrrrrr prrrrrrrrr," purrs Larry.

"Well, I'm glad somebody is happy!" huffs Fleur.

"Oh, c'mon. Things aren't that bad," snaps Claude. "It's nearly summer vacation," she chirps.

"Same miserable life, just hotter," snaps back Fleur.

We all sit in silence a bit longer. Eventually Fleur speaks.

"So, what excuse did your mother trump up to ban you from Astlebury?" she asks Claude.

"Mmm, well . . . I didn't really ask in the end . . . ," Claude mumbles.

"YOU DIDN'T ASK!" Fleur and I shout, hurling assorted teddy bears and pillows in Claude's direction.

"There was no point! Mum didn't let my big sister, Mika, stay out all night till she was almost seventeen. You know what my mother is like. She likes us all at home, present and correct. She doesn't even like pajama parties, in case some freak accident happens."

Claude isn't exaggerating, her mum is really protective. I think it's because there's only the three of them.

"Oh, dar-link . . ." Fleur laughs, being about as patronizing as a girl bleaching her mustache can manage.

"Your sister, Mika, stayed out at sixteen . . . therefore . . . the international rule of the younger sister is to push back that boundary to fourteen! You are so lame," mocks Fleur.

Claude looks slightly hurt.

"Well, fat lot of good that rule did you, huh? Are Joshua and Daphne not both older than you? And remind me again where you're going to this summer? Oh, that's it. NOWHERE," Claude eventually snaps back.

Hmmmpgh, I think to myself, *I really wish I had a flipping big sister or brother . . . or a younger one for that matter . . . or anyone to take the heat off me at home.*

I've tried complaining about my tragic only-child status to the LBD on many occasions: It gets me precicely nowhere.

Fleur always points out that for the last fourteen years of her life, the most meaningful interaction that's occurred between herself and Joshua, her seventeen-year-old big brother, has been when he farts into his hand, shoves it in her face, then runs off laughing like a drain. Fleur's nineteen-year-old big sister, Daphne, however, is certainly someone more to be proud of. She's taking a year off before university to work in Nepal, which is like a total adventure. Some of Daphne's friends have probably even been eaten by lions and trampled by elephants, which is really cool in a morbid way. Well, it is for me. I live a low-excitement life in only-child solitude. It's a big deal in my family when the Fantastic Voyage gets a new-flavored box of potato crisps in.

"You could have AT LEAST asked!" nags Fleur.

"Well, none of us are going anyway, so it makes no difference!" screams Claude, eventually losing patience.

"And I've got no boyfriend now either," moans Fleur, checking her phone again, hopefully. "I've got nothing to look forward to. Not even Blackwell fete." Fleur's bottom lip is really wobbling now.

"That music festival was going to be the highlight of my whole life," she sobs.

Okay, Fleur has a point here.

"Well, fine!" shouts Claude. "But if we want to see some live music, and we want to meet some live music fans . . . and we're not allowed to leave the city limits apart from on supervised walrus fact-finding missions . . . why don't we stop feeling sorry for ourselves and DO SOMETHING proactive and positive about it?"

"Like what?" sulks Fleur.

"Well . . . why don't we put on our own little music festival? You know, like in place of Blackwell fete?"

Claude sits back on the bed, looking very pleased with her idea.

We both stare at her in utter disbelief.

"Huh?" grunts Fleur after about thirty seconds. "And who would play at this festival?" she mocks. "Spike Saunders? Or will he be busy that day?"

"No, not Spike Saunders," says Claude firmly. "But Jimi Steele's band are pretty good. Aren't they, Ronnie?!"

"Er . . . yeah, they're great," I say, remembering the time they played a few songs in assembly and Jimi wore a tight T-shirt that showed off his perfect brown six-pack and slightly outy belly button. I'm warming to Claude's idea now.

"Er, and what about Catwalk, Panama Goodyear's group?" Claude continues.

"Oh, God, they're so popular. They sing and dance and everything," I say, rolling my eyes.

Catwalk, in case you've not heard of them, are a Year 11 pop group made up of the irrefutably beautiful Panama plus four of her equally jaw-droppingly perfect-looking chums: two boys and two girls. In Panama's spare time, when her diary isn't too hectic with essential school-bully duties or bragging about her modeling career, she's working on her destiny as an international pop starlet. No end-of-year party or school gathering is complete without a quick number or five from Catwalk. Panama's group started as a little after-school project; before we all knew it, they were set to conquer the world.

"We've had a lot of interest about our music from some important people," Panama always brags to anyone who will listen.

"Yeah, like the Noise Pollution Department at the Town Council," muttered Claude after sitting through another all-singing, all-dancing presentation. What Catwalk lack in actual talent, they more than compensate for in cute looks and designer wardrobes. I hate to say it: Lots of people really really love them.

"Yep, the Blackwell crowd love Panama's band, they'd be a definite to play," I admit.

"Tell you who I'd like to see," cheeps Fleur, surprisingly upbeat for a girl who thinks Claude's idea is poo. "Ainsley Hammond's band Death Knell. I've no idea what they do, but apparently it involves an electric guitar, a steel drum and a glockenspiel."

"Interesting!" Claude smiles, putting her and Fleur's quarrel behind them in seconds, in true LBD fashion.

"And if they're the Blackwell bands that we know about, there's bound to be more that we don't know about," says Claude triumphantly. "We could hold auditions."

"Ha ha, good idea, Claude . . . ," says Fleur.

We can all sense a "but" coming.

"But . . . how on Earth are we going to convince old Prozac McGraw to let us hold a music festival in his school grounds?

That's impossible, isn't it?" Fleur says, furrowing her pimple-free brow. "The bloke loathes music, hates his pupils, doesn't like crowds of people and isn't very keen on any type of fun at all!"

"Ah, Fleur." Claude smiles mischievously, rubbing the top of Larry's furry head until he almost explodes with pleasure. "Why don't you just leave our good friend Mr. McGraw to me?" She chuckles.

Chapter 3

the thlot pickens . . .

~~~~~~

So it's 9:25 and I've just arrived at double science.

It's the fresh dawn of another of "The Happiest Days of My Life," which is how Mum refers to Blackwell School as she's prodding me out the door every morning.

I find this description ironic in view of Granny informing me that Mother was a terrible truant back in the 1980s, who only attended lessons if chased there "with a swishy stick." Nevertheless, despite being extra snug as a bug in a rug under my duvet earlier this morning, plus one very good go at feigning glandular fever, I'm here at my bench, eager to embark on some vital Bunsen burner and pipette action.

This is more than can be said for Mr. Ball, our science teacher.

Eventually, at 9:35, following a good gossip with Fleur and Claude about which shoes we might buy next term (to heel or not to heel? That is the question), the door to the science lab creaks open and the upper half of Mr. Ball's body swings into view.

Ball's forehead is all wrinkly, he looks confused.

"Er . . . have I got you lot now?" Ball asks, peering at his watch.

"No, sir," lies Liam Gelding.

"Oh? . . . Right. Sorry," says Mr. Ball, closing the door again.

Through the windows we can see Ballsy disappearing off along the lower school's main corridor on the trail of his lesser-spotted science class. All thirty-two of Ball's pupils dissolve into sheepish giggles. It's got legs, Liam's little joke, it's run and run since first year. It doesn't take much to confuse Mr. Ball, so the kids tend to have a little fun at his ditzy expense.

You see, if you needed to know about quantum physics, or the lowdown on moon landings or man's evolution from an ape, Mr. Ball is the right man to ask, he'll truly wow you with his big scary-scientist brain capacity; however, ask Mr. Ball which class he's teaching next period or even where he parked his car that morning, well, now you've got him bamboozled.

I like Mr. Ball, though, it's good to be a bit ditzy, I reckon.

"You're evil, Liam Gelding!" hisses Claude, shaking her head, trying not to smile. "Go and chase up Ballsy and tell him he's got us until ten thirty-five."

Liam Gelding, with his pale green eyes, brown cropped hair and rather sexy silver earring, has, for some bizarre reason, become a whole heap more attractive and fragrant this term; however, at this precise moment he's spoiling the effect slightly by excavating his left nasal cavity with his finger. Liam's desperately trying not to meet Claudette's eye as he knows she's absolutely right.

"And he'll be in the admin office getting a right roasting off

Edith now too . . . she was exceptionally irate when I was passing by her hatch this morning. Poor bloke," nags Claude.

Liam gazes straight ahead, his index finger buried almost near to the knuckle.

"And he was off sick with flu last week as well," Claude adds in a melodramatic way. "He must feel terribly weak."

Liam's willpower is cracking, he begins to stand up.

"Okay! Okay! Cassiera, you win! I'll go and get him." He laughs.

It's incredible how readily the boys cooperate with Claudette's wishes ever since she sprouted that stupendous C-cup bosom.

Too late, however. Mr. Ball has returned, he must have found his timetable. Mr. Ball, I always think, looks a touch like a scientific teddy bear: He's short and plumpish with a furry beard, a tufty mustache and an abundance of chest hair, which creeps from the top of his creased white lab coat. None of Mr Ball's lab coats quite fit; the top three buttons are traditionally left unfastened, displaying several unattractive inches of graying string vest. As ever, Mr. Ball is completely unfazed by Liam's little gag.

"Are you guys Year Nine or Year Ten?" he asks, still not quite up to speed. "Year Nine!" we all chorus.

Ball grabs the exercise book belonging to one of the kids on the front bench and flicks to the last written page.

"What were we doing last time we met?" he inquires. "Crystals or locusts?"

"Crystals," we all shout.

The locusts, lazing about in their cages at the rear of the lab, breathe a collective sigh of relief.

"Ahhh, I know where we are now!" announces Ball, a broad smile breaking through his beard. We all give him a little cheer and round of applause.

Quickly, Mr. Ball springs into action, gathering all the class, including me, Fleur, Claude and Liam, around the demonstration bench to watch his latest trick.

Now, last time, as far as I can recall, we were distilling some light blue—or, hang on, it could have been dark green—fibers in a conical flask with some other sort of white powdery stuff.

I think.

Then . . . after heating the contents of the flask, we discovered that the clear liquid (I didn't quite catch its name) that Mr. Ball dropped the fibers into had changed color. It turned either blue or green.

(I'm not quite sure which.)

Mr. Ball's experiment proved without doubt that . . .

Oh, God, I'll admit it: I HAVE NO IDEA WHAT THIS PROVED. I wasn't listening. I'm not even listening this time either, despite the fact that Mr. Ball seems to be frothing-at-the-mouth excited about the formation, over the previous seven days, of turquoise crusty bits on the sides of his conical flask.

"This chemical reaction," Mr. Ball announces, "denotes something very very interesting indeed!"

In truth, I'd be more interested hearing Mr. Ball explain how I have now been sitting in science for what seems like over four hours while the clock on the lab wall still insists on reading 9:51.

I really wish I could like science, but it really doesn't float my boat at all. It didn't seem to matter in Year 7 and 8, but now I can feel that I'm slipping behind and I don't even know how I could begin to catch up. What do I do?

If I tell Mr. Ball, he'll just make me do extra science tuition, which is like signing up for extra medieval torture or something. He might even make me go and sit in Room 5 in the "special tuition" center, which isn't something anyone wants to be seen doing. Liam Gelding had to go to Room 5 for English and maths for a while last year, then when he came back afterward to join us for his other lessons, everyone in the class would sing, "Special needs, special needs, spesssshhhhel needs!" to the tune of that old song by the Beatles "Let It Be" until Liam's face flushed scarlet.

Kids can be cruel, eh? That's what grown-ups always say. Unfortunately most Blackwell kids mistake this for one of the school rules, i.e., "Kids are required to be cruel at all times during the school day and even more so at breaks and lunchtime."

Okay, between you and me, what terrifies me most about asking for help is being officially certified "dumb." Don't tell me it doesn't happen, I've seen the special stickers they put on your personal files to signify "borderline retarded." I've skated pretty close to this with a few school reports too. Not in cool lessons like English or religious studies, no, I tend to A grade them. I'm talking about maths and science. That's where I blow, big time. Those snidey little remarks written on my end-of-year report cards really keep me awake at night:

"Ronnie is a capable girl but loses all interest when the

43

going gets tough. Grade: D," my science teacher bitched last year.

"Pah, that's what you're like with everything. You've always been a quitter," snapped my mother helpfully.

"*Gnnnngn,*" I grunted, grasping around for one really difficult thing in my life I've actually finished. And failing.

I am such a loser.

Worse still was my maths card: "Veronica is quite simply a waste of my time and her own in this lesson. I have grave concerns for her future employment if she persists on lagging behind the year group. Grade: E."

I cried when Mum and Dad got home from that Blackwell's report evening. Because at some points during that term I'd even tried, a bit. Eventually Loz came upstairs and told me not to fret because if I ended up with no qualifications at all, I could get a job with him as a barmaid. "Those new computerized cash registers work all the sums out for you," he said.

This made me cry even more.

But I'm certainly not telling anyone I can't understand science, it's not worth the hassle. One good thing about science lessons, I suppose, is that Mr. Ball is typically so busy distilling stuff, pipetting and mucking about with test tubes that you can usually grab a good, lengthy, albeit whispered, chatter. Today, however, I'm feeling more than a little subdued. I'm glad I've got the LBD there so I can get a few things off my chest.

Something fishy is afoot back home at the Fantastic Voyage, I tell Fleur and Claude as we crowd around the microscope, looking for whatever it is we're looking for. I'm more than slightly bummed that neither Mum nor Dad will tell me what's going on. I know for certain they're not speaking to each other, that's for deffo, not that I've even seen them in the same room over the last week to confirm their silence.

I can just tell. Despite my scientific deficiencies, I'm flipping cleverer than they give Ronnie Ripperton credit for.

Take last night, when I moseyed home from Fleur's and was rooting around in the laundry room for a clean school shirt to iron. Innocently I yelled through to Mum, who was prepping parsnips in the kitchen: "Oi, Mum! Do you know where my short-sleeved school shirt is?"

"No . . . not really sure," Mum shouted back. "I know where all of your long-sleeved ones are, they're over the drying horse. Why do you want the short one?" she asked.

All was well so far.

"Well, Dad says it's going to be red-hot tomorrow—"

Big mistake! Blastoff! Mum's lips puckered, her nostrils flared and her eyes thinned to venomous slits.

"*Hmmmph* . . . well, you had better listen to *your father* then, seeing as he's got that hot line to the BBC meteorological department," she sniped, hurling silky slithers of parsnip into a vast pan of bubbling water.

Whenever Mum and Dad row, "Dad" suddenly becomes *"your fath-er,"* almost as if Loz hatched me all by himself in a bin around the back of the Fantastic Voyage and Magda had nothing physical to do with the whole process. It's almost as if Mum can distance herself from him, and by default from us, the Ripperton clan, with just a few strangely chosen syllables. This time, however, seemed far more serious; there was a real hurt in her eyes, like Dad had done something so heinous that I wouldn't even want to know.

This really gave me a jolt. It was at this point I realized that home has been pretty weird and miserable over the last week. And that I'm not coping very well with my parents' long morbid silences and blatant irritation at each other. Or their midnight mumblings and shoutings the very second they notice my light is switched off. I even had a stupid nightmare last night that Dad had died suddenly, and I was running about trying to plan a funeral while Mum was laughing maniacally and making a fancy cake. That was hideous.

But whatever is going on, neither side are giving anything away.

"What's up, Mum?" I said, anyhow.

"Nothing," she said, forcing a thin smile. "Nothing at all. If you want me to iron a shirt, then leave it on top of the dryer, I'll do it once we've sorted the cash registers out."

"Yeah," I said, "but what is up with—?" But I was interrupted by the kitchen order phone ringing.

Then, earlier this morning, on my way out of the pub to school, I tapped Dad for my lunch money. Dad was sitting in the saloon bar, still in his pajamas, slurping a big mug of tea, reading *The Daily Mirror*. I had decided to forgive him for his Jimi faux pas yesterday, on account of his extreme cack-handedness in most social situations like that, it's all I can expect, really. Oh, and the fact that I wanted my lunch money with minimum fuss.

"So, Ronaldo," he asked. "What's on the agenda today?"

"*Phhghh* . . . double science," I sighed. "And then I think I've got religious studies . . . dead boring. We're doing theology at the moment. Y'know, the meaning of life and all that."

"Ooh, the meaning of life? How good's that, eh?!" muttered Dad as I slung my schoolbag over my shoulder, trudging toward the door. "Hey, Ronno, do me a favor," Dad shouted. "If you find out that meaning of life thing by, say, four-ish, give me a quick call on my cell phone, will yer?"

"Will do, Pops," I yelled. "See ya. Love yer."

Dad continued in a voice only just loud enough to hear: "It'll give me something to think about in prison after I've strangled your mother. . . ."

At some level, I think Dad was only half kidding.

"Ooh, that's awful, Ronnie," squeaks Fleur, tweezering turquoise crystals under a microscope so we can all share in its holy wonderment. Mr. Ball is hopping from bench to bench, trying to prevent the stupider kids from tasting the crystals as they're, like, poisonous.

"What you need is some counseling," whispers Fleur earnestly. "You're, like, practically an abused child. Do you find that Loz and Magda take their aggression out on you when they're arguing?" she asks. "You might need a social worker."

"No, not really," I say, shaking my head, gazing out the window at the pouring rain. Dad's hot line to the BBC weather department must have been faulty. "In fact, I got five pounds lunch money this morning instead of two fifty. Dad told me to go spend his profits on false eyelashes for all he cared. I don't think that's really child abuse, Fleur."

Fleur looks disappointed.

"You might still need a bit of therapy, though," Fleur says hopefully. "Like that sort where you swim with dolphins in Israel and cry a lot. I saw it in *Marie Claire* magazine."

"What you need," interrupts Claude, "is to just let your mum and dad get on with it and try to keep yer shneck out of things."

(NB: *Shneck* is the LBD's word for nose. Say you see someone with a big nose. It's the LBD rule that you've got to go "Sherrrrneckkkkk!!" really loudly in a squawky way . . . praying that the person in question with the "biggen shnecken" isn't conversant in LBD.)

"Mmm . . . I know what you're saying," I reply. "Probably I should."

Claude looks extra authoritarian at the moment in her lab specs.

"Definitely," says Claude. "They're having a row, just let them argue it out. Your mum and dad are a right pair, Ronnie. They love each other to bits, anyone can see it. This time next week they'll be trying to dump you at your granny's again because they want to go on one of their romantic weekends."

We all giggle then, fake putting our fingers down our throats, grimacing. I don't even want to contemplate what my parents get up to on the "romantic weekends" they occasionally take in Parisian hotels and suchlike, but I hope it involves a lot of examining the in-room trouser press and looking at the River Seine and NOTHING too "romantic." *Bleeeeeughhh.*

"Anyhow, I need your full attention over the next week. We've got a *very* full schedule . . . you're going to be my right-hand chick."

Oh, dear, I know EXACTLY what Claude's talking about here. I knew she wouldn't leave our little LBD conversation about the Blackwell fete last night as pie in the sky for too long. That's just not Claude's style.

"Oh, Claude, we can't," I say.

"You're not being serious?" says Fleur with a look of growing anxiety.

"It's impossible . . . isn't it?" I say.

But Claude has that scary, unstoppable look in her eyes.

"It IS possible," Claude affirms. "We're going to see Mr. McGraw at first break to put our plans to him about Blackwell Live."

Claude pauses a moment to enjoy the sound of her new title; she invented the phrase "Blackwell Live" at 3:15 A.M. this morning, sitting up in bed at Flat 26, Lister House.

You see, late last night, long after the LBD had giggled, fantasized, danced and gossiped till we were exhausted about how totally, unbelievably fantabulouso it would be to turn Blackwell fete into a full-scale local pop/rock extravaganza; long after I'd toddled home, encountered Magda and fallen asleep; and hours after Fleur had finished her vitamin E deep-impact face pack and turned on her *Whale Sounds Power Snooze* CD, Claudette Cassiera was awake until at least 4:00 A.M. . . . plotting. As you can imagine, Claudette plotting is a very scary thing indeed. It involves numerous sheets of paper, spider diagrams, doodlings

49

and scribblings out. It also involves the emergence of one of Claudette's infamous "THINGS TO DO" lists.

Oh my Lord. I can see one being produced from Claudette's rucksack right now. Point one says:

1. Make appointment with McGraw to discuss Blackwell Live.

It has a big tick against it. She's only gone and done it!

"Oh, I have GOT to see this one." Fleur smirks.

"That's good," retorts Claude, "because you're coming along too. I need full LBD backup to swing this one in our favor."

That wipes the smile right off Fleur's chops.

"Of course, Fleur," continues Claude, "this will require you to act pleasantly, schoolgirlish and, well, almost like a normal human being for over twenty whole minutes . . . Swanno, can I count on that?"

Fleur giggles and sticks her tongue out. "Huh. It'll take a lot more than me saying a few pleases and thank-yous for McGraw to start liking me again." Fleur laughs.

"Perhaps," says Claude. "But it wouldn't hurt to try."

"Do you think I should apologize again for that massive bill he got from . . . ooh, what was it called? . . ." Fleur thinks deeply. "Oh, yeah, Castles in the Sky, the bouncy castle company?"

"Well, yes, you could . . ." Claude stops, then changes tack. "Actually, Fleur, I've thought about that now. DON'T mention the bouncy castle incident. In fact, Fleur, don't speak at all. Just smile."

Fleur crosses both eyes and gives a big smile with all of her teeth and gums showing, made all the more eerie by the fact she has plum-colored lipstick smeared on her front teeth.

"That's very pretty, Fleur," says Claude. "Very genuine."

Claude turns her attention to me.

"Right, Ronnie, you're my only hope here. Once we're all in McGraw's office, we have to work together tightly to get the outcome we want."

"What, like a Good Cop–Bad Cop sorta routine?" I ask, suddenly feeling very devious.

"Well, no," corrects Claude. "More like Nice Schoolgirl–Even More Crawly Bumlicky Schoolgirl."

"Oh, well," I say. "Can I be the first one?"

"For sure." Claude smiles.

As far as an LBD planning meeting, this is highly civilized.

We've got a smidgen of a plan together, and no one has felt the need to call each other a "total durrbrain" or get personal about the other girl's hairstyle. Sadly, our good progress is brought to a halt by minor classroom chaos.

Mr. Ball has left the front of the classroom and is striding around the benches, inhaling deeply.

"Has somebody got sweets?" he says. "I am certain that I can smell chocolate. And it's a milk chocolate too."

Mr. Ball's highly sensitive nostrils are twitching.

"C'mon, hand 'em over, whoever you are!" says Ballsy. "You all *know* how I feel about sweets in the chemistry department."

Yes, Mr. Ball, we all know how you feel about sweets in general. You adore them. It's rumored that the local newspaper seller Mr. Parker bought a new Volvo last year on the strength of your minty humbug, chocolate raisin and cola cube addiction.

51

Poor Sajid Pratak, a tiny pip-squeak of a boy perched on one of the back benches, is caught mid-chomp.

"Sajid!" yells Mr. Ball.

"*Mggghp* sir!" goes Sajid.

"Bring those sweets up here," Ball instructs.

Sajid trudges to the front of the class, surrendering his crumpled bag.

No sooner is Saj reseated, Mr. Ball is pointing at the blackboard with one hand while his other furry hand begins foraging amongst the sweeties, making them disappear into a clearing in his face forest.

"Sweets are forbidden in the chemistry lab, Sajid," Mr. Ball says. "*Mmeghg*-specially"—chomp, chomp—"delicious chocolate-coated *mgh*Turkish Delight *sugch* as this. You children could have any manner of hazardous chemical on your hands when you're eating. Your innards could dissolve!"

Sadly, this is what always happens when weak-willed Mr. Ball finds sweets in his classroom. Firstly he confiscates them as he's "paranoid we'll get poisoned," then he ends up scoffing the lot. Afterward, Mr. Ball feels wracked with guilt about pilfering confectionery from victims under five feet tall, so he ends up buying the pupil more sweets in return next lesson. The LBD all roll their eyes and giggle.

"Stop moaning, Mr. Pratak," says Mr. Ball. "Just you get on with writing up that experiment till the end of the lesson."

BBBBBBBBBBRRRRRRRRRRRING goes the school bell.

"Which is now!" Mr. Ball smiles, relieved.

We all start packing our bags.

"Good-bye, Year Ten!" shouts Mr. Ball, making a sharp exit

for the staff room before some pesky student teacher nicks his comfy chair by the radiator. "See you soon!"

"Year Nine!" we all shout.

And then he's gone.

in search of great craic

"But what are we going to say to him?" I ask Claude anxiously as we head toward McGraw's lair.

We're weaving through the morning breaktime crush of a thousand Blackwell bodies. Agghh . . . I spot Jimi standing just inside the school yard with his two mates Aaron and Naz. Thank God Naz is doing something extremely impressive with a football (spinning it on one finger, since you ask), meaning I can slip by without Jimi seeing my face. I flinch again when I see Panama and two of her clique, Abigail and Leeza, hovering around one of the doorways that we need to pass through. As tradition requires, the girls all flash filthy looks at Fleur simply for being taller and naturally prettier than they are. They're mumbling some rubbish about Fleur being a "lanky cow," their usual route of attack. Most girls would crumble under such abuse; however, Fleur seems oblivious. Fleur Swan really is bully-proof—just like her name suggests, she glides right through trouble with her nose in the air, which just seems to make her tormentors more determined. It doesn't matter today anyway, we're moving pretty quickly. Fleur and I have to hurry to keep step with Claude's increasingly purposeful stride. We're now drawing dangerously close to the doors of the administration corridor, a sort of Blackwell inner sanctum situated in the center of the school, home to the offices of McGraw; Mrs. Guinevere, deputy head; plus Edith, school secretary (and part-time fire-breathing dragon).

I cannot flipping believe Claude is taking us here.

Nobody chooses to walk down this corridor via their own choice.

No, this is a corridor that you're sent to, well, to be more accurate, frog-marched to, when you've been caught slap-bang in the midst of being a social nuisance.

Actually, for such a scary place, the admin corridor is really rather beautiful. In general, Blackwell's decor is a fetching hue of sludge green, earwax yellow and incontinence brown; however, this 100 meters of space boasts pristine white marble floors that are polished daily, fresh pale turquoise walls and opaque patterned glass lamp shades. It's almost like a TV home makeover team turned up, blew all their budget on the admin corridor, then decorated the rest of Blackwell for £14.29.

"Er . . . well, I've not really planned *exactly* what we're going to say, as such," says Claude, knocking on Mr. McGraw's polished teak door. "And anyway, it's not just McGraw. I forgot to tell you, it's Guinevere as well. I said it would be better if they both were there. Y'know, kill two birds with one stone?"

Fleur and I look at each other in sheer horror.

I suddenly feel a terrible urge to go to the toilet.

But it's too late, the door has opened.

"Ah, Claudette Cassiera. Come in, come in," McGraw says, his gray face alive with delight. This is about as enthusiastic as I have ever heard McGraw being about anything, including last winter when he appeared on local radio saying the school was flood-damaged and closed for the week.

"And Veronica Ripperton too?" he adds, with a weaker smile, probably clocking that I'm wearing cream ankle socks instead of regulation three-quarter white ribbed ones.

"Oh, and it's you. Fleur Swan. What a lovely, er, surprise," McGraw lies, clearly remembering bouncy castles, Bovril and a whole string of other minor offenses he could be taking into consideration.

Claude nudges Fleur, who, on cue, gives a big broad smile from ear to ear, sort of twinkling her fingers at him. She looks like she should be dispensing dinners on a Virgin Airways flight.

We all file into the office, then stand rigidly in an arc facing McGraw's desk.

"Oh, please, young ladies, do have a seat," says McGraw, flourishing his hand around the room, pointing out chairs usually reserved for parents.

A seat?

A SEAT!?

Ha ha! How flipping different is the McGraw Office Experience when you're not there for Bovril-related wrongdoing?

Unbelievable!

Suddenly there's a further knock on the door. Mrs. Guinevere slips in behind us.

"Sorry I'm late, Sam, er, I mean Mr. McGraw," she says in her rich Dublin accent.

Mrs. Guinevere looks almost regal in a long black velvet

skirt, an ornate flowered waistcoat and a crisp white linen blouse. Her cropped auburn hair is flecked with strands of gray, which shine like platinum.

"Mrs. Guinevere, please have my seat," says Claude, spotting the chair shortage and leaping up. Quickly she's taller and slightly more powerful-looking than anyone else in the room.

Very cunning.

"So, Claudette, what can we do for you?" asks McGraw. "Something about a special concert you'd like to help organize?" McGraw is looking down at a slip of paper with Edith's swirly writing across it.

"Yes, sir," begins Claude. "An open-air music event for school musicians. You know, like a real chance for local talent to perform? Plus, an opportunity to raise money for local charities too . . ."

Jeez, Claude, when you put it like that, I think I'll be busy hand-washing my thongs that day. Still, five minutes into the meeting and we've not been ejected yet.

"And what musicians do you have in mind?" probes McGraw. "I know that the Blackwell Bellringing Society has suffered a huge drop in support since Mr. Cheeseman left for his new teaching job. . . . Yet still they ring on, spreading joy. Would they get a slot on the bill?"

"Er . . . well—" Claude winces.

"And I DO know that Miss Nash from the music department has been teaching her lunchtime choir group some wonderful Elizabethan close-harmony madrigals," McGraw continues.

"Veronica, make a note of that," says Claude, simply for effect. "They sound very promising."

BUGGER OFF, I write on my notepad, showing both Claude and Fleur. Fleur almost giggles, but at the last minute turns it into another big smile. McGraw and Guinevere peer at us all intently.

"But, really, it would be a celebration of all things musical and rhythmic," says Claude, stepping up her campaign. "You know, like singing and rapping, and dancing . . . and we'd have rock bands and pop music and—"

"Pop music?" says McGraw.

In the same tone as you'd say "Dog poo?" if you found it on the bottom of your flip-flop.

"Yes, pop music," says Claude. "And other stuff."

Claude, to give her due, then follows this up by making some dead grown-up points about "school morale" and "making Blackwell a household name." But by this point I don't think McGraw is listening.

He's staring out of the window mournfully, probably imagining Blackwell School filled with marauding youth, all of them dancing, stage-diving, playing loud guitars, snogging each other and having a really fantastic time. Ironic, as this is exactly what we can see slipping away from us.

"Well, girls," McGraw says, drawing a red pen line through the slip of paper before him, "I really don't consider Blackwell School grounds a fitting location to hold an event such as—"

McGraw begins what sounds like it might be extended grumble, but he doesn't get too far.

"I love it," says Mrs. Guinevere. Her eyes are all twinkly. "It would be like a little mini local music festival!" she enthuses. "What an exciting idea! That sounds like great craic!"

Mrs. Guinevere says the word *craic* to sound like *crack*. In this context none of the LBD are that sure what it means, but it sounds like a really good giggle nevertheless.

We all flash Mrs. Guinevere our largest, most relieved smiles.

"We think so too!" I say. "It would be totally fantabulous!"

"I'm sorry?" says Mrs. Guinevere.

"It'd be good fun," explains Claude.

"Ahhh . . . I get you now!" Mrs. Guinevere laughs.

Mr. McGraw huffs, puffs, then places his left elbow onto the desk, resting his head forlornly on his hand, directly beside a framed black-and-white photograph of his depressed-looking self standing with Myrtle, his equally gloomy wife. Our headmaster then sighs again, in a tired-of-life way, this time from the very bottom of his belly.

"Look, what you're suggesting isn't some picnic in the park, you know, girls?" moans McGraw. "It will require a lot of long, arduous, complex planning and hard work . . . and a lot of responsibility heaped on your young, inexperienced shoulders. I really don't think that three Year Nine girls are up to this task." McGraw shakes his head. "I mean, how will you even manage to . . ."

I hate to admit this, but I think he could be just a teensy-weensy bit right. We could really mess this thing up here. Well, all right, it's most likely to be me, *I could really mess this up.* This whole thing seems like another fab opportunity for me to prove to the teachers that I'm a burnout who "doesn't see projects through till the end" and "flakes out under responsibility."

Wonderful.

Okay, this might just be nerves.

Don't get me wrong, I really want Blackwell Live to happen, it's just the potentially hideous, snowballing sense of personal failure that I'd rather avoid.

"I'll help them," interrupts Mrs. Guinevere. "I don't mind, in fact I'd love to get involved! We put on many a play and concert without too much strife when I was a young girl at St. Hilda's in Dublin."

Mrs. Guinevere breaks out another big grin, even just remembering it.

"It'll certainly be a challenge, but I'm confident these girls can rise to what's needed of them."

You go, Mrs. G!

"Anyway, the girls can report in to me with their day-to-day progress," Guinevere adds. "So I'll know if they've tried to sell the school to the sultan of Brunei or blow up the playing fields . . . oh, I'm sure it will be fine, Mr. McGraw."

We all flash our best angelic smiles in Mr. McGraw's direction. He wrinkles his nose back at us.

"Well, think about it at least," Mrs. Guinevere says.

McGraw stares once again out of the window; he must love this, knowing the whole room hangs on his every word.

Following a long silence in which I notice that Mr. McGraw has been doodling a picture of a tree on his phone message pad, King Doom eventually speaks.

"Money," he says, placing both hands behind his head, satisfied with the stumbling block he's conjured up. "How are you planning to pay for all of this? Are your piggy banks going to stand the strain, or are you all doing double paper routes at the moment?"

McGraw smirks. He's found, so he reckons, the chink in Claude Cassiera's armor.

"Well, I thought we'd sell tickets," answers Claude. "The concert will take place over the weekend, after all, so people would probably expect to pay a little entrance fee just to cover costs, wouldn't they?"

Claude does seem to have a good answer for everything so far. I'm so glad nobody's asked me anything yet, or Fleur, who looks about ready to tell McGraw to stick his school fields up his bum. Or worse.

"Oh, deary me," mocks McGraw. "You're going to invite pupils to show up at Blackwell over the weekend? . . . And you're going to make them pay for the pleasure?! Come now, Miss Cassiera. If I thought that was feasible, I'd be holding this conversation with you via conference call from the Happy Coconut Beach Bar in Honolulu! I'd be a millionaire by now."

Okay, McGraw's joke is slightly amusing, but no girl gives the big spoilsport the pleasure of a chuckle, especially not Mrs. Guinevere, who is possibly even angrier than Fleur at this point.

Claude is rustling about in her folder. She produces a single sheet of paper covered in what looks like percentages and equations.

"Okay, I understand your concerns, Mr. McGraw, but if I can refer you back to the results of the Blackwell questionnaire that we filled out last year." Claude waves her piece of paper. "It seems that pupils probably *would* pay to see music, if we put on a good enough show for them, that is."

"Questionnaire? What questionnaire? We've never done a . . . ," argues McGraw, looking confused.

Mrs. Guinevere catches Claude's drift.

"Ah, Claudette's talking about the physical and social education department's life science questionnaire. You know? The one we gave out to all one thousand Blackwell pupils to fill in last June?"

"That's the one!" Claude smiles. "Do you not remember it, Mr. McGraw?" she says.

"*Pgh, splagh* . . . Of course I remember it . . . ," mutters McGraw. "We wanted to . . . er . . ." McGraw admits defeat. "Oh, remind me again what we wanted, Mrs. Guinevere?"

"To find out Blackwell pupils' likes, dislikes and attitudes toward school and home lives," prompts Mrs. Guinevere.

"Ah, yes, I remember it now. I was just a little, er, confused for a second," snaps McGraw, dredging the darkest corners of his memory for any info whatsoever about that PSE project. Eventually tiny bits start seeping back.

"What's this got to do with anything?" he says. "All I can recall is several pupils filling in a lot of insolent remarks about my tie collection and some bright spark suggesting we build a Blackwell Tarzan Swing. Pah! It simply underlined to me the percentage of utter buffoons I'm employed to baby-sit between eight A.M. and four P.M."

"Actually, we did gain a lot of useful info from that questionnaire," says Mrs. Guinevere patiently, turning back to Claude, who's waiting to read from her sheet. "What did you find out, Claudette?"

"Well, according to official Blackwell statistics, it seems that ninety-five percent of our pupils said that one of their main pocket money and Saturday job wage expenditures was . . ." Claude pauses for effect. "Music."

Mr. McGraw's face is an absolute picture. He looks a bit like a lottery winner who's just discovered he's boil-washed and tumble-dried his winning ticket.

"Oh," he grunts.

Claude continues, "They buy CDs, concert tickets, dancing and singing lessons, guitar strings, ballet shoes . . . they download MP3s off the Net, rip CDs . . . that sort of thing . . . it seems that Blackwell is sort of united by a common love of music."

Claude places the piece of paper back into a folder she has rather presumptuously felt-tipped *Blackwell Live* across.

"Riiiiiiiight," says McGraw crossly. The one thing more annoying than thick pupils, he's just discovered, is flipping smarty-pants pupils, they must drive him mad.

"Oh, dear, is that the time?" announces McGraw. "Sorry, girls, your time's up, I've got a class to supervise in two minutes."

Our headmaster rather abruptly winds up our appointment; obviously he's heard quite enough. "We'll get back to you forthwith on this matter," he says, nodding toward the door. "Off you pop now, you don't want to be late for third period."

There's nothing much else we can do now, well, aside from claim squatters' rights and refuse to leave his office.

Claude looks crestfallen; she packs her orange folder into her little black rucksack, thanks both the teachers for their time and makes toward the door; Fleur and I follow closely behind. However, as Mrs. Guinevere holds open the door, directing us three disheartened LBD members through, she whispers under her breath, just loud enough for us to catch, "Don't hurry away, ladies, wait outside for a moment," before snapping the door shut, leaving us on the other side.

"I thought I had him there for a minute," says Claude, her eyes seeming a little bit red-rimmed. "He was on the ropes, I just needed a few more jabs at him . . . ," she says.

Fortunately for the LBD, however, behind the door, the bell for round two seems to have already dinged and donged.

At first, we hear Guinevere and McGraw having a civilized discussion . . . but this turns quickly to just Mrs. Guinevere's voice, its volume increasing with every sentence. We can't hear every word from where we are in the corridor; however, the LBD can still make out a few fantastic sentences.

"I cannot believe you sometimes, Samuel!" Mrs. Guinevere says, followed quickly a few moments later by: "You need a rocket placed *you know where* to get you moving, that's what you need!"

Claude and I look at each other, our eyes wide with excitement. I'm really hoping Mrs. Guinevere doesn't suddenly fling open the door, because Fleur has her ear pressed so firmly against it, she'd certainly fall in and end up perched upon McGraw's lap.

But the next part we overhear is the very bestest bit of all: "I can leave anytime!" Mrs. Guinevere screeches, obviously not realizing that we can hear her. "I'm not the only staff member combing the *Guardian* job section for a one-way ticket out of Blackwell, you know!"

The LBD all place our hands over our mouths at the same time, suppressing fits of giggles.

After that, everything inside McGraw's office goes suddenly very silent, the next few minutes dragging by extremely slowly. Claude turns to me with an anxious expression.

"Maybe Mrs. G's got the sack?" Claude whispers. "It's very quiet in there now, isn't it?" Claude gazes down at her polished black shoes, then looks me straight in the eye.

"Oh, God, this is all my fault," she says.

Just then, the door opens and Mrs. Guinevere appears with a calm, triumphant smile. She claps her hands together in a businesslike manner, then places one carefully manicured hand onto Claude's shoulder.

"Right, ladies. We're in business," our deputy head announces. "You've got four weeks to kick this thing into shape. I'm suggesting Saturday, July twelfth for the concert, that's end of term. Let's kick summer vacation off with a bang, eh?"

We all stare at her in disbelief.

"But you've not got a lot of time, so it's all systems GO from this moment on . . ."

I wish one of us could think of something to say back.

"What did you call the concert on the front of that folder, Claudette?" Mrs. Guinevere asks. "Blackwell Live, wasn't it?"

"Uhhh, yes, miss?" Claude replies, smiling widely.

"Blackwell Live!" repeats Mrs. Guinevere. "I like that name, it has a ring to it, doesn't it? So as I say, ladies, get shaping with a plan, have a root around for some bands, singers and, well, whatever you can come up with, then give me the latest news in a few days' time. We'll take it from there."

Mrs. Guinevere turns on her heel and clip-clops away down the administration corridor.

"I'm sure it will be great craic, girls . . . great craic!" she says as she walks away. "The best of luck with your planning!"

And then she's gone.

"Did that really just happen?" asks Fleur, grinning not just from ear to ear, but somewhere around the back of her head too.

"OH. MY. GAWWWWWD," I squeal. "That was a yes! It was a yes!! . . . Hang on, that was a yes, wasn't it, Claude?" I double-check.

"Too right it was a yes!" says Claude. "We're putting on Blackwell Live! We're going to do it, just like we talked about last night!!"

SCREEEEEAAM!

After confirming and double confirming that Jimi Steele isn't anywhere in close proximity . . . I throw my arms in the air, wave 'em like I just don't care, holler, whoop, then join with the LBD in a celebratory Funky Monkey dance routine right along the administration corridor, through the middle school cloakrooms, then twice around the school pond. Life has taken a fantastic, brilliant, amazing upturn!

How glad am I now that, when I put the oven on last night and threatened my dad that I'd commit suicide by sticking my head in if he didn't allow me go to Astlebury, I changed my mind at the last minute and just made a baked potato instead? Imagine if I'd have missed this!

and there's more

I'm back home at the Fantastic Voyage now. I've just finished playing a few rounds of "Guess My Mood Today" with Mum (today's answer, in case you're wondering, was Distant and Angry). But this won't depress me tonight, not after so many amazing things have happened today.

For example, the bit when McGraw spotted the LBD stacking our trays in the dining hall after lunch and was forced to, through Britain's tightest lips, tell us he was "really pleased" to see us "taking on such a worthwhile project." That was great. Especially as it was quite clear that it was giving McGraw physical pain similar to hemorrhoids to say so.

Another fab bit was sticking up our first Blackwell Live audition posters, just outside the assembly hall, and watching the first small crowd of looky-loos gathering to read all the details. How cool is that?

By the way, our posters say:

CALLING ALL BLACKWELL SINGERS, MUSICIANS, DANCERS, ROCK BANDS AND BUDDING POP IDOLS!

We need you for Blackwell Live on Saturday, July 12th—
Blackwell School's very own

MUSIC FESTIVAL

Auditions are this Monday, June 23rd, 4:00 P.M. in the gym.
Speak to Claudette Cassiera, Veronica Ripperton or
Fleur Swan for further details or simply show up and
show us what you can do.

Within less than an hour, people began stopping the LBD in the corridors, in the school yard and on the playing fields to ask us what the devil we were playing at, or even funnier still, to sing us a few verses of their favorite songs, do a bit of break-dancing, or tell us about the Grade 3 piano exam they'd just passed! One lad even jumped out from behind the geography shelf in the library and serenaded me at the top of his voice:

"Has anyone ever seeen my bay-beee?
The one with the beautiful eyes
Cos there ain't nooooooo dis-guisin'
The way I luuuuurve her!"

Then he did a bit of a tap dance . . . which would have been quite flattering, except that the lad was Boris Ranking, a sturdy fourth-year lad with bright orange hair and amazing tangerine lashes who looks exactly like a Highland calf.

By the time we'd arranged with Johnny Martlew, the Year 13 lad who designs the Blackwellschool.com website, to post the details on the Latest News page, then persuaded Edith to stick a note into the class registers so that form teachers could tell every class, we'd started to feel a bit like pop stars ourselves. In fact, by about 4:00 P.M., everybody was talking about the LBD. It was brilliant!

However, better than all of this was what occurred at about seven o'clock this evening, just as I was lying down on my bed to do my French homework.

Okay, I'll admit that I'm not usually a big homework-done-on-time sorta lady, and let's face it, I had a lot more than feminine and masculine pronouns on my mind after today's events, but I had to get this stuff learned. You see, I've got one of Madame Bassett's legendary vocabulary tests tomorrow morning and I cannot fail.

No way.

It's simply not worth the hassle of giving M. Bassett a less than 50 percent result. She'd probably just pick on me for the entire double period, making me stand up and describe, in French, the complex details of planning a music festival or something equally horrendous. Can you imagine?

"Errr . . . *J'aime beaucoup le,* sorry, I mean, *la musique . . . et, ooooh la la . . . Je n' sais pas* . . . er . . . *Et j'ai besoin d'une tente.* . . . Errr . . . and *j'aime le veggie burger* . . . Oh, God, pleeeeease can I sit down now?" *(Dissolves into tears.)*

She would love that, Madame Bassett would.

La bitche.

So anyhow, I'd just opened my Tricolor textbook and was becoming quite engrossed in a very interesting story involving a man from La Rochelle named Monsieur Boulanger who, rather spookily, also worked as a baker (fancy that, eh? What a coincidence) when a loud noise reverberated through my floorboards, almost shaking all of the teddy bears off the top of my wardrobe.

This kinda made me angry.

You see, not only was I the last to arrive in this family, therefore I got the bedroom which is the size of a gerbil hutch; worse still, I'm also situated directly above the Fantastic Voyage's function room; hence, I've got to endure being woken up some Sunday mornings by noisy christening parties, or even kept awake some evenings by tipsy lunatics singing "I Will Always Love You" over the karaoke.

(Hang on—maybe I am an abused child after all?)

Okay, to be fair, Dad hardly ever hires the function room out these days as he says it's not worth the bother (I think he means my moaning), but it certainly sounded like something was going on down there now.

KEEEEEERRRRWWWAAANNNNNNNNG!!!!

Yep, that sounded like a great big noisy guitar riff to me.

So, after a lot of sighing and throwing myself about my room, blaming my father for my inability to break out of Ability Stream 2 for French, I popped down to stick my shneck around the function room door . . . only to find something so wonderful and unbelievably cool that I fully plan to bore my grandkids senseless with the memories of it when I'm a white-haired, false-hipped old nana.

Jimi Steele and Lost-flipping-Messiah were practicing underneath my bedroom!

I didn't know Dad had said yes to this!

I was frozen to the spot for the first few moments. I even considered running back upstairs, having a shower and ironing my best going-out clothes, then appearing back downstairs in full makeup. But even I could see the vague lunacy in that plan; they might have gone by then. So I stood at the back of the room, watching Jimi and Naz tuning up their guitars and arguing over chords. Now, okay, I *do* remember what I said about becoming a stalker, so I was trying to be cool about it, but heck, I was there long enough to notice how Jimi's sandy hair seems to have acquired gorgeous honey-blond highlights since summer began. (These are certainly, I feel, naturally bleached through all those long outdoors hours Jimi spends in search of nice waxy benches and handrails to skate along.)

Oh, God.

I really do find Jimi so unbelievably gorgeous that I almost feel sick every time I look at him.

Is this normal?

Yes, I know "love hurts," but does it also make you puke and want to sit on the toilet a lot too? Or am I a freak?

The worst thing is, I can't even put my finger on what I actually want to do with Jimi. Do I want to snog him? Or just hang out with him and make him laugh? Or lock him in my room and make him listen to CDs with me? Or maybe I just want to be seen kicking about with him, holding his coat while he practices skating or helping him with his crutches when he has a fall, so all the other Blackwell girls say: "Oooooh, look! That Ronnie Ripperton's going out with Jimi Steele! I'm sooo jealous."

Is that it?

I really don't know, I just know I want to be somehow more part of Jimi's life than I am right now. Anyway, whatever it is I want to do, when I found Jimi actually standing in my home, I settled for standing gazing at him without blinking for so long that my eyes became all dry and fuzzy, like old sweets down the back of the sofa.

Not a good image to portray.

"Hey, Ronnie!" shouted Jimi.

Gulp.

"Oi, oi, it's the landlady!" yelled Naz. "Hey, what do you

think of the show so far, then, Ronnie? Not bad, eh? Considering our singer's tone-deaf, eh?"

Everybody, including me, giggled. Jimi blushed a bit and told Naz to shut his mouth.

"Well, as far as I could hear, you've just sounded like a car crash for the last hour," I chirped. "Have you lot got any actual songs, or just . . . noisy noises?"

"Ooooooh, get her!!!" Naz laughed. "She means you, Jimi, of course."

"I meant all of you," I said, grinning cheekily. "I thought there was a fight going on down here, or something."

I'm not really this cool, I don't need to tell you this, I was just pretending to be cool, and somehow it was working.

"We'd better practice a bit harder, then." Jimi smiled, staring directly at me.

Uccckkk—he was giving me that "nearly hurl" sensation again.

I took the practice bit as my cue to leave, but just as I reached the door, Jimi shouted after me, "And you're in luck, Ronnie, I've checked with our manager. Turns out we ARE free on July twelfth to appear at Blackwell Live. Lost Messiah can be your headline act, eh?"

Jimi flicked his hair out of his eyes and played a loud B chord, shaking the foundations of the room, while Naz looked at him, sort of confused, trying to work out when in the last few hours Lost Messiah had acquired "a manager."

I waited until the sound subsided, cocked my head to the side and said rather cutely, "Well, first you best make sure you're free this Monday after school, cos you'll have to come to the auditions. You know? Exactly the same as everybody else." Then I took a few steps away, turned and added, "Oh, and you better get some singing practice. Because, well, standards are going to be very high."

Then I shimmied out of the door, back up to my bedroom, to further screams of "Ha ha ha! She told you, Steelo, didn't she, eh? You Muppet!" from the rest of Lost Messiah.

What a triumph, eh?!

And, yes, I did remember to pull, not push, the pull door this time.

Chapter 4

the best of times . . .
the worst of times

After all the high spirits and jolly hoo-hah of the past few days, at precisely 3:00 A.M. this morning, I discovered what Mum's been wittering on about all my life when she says: "Things always seem blackest in the middle of the night."

Silly old me thought this was Mum stating the bleeding obvious, like durrrrrr, *of course* it's dark at 3:00 A.M., or else we wouldn't need bedside lamps, would we? And how would we know when to go to sleep? Of course, now I realize that Mum was being "deep and meaningful" and she was actually meaning: "When your worries wake you up in the middle of the night, suddenly they seem bleaker than you could ever imagine."

This is soooo true.

I slid under my duvet last night as a funky, sassy, music-festival-organizing chick who was over the moon with what we'd achieved. But at some point during the wee small hours, the bogeyman crept in, shoveling sackfuls of self-doubt down my earhole.

I tossed and turned for the best part of an hour, sighing,

huffing, then rearranging my pillows thirty-six times, letting Blackwell Live stew in my half-sleepy brain.

Big mistake.

Before long, I wasn't simply terrified. Oh, no, I also became rather irate with the LBD for getting me into this mess. Especially that aggravating Claudette "Venn Diagram" Cassiera. Why can't she just leave things alone? Why is she like a dog with a bone when she has a plan? And why does she ride rough-shod over all my concerns and insecurities? Maybe I didn't really want to do this Blackwell Live thing . . . but now I *have* to!

Grrrrrr.

And as for that Fleur "Microbuns" Swan, this is all her fault too. If she wasn't so ditzy and shallow when it comes to lads, she'd have seen Blackwell Live for the awesome failure it potentially is. And not just as "a really good chance to snog some boys." There is more to life than lads, Fleur Swan! (I hope.)

That's it, I thought. *As of Monday I am resigning from the LBD and commencing kicking about with the Archery Society dweebs. Or I'll be a school loner. Far less trouble.*

But I'm also blaming Mr. McGraw for my worries.

It was ol' gray chops who introduced me to imagining the worst-case-scenario outcome in every situation, including Blackwell Live. I didn't even know what *worst-case scenario* meant until I began Blackwell School and learned that *every single path* you choose to walk in life could have a W.C.S. if you're unlucky.

Say, for example, Blackwell enters a cross-country team in the local championships. Sure, we *might* win loads of medals and get our photo all over the local papers, it *could* be wonderful. But, wait for it; the worst-case scenario would be that we trail in last to every other school, we get our gym kits stolen by local sneak thieves, and then the minibus gets a flat tire, so we have to get towed home.

You didn't think of that, did you?

Bummer, eh?

Or, say in geography you were learning about Jamaica, about its lush tropical climate, local carnivals and gross national productivity. Well, if Mr. McGraw was taking that lesson, he'd point out the strong potential for freak weather conditions, causing the banana harvest to shrivel and a mass typhoid outbreak.

Getting the picture? Life sucks sometimes; get used to it.

So, anyway, at 3:14 A.M. on Saturday morning, I woke up needing the loo, but somehow started contemplating just what the LBD had got themselves into.

Not only had we promised McGraw and Guinevere, as well as the whole school, that we would put on an amazing Astlebury-style music festival with live bands and cheering crowds; we'd also stuck audition posters up and posted it on the World Wide Web too! Everyone was talking about it. There really was no turning back.

Now, every time I closed my eyes, all I could imagine was a big empty playing field and a tearful, disappointed Mrs. Guinevere. Nobody would want to buy our stupid tickets. In fact, as far as I could see, no bands would offer to play our idiotic concert anyhow.

My palms were beginning to sweat.

I mean, imagine if nobody turned up at the auditions?

What if it's just the LBD sitting in the school gym on

Monday, all by ourselves, playing I Spy for an hour, then doing the "walk of shame" through the streets home? We'll never live it down! Okay, I'll admit I wasn't so bothered about looking like a loser in front of McGraw, sheesh, I've had three years' practice doing that.

BUT WHAT ABOUT IN FRONT OF YEAR 11? What about in front of Lost Messiah (who have now started practicing in our function room so I can't even escape their ridicule out of school hours)?

"Aaaaggghhh!" I eventually whispered out loud. "We're going to be the laughingstock of the whole school!"

(NOTE TO SELF: Find out exactly what is "the laughingstock." I have no idea what this means. I just know Magda often threatens people with being it and it's a very bad thing to be.)

So, as you can see, by 3:30 A.M., I'd got myself worked up into a right pickle. In fact, by 4:00 A.M. I'd decided that my only option was to raid the Fantastic Voyage's safe, buy a one-way ticket to Negril in Jamaica, and set up an assumed life under a false identity. (Knowing my luck, I'd get there just in time for all the shriveled banana and typhoid fun.)

How the devil did this happen?

Blackwell Live was the best idea in the world five hours ago!

I texted Claude on the off chance she was still awake (y'know, brokering a Middle East peace deal, or whatever the heck Claude Cassiera does when she stays up all night), but Little C wasn't responding.

Eventually I decided to turn on my TV and see if there was some trashy nighttime movie to take my mind off my woes.

Big mistake.

All that was on at this stupid o'clock hour was the all-night news program on BBC, playing world headlines. They were NOT a barrel of laughs. There was a factory closing in Scotland and five thousand workers were destined to be jobless and penniless; a river had burst its bank in Russia and loads of people had been swept away . . . oh, yes, and a giant panda in Miami Zoo was refusing its meals due to its partner dying.

Grrrrreat.

I felt worse than ever then.

McGraw clearly has got a second job at the BBC producing the Worst-Case Scenario headlines.

Misery really does love company, so at about 5:00 A.M. I was pleased to hear Mum padding about the house, traipsing backward and forward to the loo about four times, then downstairs to the kitchen, where she had a good effort at waking the entire high street up making a snack. I heard a plate smash, some very loud rude words echoing up the stairs, then eventually the TV in the living room springing to life.

Excellent! Mum was up for the day.

I pulled a hooded top over my jimjams and went to tell her that my life was terrible and I needed to leave the country.

Unfortunately, Mum was having an attack of the nighttime blues herself. She was slumped on the sofa, dressed in a big chunky cardigan and tracksuit bottoms, her long brown hair scraped off her face in a high ponytail, watching the same depressing news program as I'd been. On Mum's lap was a plate holding a huge, clumsily made sandwich. Her eyes were a bit red-rimmed, like she'd been crying.

"You're up!" I said.

"Can't sleep, darling. I was, er, a bit hungry," Mum said.

I sat down beside Mum, noticing that her towering sandwich was made from both crusts of the loaf. Banana slices, salami *and* cucumber were escaping from the sides of her culinary creation.

Bleeeeeugh.

Mum was staring at the TV forlornly.

"Stupid panda." Mum sniffed. "He won't eat his bamboo."

Mum nodded toward the screen, which showed a flurry of khaki-clad zookeepers, all shaking their heads, offering a sulky-faced panda various succulent-looking branches.

"I like bamboo shoots," Mum continued, sounding like she was going to start sobbing. "They're very tasty in a hoisin sauce."

Oh, dear.

I wasn't the only one looking for someone to make them feel better. Mum looked terrible, although it had to be said, from the noise she was making with her sandwich, it was making her feel a tad happier. (Especially the layer of marmalade.)

"*Mghhhph,* so what's keeping you awake, young lady?" asked Mum, taking another big bite. "Is this you having a late late night or an early early morning?"

"I've been to sleep," I said. "But I'm awake now. I'm reeeeeally stressed."

Mum sort of laughed.

"Huh, what exactly have you got to be stressed about?" she said. "You're only fourteen!" Then she quickly corrected herself as we've had, like, a hundred arguments before about how stressful it is being me sometimes. "Sorry. Sorry. I mean, what's stressing you out *now?*" Mum said. "I've lost track of where we are. . . . Do you still hate science?"

"Yeah, I hate science."

"But you're trying, aren't you?"

"Of course I'm trying," I lied.

"So it's not *that* you're stressed about?"

"No, I'm reeeeally stressed-out. Science just makes me depressed, that's different."

"Ahh, depressed too?" Mum chuckled. "Depressed *and* stressed? Well, good to see that we made the right choice sending you to Blackwell." Mum wiped her finger across the plate, picking up the last trails of marmalade. "You do know some families actually move house to qualify their kids for your school, don't you?"

"Mmmmm, yeah, you always say that," I said.

Mum *does* always say that.

Mum and me have had some conversations so many times over, like this one about "how lucky I was to get into Blackwell," that we've got this joke that we should just give them numbers and shout them out instead.

"It's not my fault I'm old and senile," Mum says, pretending to be upset.

True, she is quite old, she's almost thirty-nine.

"C'mon then," Mum said. "Tell me the whole story." So I did. I told Mum all about how the LBD really really wanted to go to Astlebury, to which Mum said, "Well, you're not," to which I said, "Ha ha, I already knew that, we're on to plan B now anyhow."

So Mum said, "Why didn't you ask me anyhow? You asked your dad! You think I'm an ogre, don't you?"

So I said, "No, no, you're not . . . you're just a . . . It's just that . . . Oh, God, yes, you ARE an ogre sometimes."

This made Mum look sadder.

So then I told her all about Blackwell Live, and about Claude's plan, and about our meeting with McGraw, then about Guinevere shouting at McGraw. This cheered Mum up loads.

"Ha ha ha . . . *Rocket up his you know where!*" Mum repeated. "That's pretty terrible. You girls shouldn't have heard that, really, y'know? Mrs. Guinevere would get into trouble. . . . Still funny, though." She laughed.

Then I told her about the auditions and all about Lost Messiah, and the website and the tickets . . . by this point I was rabbiting away really quickly, and my palms were sweating again.

"I'm really scared, Mum," I eventually said.

We both stared at the TV again.

When I looked at Mum next, she really was crying, vast rivers of tears flowing down her cheeks.

"I think this is all great!" Mum sniffed.

"You do?"

"Yes, it's a wonderful idea, I'm really proud of you."

"I've not done anything yet . . . and we might mess it all up," I said.

"I'm sure you won't," Mum said. "This is so great. . . . I mean . . . when I had you, I was always worried that . . . well, you know, what if something bad happened to me when you were little? You, well, you'd not be able to look after yourself.

And that used to upset me . . . but now I look at you, and you're like a young woman, you're taking the initiative to do all this great stuff . . . you know? You're doing your own thing. That makes me really happy."

I'd like to be able to say that this was one of those important mother-to-daughter chats, one I'll be able to look back on in years to come, but I'll be honest with you: I didn't have a Scooby-Doo what Mum was blathering on about.

Mum was sitting there peering at me.

"What I'm saying is," Mum continued, "it's not easy being a mum, and the world is such a horrible place to bring a little girl into . . ." *Sniiiiiiiiiffff.* "And I used to worry all the time that sometimes I don't make a very good job of things . . . but then I look at you, and I hear about the things you do . . . and I know that I did all right."

Mum produced almost an entire man-size box of Kleenex from her pocket and blew her nose really loudly; in fact, so loudly that she could have blown a bit of her brain out.

"I've not been a bad mum, have I?" Mum said suddenly. Like my opinion at this moment really mattered.

"What? Of course you've not been a bad mum," I said. What a stupid thing to ask. "Mum! You've been a top mum . . . hang on, you *still are* a top mum. What are you talking about?"

Mum continued, looking at me with her head slightly tilted: "I've just been wondering lately. What kind of a world is this to bring babies into? That sort of thing."

"That's really, er, heavy," I say, rather uselessly.

Mum must be taking this row with Dad really to heart if she's thinking all this crazy rubbish.

81

"Mum, you're being dead silly here. I mean, you're wrong. Totally wrong . . . I mean, I know that me and you fight a lot these days, but most of the time we have a brilliant laugh. You're, like, the coolest mum out of my whole class."

Mum cheered up when I said that.

"How am I *cool?*" she said, dabbing her eyes.

"You just are," I said. Mum creased her brow slightly. "Right, okay . . . ," I said. "Well, you were the only mum I knew when I was a little girl who would flambé my rice pudding at the supper table with a proper chef's blowtorch like on TV cooking programs. Like, *woooooosh!* On fire!"

"Yeah, that was kind of cool," Mum admitted, chuckling. "Probably not very safe, but cool."

"And we used to bake loads of pies and cakes together when I was little. That was excellent . . . I mean, I know we don't bake together that much now, cos it's a bit, well, babyish. But, hey, we can do that sort of thing again if you want?" I said. I felt a bit bad now for always trying to be so independent. Those days were good fun.

"I'm sure we can," Mum announced, smiling. "There'll be more time for babyish things, I'm sure. Everything doesn't have to be serious in this house."

"Nah," I said, grabbing the remote and flicking the channel on to cartoons.

"Ronnie, I really think things are going to be fine with your festival," Mum said. "You're a very competent young lady."

Even though it was Mum saying it, this was still one of the best things anyone has ever said to me.

Then she stood up, announced the kitchen was opening early and padded off.

Next time I saw Mum, later on today, she was throwing around a lump of dough as big as her head and shouting at Muriel, our sous-chef. She seemed to be quite enjoying herself.

Weird.

paddy needs a chill pill

It's now Sunday night. This weekend has totally dragged.

Both Claude and Fleur have been busy doing family stuff. Claude had to go to her cousin Gerrard's house for her great-uncle Leonard's birthday party (*party* is not the term any of the LBD would use to describe such events). Fleur, on the other hand, has had a huge row with Evil Paddy over the family phone bill. She's been addressing this debt by polishing Paddy's BMW and accompanying him to see her gran in the old folks' home. Miss Swan insists she doesn't give a hoot about Paddy and how he feels about her, like she's so rock 'n' roll that Paddy's just a housemate she'd rather be rid of; likewise, Paddy treats Fleur like his evil nemesis, always on the prowl to rid him of his wages. Nice ruse, fellas, but I don't buy this at all: They're as thick as thieves really. They actually enjoy kicking about together, especially at the old folks' home, which is not a barrel of laughs.

Fleur says that when she visits her gran—who is mad, blind, and has only two subjects of conversation, the Second World War and the escalating price of canned peaches—well, it's difficult to work out who in the room wants to be dead the most.

That's really sad, isn't it?

I don't want to ever get that old.

Being abandoned by the LBD sucks. I've tried to occupy my time usefully (I sorted my CDs into alphabetical order and made a list of other CDs I need to buy), I've listened to my new Spike Saunders CD *To Hell and Back* about twelve times and learned all the words to a few tracks, and I've tried my very best to keep my mind off my worries.

Somehow I'm still a heady mixture of anxious and bored rigid.

The thing is, it's tricky trying to be bored at the Fantastic Voyage. If you make it too obvious, there's a good chance Loz or Magda will find you something useful you could be doing. Something like hosing down the cellar, or polishing various brass fixtures and fittings in the saloon bar, or even cleaning the front windows in full view of the high street traffic jam.

You DO NOT, repeat, NOT want that.

Especially not the windows option. Believe me, so many Blackwell kids will travel past you on the bus, grinning their heads off and waving, you may as well place an advert in the school newsletter announcing you're changing your name to Billy No-Mates.

My saving grace has been that it's drizzled all weekend, meaning at least I could skulk alone in my room without my parents harassing me too much. Lordy, if the weekend had been sunny, it would have been a different matter entirely. I've noticed, over the past fourteen years, that the moment the sunshine appears, grown adults seem to become totally obsessed that young people are "making the most of the sun." (Ah, there's a sentence that fills me with dread.) Oh, yes, if the sun even pokes its head from behind a cloud for ten minutes above the Fantastic Voyage, rest assured my parents are straight into my room, poking me with a stick, nagging me to "go out and enjoy the heat wave" and "stop missing the best part of the day" or even "go to the shop and buy ice cream cones for me and your dad."

But as I say, it rained this weekend anyhow and, rather ingeniously, on Saturday morning I took a can of furniture polish and a feather duster into my bedroom, then lay on my bed watching crappy TV with it close at hand. Every time Loz or Magda knocked, I jumped up and pretended to be polishing the same fifty centimeters of window ledge. This has kept them satisfied for the last forty-eight hours.

BRRRRRRR BRRRRRRRR!

Is that the house phone?

It certainly *sounds* like our house phone.

Well, it's not for me, anyway.

Nobody calls me on the house-phone line, not now that I've got my cell phone.

Phhhh, I'm not answering it.

BRRRRRRR BRRRRRRRR!
BRRRRRRR BRRRRRRRR!
BRRRRRRR BRRRRRRRR!

I'm still not answering it. It can ring as much as it likes.

BRRRRRRR BRRRRRRRR!
BRRRRRRR BRRRRRRRR!
BRRRRRRR BRRRRRRRR!

"Ronnnnnnnnnieeee! Answer that flipping phone! We've got a full bar down here! I know you're up there, you lazy little sloth," shouts Dad.

Damn, better answer it.

"Hello," I say. "The Fantastic Voyage Public House and Torture Chamber. Can I help you?"

"Yes, you can, Miss Ripperton, it's Miss Swan here," says Fleur.

"FLEUR!? Why are you calling the house phone?" I say.

"Can I put you on hold a moment?" says Fleur.

"Eh?" I say. I can hear Fleur pressing buttons on her phone.

"Hello, Ronnie, this is Claude," says Claudette's unmistakable voice.

"Excellent!" squeals Fleur.

"Claude, what is going on? Are you both at Fleur's house?"

"No, I'm at my own house!!" says Claude.

"And I'm at my own house too!!" shouts Fleur. "Paddy has had a conference call service fitted to his study phone line! Now we can all talk at once!!"

"Ha ha ha—heeeeellllllllllo!!" we all shout, giggling.

This is truly a momentous occasion. I'm experiencing the full splendor of an LBD meeting from the comfort of my own living room. I need never leave the house again!

"Soooo . . . Good weekend, Ronnie?" asks Fleur.

"Sucky weekend," I correct her.

"Oh, dear, well, what about you, Claude? Fun at Uncle Leonard's?" Fleur asks.

"Hmmm . . . It was a family dinner," grumbles Claude. "Everything was okay till we sat down to eat . . . when I discovered that I'd been put on a separate coffee table in the living room to eat with all the other 'little people.' "

We all groan.

"I spent an hour trying to dissuade my six-year-old cousin from sticking butter beans up her nose."

"Bummer," I say.

"Hang on, Fleur," interrupts Claude. "Weren't you actually grounded this weekend *because* of the phone bill? Should we really be conference calling?"

"Ooooh, no, I wasn't grounded because of how much the phone bill was," sighs Fleur. "Well, not as such. It was something else . . ."

Fleur leaves a long pause.

"Oh, you know what my dad's like," she continues. "He's a total schizoid. Actually, he's downstairs cleaning his guns, declaring war on the Swan family right now, just cos Josh has knocked a side mirror off Mum's Volkswagen." Fleur tuts. "He needs to chill out."

"So, what did you do to get grounded, then?" asks Claude.

"Oh, right, yeah, well, Paddy got this letter through from British Telecom about his private study phone bill," says Fleur. "They said he'd been entered into a sweepstakes for a Special Sunshine Holiday in Martinique—"

"He grounded you for that?" I ask idiotically.

There's bound to be more to it than that.

"Well, no, he was pretty psyched about that, actually. But the letter said that the holiday was for nine people: Paddy and his top eight Friends and Family Numbers," explains Fleur.

"What a totally cool competition!" I say.

"What are Friends and Family Numbers?" asks Claude.

"Oh, something boring about you choosing the people who you spend the most money talking to," says Fleur. "Then you register them with phone company bods and get a discount on the calls."

"Ahhh, I get you," says Claude.

"Well, ahem, except Paddy didn't," says Fleur.

"Does Paddy not like any of his friends and family?" I ask.

"Not enough to call any of them," says Fleur. "So he didn't register any of his numbers."

"So, why are you in trouble?" I ask.

"Well, the stupid phone people automatically registered some for him, going by who he calls the most. So, ahem, this morning Paddy received a letter saying he could be going on a Special Sunshine Martinique Holiday with, ahem, both of you two, Junior Watson, Dion, Johnny Goodman from the lower sixth, oh, yeah, and that lad from Shrewsbury that I snogged in Rimini last year."

"Ouch," we both say.

"No, no, it gets worse," says Fleur. "Also on the list was Paramount Pizza Home Delivery and Lucky House Cantonese Noodle Bar. I've been, ahem, sort of using his study phone when he wasn't looking."

"Noooooooooo!" we both squeal, cringing.

"You are so busted!" I say.

"Tell me about it," sighs Fleur. "I've never seen him so angry. He couldn't speak for about twenty minutes. Then he said I was a luxury he couldn't afford and he was handing me over to social services."

"What did your mum say?" asks Claude.

"She was a proper star, actually." Fleur giggles. "She kept him in his study for about an hour and sent me off around town on some errands. Y'know? Just to calm things down. I could still hear Dad yelling at the end of the road about there being a 'dire mix-up fourteen years ago at the maternity ward' and that he wanted 'his real daughter back.' Ha ha ha!"

Paddy's emotional breakdown has been somewhat lost on Fleur.

"Aww, I feel sorry for your poor dad," announces Claude charitably.

"I do too," agrees Fleur. "He's a lunatic."

"Maybe we should put the phone down and chat tomorrow at school?" I suggest.

"Oh, don't worry, we've only been on the phone about a minute," says Fleur. "Anyway, this is what I was calling about: Blackwell Live."

"Yep. Auditions tomorrow!" chirps Claude. "How cool is that?"

"Really cool!" says Fleur, almost outchirping her.

"I can't wait to see who turns up," squeaks Fleur.

"Oh my God, I hope there's a good turnout. Loads of people promised to come, didn't they?" says Claude.

"Yeah, only like the whole school!" Fleur giggles. "Er, are you still there, Ronnie?"

Silence.

"Ronnie?" says Claude.

"Murrrrrr," I sort of whimper.

"What's up?" my LBD compadres ask.

"Nothing," I say.

"What are you *murrrr*ing for?" asks Claude.

"I'm a bit . . . sort of . . . well, I've been thinking," I begin.

"Oh, dear, what have you been thinking?" says Claude.

"Well, I've been worrying about the whole thing," I say in my feeblest voice. "Maybe nobody will turn up tomorrow and . . ."

I stop my bleating just there.

I don't want to delve into the deepest, darkest caverns of my mind and confess to the LBD what I've been worrying about. Some of it has been plain hideous. I mean, at one point, for example, I was worrying about a faulty speaker setting the Blackwell Live stage ablaze. Bearing in mind that we haven't even got any performers yet, let alone speakers or stages, maybe I'm being a bit daft. I do tend to jump the gun slightly when I'm worrying.

"Oh, Ronnie," sighs Claude. "Don't you dare start being flaky, you know you wind me up when you do this."

"I'm not being flaky," I say, flakily.

"Look, don't fret about the auditions!" says Fleur. "I haven't told you what happened yesterday on my little jaunt down the high street, it was sooo cool, this will stop you worrying."

"Spill it!" commands Claude.

"Well, I set off down Disraeli Road on Saturday morning. I was feeling a bit sucky, but anyway, I got as far as the corner of the high street when something cheered me right up. I saw these Blackwell lads walking toward me, I think they were about Year Seven, they were quite teeny. So, as they got closer, I noticed they were waving and smiling at me."

"Did you know them?" I ask.

"No. But they seemed to know me. They were saying 'All right, Fleur! See you on Monday, we've got something dead good to show you!' Then they ran off laughing and singing."

"That's cool," says Claude. "Ooh, I hope they meant at the auditions. All Year Seven boys usually want to show you are their nose-bogeys."

"I know. But it gets better. So I'm walking down the high street and I spot lots more Blackwell bods like Benny Stark from Year Ten, who was just off to buy drumsticks to practice his new songs, and some Year Eleven gothy, nu-metal types that hang about with Ainsley Hammond. They asked if they could bring BOTH their steel drums to the auditions."

"Ha ha! Did you say yes?" I ask, cheering up right away.

"I said they could bring whatever they wanted." Fleur laughs. "So next, I popped to the dry cleaners to pick up Mum's skirts, and ended up in a long chat with that totally gorgeous Year Eleven lad Christy Sullivan. You know? The lad who works the cash register there on a Saturday? Big eyes? The one with the kind of flared nostrils and the denim jacket?"

"Yeah, I know who you mean, his mum and dad are Irish, they come in the bar sometimes," I say. "He is fairly lush."

"You were talking to him?" says Claude.

"For about twenty minutes. Until that weirdo manageress with the out-of-control perm got annoyed with us. Anyway, he was telling me about how he loves doing karaoke. . . . Oh, and by the way, he was sooo flirting with me, I mean it was embarrassing how obvious he was making it. . . . But, in brief, he said he might pop down to do the Frank Sinatra song that he always does at family gatherings. . . . Cool, huh?"

"Really cool," we both agree.

"Anyway, whatever, by the time I left the dry cleaners and had walked back through the shopping center, bumping into folk all the way along who wanted to talk about Monday, I was beginning to know what celebrities feel like! Honestly, the constant attention can be sooo exhausting." Fleur pauses, then announces triumphantly, "Honestly, birds, EVERYBODY is talking about us!!"

"We'll have to start signing autographs ourselves soon!" jokes Claude.

"Mmm, I know," agrees Fleur. Not at all joking. "I've been having a bit of a practice on the telephone pad."

"So it's going to be a chaotic audition tomorrow, then . . . ," begins Claude with a mild note of anxiety in her voice, probably reaching for her clipboard and notes to begin planning.

"I forgot the best bit!" Fleur says. "I went into the Music Box to buy some CDs!"

Ahhh, the Music Box CD and Vinyl Boutique. On Arundel Road, just behind the shopping center. Little red door, really dark inside. No shopping trip would be complete without it.

"And I saw Jimi Steele and Naz," says Fleur. "And I spoke to them too!"

"What about?" Claude and I ask.

"About the whole Blackwell Live thing. And this really is the best bit . . . they're coming tomorrow and they've written a special song. A special song for us."

"That's fantastic! But hang on, the song's not really for us, though, is it?" Claude laughs, trying to establish some reality into the conversation. A tough call, as Fleur sounds about ready to hyperventilate.

"Well, okay, not 'us,' perhaps," says Fleur. "More especially for Ronnie. I think it's a song for you, Ronnie."

"Fleur, have you been eating extra idiot pills again?" I ask. "What are you talking about?"

"Well, stop me if I'm reading too much into this . . . but right at the end of the conversation, Naz said, 'So, we'll see you on Monday, then?' Naz was being quite cool and acting like he was just saying it in a normal way, like he doesn't fancy me at all. Which, to be honest, I find VERY difficult to believe, but nevertheless . . ."

Claude and I sigh. Fleur continues.

"But then Jimi Steele suddenly blurts out, as if his mouth had started working separate to his brain, 'What about Ronnie, she'll be there, won't she?' Then his face sort of flushed red, cos he realized exactly what he'd said. Y'know? Like it really mattered to him if you were going to be there?"

"Did he?!!" I say, going a bit red too.

"Yep," says Fleur. "And then Naz kicked Jimi's leg and said, 'Oooh, subtle, Jimi! No one would guess you fancy her now, eh?' "

"He did not!" I say.

"He totally did," argues Fleur. "Fact."

"Then what happened?" Claude asks.

"Oh, I sort of walked off, leaving them both giving each other 'dead arms.' I lose interest when boys decide to have play fights. I mean, you'd think Jimi and Naz would have got over giving each other wedgies and Chinese burns by now," sighs Fleur. "Still pretty freaking cool, huh?"

"I'm sure it means nothing," I say (really really hoping this all means something).

"Yeah, I'm sure it means nothing too . . . ," says Fleur, extra-sarcastically.

"You great big premier-league dweeb! OF COURSE it means something! Get off the phone this moment and go and do a face pack, you need to look like Miss Dish Delish for four P.M. to-morrow."

"I hate face packs . . . ," I begin to protest.

But suddenly Fleur lets out a gasp similar to someone in a horror movie who has just realized that Mr. Axe Murderer is in the building with them. "OH MY GOD, FOOTSTEPS! Gotta go! It's Dad! Paddy's gonnakillme. Laterz."

Click.

Bzzzzzzzzz.

At some level, Paddy Swan might have been relieved, grateful even, to know that his new conference call line was running in perfect working order, as tested for him, very kindly, by Les Bambinos Dangereuses.

It was unsaid, but we all agreed that now wasn't the time to inform him.

Chapter 5

give us a tune then . . .

Trust Claudette Cassiera to have brought sandwiches.

"Well, the auditions could go on for hours," Claude insists, drumming her fingers on the Tupperware lid of her lunch box. "I didn't want us to starve. . . . Anyway, Veronica, nobody said you had to eat any of them."

"Er, hang on," I correct her, eying up the stuffed-full box, "I didn't say that. Anyway, what sort are they?"

"Cheese and pickle," Claude says proudly. "And I also brought chocolate muffins. But don't worry, I'll eat them all myself."

"Mmm, muffins," I say, licking my lips. "Are they chocolate chip?"

"They *might* be chocolate chip," teases Claude. "They *might* not. We'll just have to see how nice both of you are to your best friend, won't we?"

Claude places the box back inside her rucksack with a satisfied smirk before jaunting off across the empty gym toward a dusty tower of school chairs.

"Er, excuse me," tuts Fleur. "Sorry to get in the way of your vital muffin discussion, but can someone tip me off to what the plan is for the next few hours?"

Fleur actually looks a tiny bit anxious. That can't be right.

"I mean, what sort of acts are we looking for, anyway?" she says.

It's 3:37 P.M. The end-of-school bell has just rung, and at this moment in time, Blackwell's gym is so deserted, our normal speaking voices are booming echoes. Aside from the LBD, there's a whole lot of nobody here. It's difficult to imagine anybody is beating a path down here, begging to audition. In fact, we might just be getting those muffins out quicker than we planned, just to cheer ourselves up.

"Well, I thought we should leave our options fairly open," Claude suggests. "But we're definitely looking for no more than six different acts."

"Why six?" I say.

"Well, that's how many we'll have time for on the day, I reckon. We're also looking for people who are, er . . . good."

"Good?" sighs Fleur. "Good . . . like, durrrrrrr, Claude . . . of course we want people who are good. What does 'good' mean, anyway? What if we all disagree?"

Claude adjusts her reading specs, exhaling deeply, resisting the urge to batter Fleur about the head with her Blackwell Live folder.

"Fleur, when do we ever agree?"

"Now and then," admits Fleur.

"Precisely," says Claude, trying to separate the top three seats from the stack without being fatally squashed by Chair

Mountain. "But somehow, some way, Fleur, we still manage to get loads of dead cool stuff done, don't we? We'll just have to compromise with each other."

Claude places three chairs upon the varnished floor, then spots the old trestle table at the back of the gym that Mr. Gowan, Blackwell's caretaker, promised the LBD we could use as long as we didn't smash it. (Mr. Gowan is one of those mumbly-grumbly grown-ups who's convinced young people enjoy breaking things just for the fun of it. "I've had that table since 1977. Try not to snap its legs off!" he'd warned us. "We'll guard it with our lives," assured Claude.)

Fleur and Claude begin wrestling with the antique table, fiddling with the pins and screws, gently persuading it to stand up straight. I busy myself wiping dust and grime off our chairs with my pocket tissues.

"What we need to look for, I reckon . . . ," I say, trying to re-call a phrase I heard somebody say on a TV program. "Now, what is it called . . . ? Ah, that's it, the X factor!"

Claude and Fleur both stare at me blankly.

"Blackwell Live's bands and singers need the X factor," I say again.

"What, like in maths lessons?" says Fleur, wiping a dusty hand through her blond locks.

"No, silly, the X factor is what good performers are sup-posed to have and boring ones don't," I explain. "It's that spe-cial thing, like a twinkle in their eye, or the way someone moves. That's what makes them outstanding, isn't it? It's the thing that makes people want to watch them instead of, er, well, doing something else."

"Yeah, I think I know what you mean," agrees Claude, nodding furiously. "Like Spike Saunders!"

"*Exactly* like Spike Saunders." I smile. "I mean, a hundred boys could sing and look cool in videos almost like Spike does, but there's something, really, like, totally . . . er . . ."

"X factor about him?" Claude says, helping me along.

"Yeah, totally X factor about him!" I grin.

"I like his bum," announces Fleur, somewhat missing the point.

"Yes, Fleur, we all like his bum," says Claude, shaking her head. "But we didn't travel two hundred miles on a bus last year and pay stacks of cash to see Spike just to see his bum, did we?"

"I did," says Fleur, winking at me.

"Oh, lordy," says Claude, trying not to laugh at Fleur, as we both know it simply encourages her.

Claude takes out a notebook and writes *X factor?* in big letters on a fresh page. Silently, I pity some of the poor souls determined to impress Claude this afternoon. Inadvertently, I've just made their job fifty percent harder.

Eventually our judges bench is erected at the far end of the gym; three chairs sit behind it, facing toward the vast empty floor. Claude has unlocked the cupboard containing the gymnasium's rather lame stereo system: a small CD player, radio and tape deck so ancient that it possibly belonged to Jesus before he kindly donated it to Blackwell School. After a few false starts, Little C soon works out how to blast tunes from the two main gymnasium speakers (a technical task that took Mr. McGraw the best part of five years to master).

"Ooh, I hope people bring CDs and tapes to sing along with," Claude worries aloud, strolling around the perimeters of the gym, checking for power sockets just in case people want to plug electric guitars or synthesizers in.

"Yeah, me too." Fleur giggles. "We can always just turn the volume up to MAX if they sound too awful."

"Fleur Swan, shame on you!" Claude says, wagging her finger.

In truth, I've tried imagining what on Earth I'll do if people are really really dreadful; cunningly I've decided that I'll pretend to get something vitally important out of my rucksack, like a new pen or something, then I'll place my entire head inside and have a good old hoot. Cruel, but necessary.

"Come on, girls, we've got to be kind to everyone, no matter how awful they are," says Claude, being the voice of reason as ever.

Jeez, Claude Cassiera really does believe all that baloney about how "It's not how good you are at something, it's the taking part that counts," which is quite clearly rubbish if you ask me. Nobody was "kind" to me last term when I trudged home last out of forty in the 400-meter race, were they?

Yes, okay, I did walk the last two laps, and sit down at one point for a rest, but nobody said, "Well done, Ronnie! You did really well for just turning up and wearing your gym knickers the right way around anyway! That was really fantastic!" No, everyone was extremely rude indeed, especially Mrs. Wood, our PE teacher. She said she'd seen three-legged races run faster, then she suggested I do it on a moped next time. Everybody almost wet themselves laughing.

If I were a cruel person, these Blackwell Live auditions could be my revenge on a school that mocks me.

Good job I'm lovely, eh?

"Now, while I remember," says Claude, "I need someone to be in charge of collecting phone numbers. Who wants to do that?"

"I can do that," cheeps Fleur enthusiastically. "When do you want me to ask for them?"

"Well, I thought," says Claude, nabbing the table's central seat and placing three notebooks and pens down, "just before a band or a singer performs, we'll take a contact number for them. Then later on, back around your place, we'll decide who's in and out and call them with the good news. That sound all right?"

"Good plan," says Fleur, raising one eyebrow mischievously. "And even better than that, we'll have loads of really cool lads' phone numbers too, won't we."

I have to laugh this time.

"Yes, we will, Fleur," says Claude. "But we won't be abusing this privilege by phoning them for other reasons at a later date, will we?"

"No, we certainly won't, Claudette," Fleur says, shaking her head.

As Claude looks for more highlighter pens, Fleur winks again at me. It takes an iron will not to giggle at her.

"Er, excuuuuse me . . . ," echoes a voice from the far end of the gym.

Our first performer has arrived!

"Am I too early? Shall I go away for a bit?"

Aha, it's Chester Walton, a sporty Year 10 lad infamous for wearing far too much hair gel, the collar of his blazer perpetually turned up and an abundance of very fragrant body splash. I can smell Chester right at this moment from over 200 meters away.

"No, Chester, it's three fifty-eight P.M.," says Claude charitably. "We can kick off a little early just for you. Please register your details with Fleur, then . . . well, do whatever you want. It's your call."

"Wonderful, wonderful," says Chester, smiling with all of his teeth. "And before I begin, can I just take this opportunity to tell you ladies how exceptionally radiant you're all looking today."

"Thanks, Chester," I groan. "So are you."

Chester swaggers up to Fleur, who immediately begins cocking her head to the side and gurgling like a drain.

"Especially you, Fleur Swan," continues Chester. "If your eyes got any bluer, I'd be tempted to change into my Speedo and dive straight into them. They're like the Pacific Ocean."

(No, he really did say this. I'm not making it up.)

"Oooh, Chester, shutttup, stopppppit, stop being silly!" says Fleur, losing all power over her brain cells. "Tee hee hee. Anyway, what's your phone number?"

"Oooh, Fleur, why do you want my phone number?" teases Chester. "Do you want to take me out on a date one night? Is that what you're saying?"

"Noooo, shuttttup, not at all, ha ha hee hee," simpers Fleur. "It's just that—"

"We want your number," Claude butts in rather harshly,

"so that in the slim chance you're not rubbish, we can contact you."

What was that Claude was saying about being kind to everyone?

"Ah, I see," says Chester, undeterred. "But I don't think you'll be disappointed in what I have to show you."

Chester walks over to the stereo, stopping midway to examine his reflection in a nearby window, ensuring his collar is extra sticky-uppy, before inserting a CD into the stereo and pressing PLAY. Suddenly, the air fills with saxophones and cymbals; it sounds like the introduction to a rather old-fashioned jazz number. After a few bars, Chester pulls a hairbrush from his pocket and begins to croon.

"This one is going out to all the *laydeez* in the house tonight," says Chester, pointing individually at all three LBD members. "And I feel so very lucky to have such a beautiful audience, to hear me sing such a beautiful song. Which goes a little something like this . . ."

"He is NOT playing at Blackwell Live," announces Claude under her breath before Chester has even sung a note.

"Ooh, wait on, Claude, this is going to be good." I laugh. "He's not even started yet, give him a chance!"

With an open mind and a heavy heart, we gave Chester "a chance."

"Sometimes when a man lurrrves a woman.
A wooman like yooooou
It's hard.
Ooh, you know it's haaaaaard?"

It wouldn't have been so hideous if Chester Walton could actually sing, but the boy couldn't find a note, let alone hold the same one for more than two seconds.

"Isn't he great?!" coos Fleur, clapping along.

Claude and I exchange withering looks.

"Thanks, Chester," says Claude as he finishes his final chorus, ending up somehow on his knees in front of the table. "We'll be in touch."

Chester stands up, blows each one of us a kiss, then makes his way through the small crowd gathered around the gym door, high-fiving some of the lucky, lucky souls who caught his performance.

"Oh my God! Are all these people here to audition?" says Claude. "There's flipping loads of them! Please make some of them better than Chester Walton."

I stand up to get a proper look. Claude hasn't spotted the long winding queue stretching right along the corridor and into the lower school cloakrooms.

"There's about two hundred people!" I say, shaking my head in disbelief.

"I told you so!" says Fleur, pocketing a spare copy of Chester's phone number.

Claude takes a deep breath and regains her cool, beckoning in the next Blackwell bod.

"Constance Harvey," announces a redheaded Year 9 girl. "I've not brought a CD or anything, I'll just sing a cappella," she says confidently.

"Ooh, go on then, when you're ready." Claude smiles.

In seconds, Constance is in full tunesome flow, bellowing

out a heartfelt rendition of an old country-and-western song called "Stand by Your Man."

Constance, to give her credit, is really putting 110 percent effort into this audition, so I shouldn't be harsh. And it's not that she's a bad singer; it's just she's not a very good one either. I'm not overly keen. I mean, call me Mrs. Unnecessarily-Harsh-Pants, but I don't like the strange half-American accent Constance chooses to sing in (when I know full well she lives four streets away). Or the fact that she keeps waggling her arms about on the choruses like a demented windmill.

Ugggggggh! I was getting that really jittery 3:00 A.M. feeling again, aided and abetted by that ever-burgeoning queue of Blackwell bods carrying xylophones, trumpets and flutes.

"I want X-factor people playing Blackwell Live," I mutter quietly to Claude. "This is a PROPER music festival. Like Astlebury. Not a circus freak show."

Thankfully, Constance sings a shorter version of "Stand by Your Man" than I remember.

The red-haired diva looks to the LBD pleadingly.

"Thanks, Constance, that was really, er, something," announces Claude without a hint of falseness. "We'll have a think and be in touch."

"Fine, suit yerself," says Constance, flouncing away with her snub nose pointed skyward.

Claude looks at her watch, shaking her head.

"Right, girls, we're going to have to get through these acts a bit quicker," she says, but her nag ends there as Fleur interrupts her loudly, leaping to her feet with both hands on her skinny-bilinky hips. Fleur sounds furious.

"OOH! LOOK WHAT THE CAT'S DRAGGED IN!" snarls Fleur, her eyes shining with anger. "IF IT ISN'T MY LONG-LOST FRIEND DION JAMES?!"

And it is too.

It is quite beyond belief that Dion—last spotted over a week ago snogging Fleur (proper snog, mind? Tongue swirly about and everything) outside her house on Disraeli Road and promising to call her to arrange another date before disappearing off the face of the planet—has the sheer audacity to make an appearance at the LBD auditions. But here he is, clutching an acoustic guitar with a stupid sheepish smirk plastered all over his unwashed face. Dion James must either be far far stupider than he looks (impossible), or he's got some weird twisted death wish.

"Awww, give me a break, Fleur," moans Dion, hopping nervously from one foot to another. "I've been meaning to call—"

"HOW ARE YOU GOING TO PLAY YOUR GUITAR WITHOUT FINGERS?" yells Fleur.

"Wah? Er, I . . . ," mumbles Dion, checking his eight fingers and two thumbs are still attached to his hands. "Fleur, I've got my fingers, look!"

"OH, YOU HAVE, HAVE YOU?" shrieks Fleur. "Well, they've obviously been out of working order for the last WHOLE WEEK as you couldn't use your cell phone, could you? You lying, horrible piece of rubbish, Dion. Take your guitar and shove it . . ."

Thankfully, as I cower under the desk, Claude takes control of this brewing, very public LBD hoedown. Gaggles of Year 7 girls and boys stand watching, totally transfixed by the unfolding drama. This is better than TV.

"Fleur, Fleur, pipe down. We've got to be professional about this," Claude says, turning stiffly to Dion, adjusting her specs with her finger.

"Now, Dion. Despite you being lower than a wood louse, and sneakier than a snake, you do have a guitar, so get on with it and make it quick."

"Cheers, Claudette," coos Dion.

Dion, looking more like a ferret than I ever remembered him, strums the opening guitar riffs to a little ditty he has penned himself.

He opens his mouth widely, displaying fawn-colored teeth, and sings the first lines.

"Bab-ee you're the one I want /
I wanna take you in my arms,"

sings Dion, looking at the floor, the ceiling, his shoes, anywhere except at Fleur.

"I wanna run with you in open fields /
And keep you away from harm."

The LBD look at each other mischievously, then glare straight at Dion, chorusing merrily and in a spectacular outburst of togetherness: "NEXXXXXXT!"

"That was lovely, Dion, don't call us, we'll call you." Claude smiles.

Ha ha ha, you don't mess with the LBD, I think to myself proudly.

Dion shuts up abruptly. Well, for a second at least, before

yelling something extremely rude that, as a young lady, I'd prefer not to repeat; then he stomps toward the door, leaving everyone in the gym giggling mercilessly.

"Thanks, girls," says Fleur, genuinely touched. "Dunno what I'd do without you."

"No problem, Fleur," says Claude simply, "never liked him anyway," before beckoning to the door: "CAN WE HAVE THE NEXT PERSON, PLEASE?! COME ON, KEEP IT MOVING NOW, PEOPLE!"

Fun? Perhaps. But despite this drama, it was fair to say that the last half hour had gleaned nothing of even slender promise for Blackwell Live.

Well, unless we planned to spend the entire festival summoning Fleur's horrible ex-boyfriends onto the main stage, then humiliating them (which, hey, I'd have bought a ticket to see, but I'd wager the rest of Blackwell probably would not).

Thank Jehovah for Christy Sullivan, who ambled in next.

True to his word, exactly as he'd promised Fleur in the dry cleaners, Christy was here, with a cheeky grin, clutching a CD of orchestral Frank Sinatra songs to his rather muscular chest.

"This is one my gran makes me sing for her every Christmas," announces Christy as the introduction blasts through the air. Just a tiny hint of a blush seems to cross his cheeks when he realizes what he's just admitted.

"Awwwww," choruses the LBD plus all the females in the gym. "That's really sweet!"

The thing is, Christy can get away with the gran confession as he's got lovely big brown eyes and he's . . . well, he's just an all-around smashing sort of lad. I mean, okay, he's no Jimi Steele in my opinion, but hey, who is? I know certainly that if anyone else admitted they sang for their gran, they'd have sounded really lame, but from Christy's lips it sounded really cool. Cleverly, Christy must have done a quick clothes changeover in the loos before he arrived, meaning he really cuts a dash from the crowds of black blazers and gray school trousers that surround him; he's wearing a tight black short-sleeved T-shirt and rather expensive-looking dark green combat trousers, showing off well-toned thighs.

Sigh.

Christy definitely has a certain special something about him. He's quite impossible to stop goggling at, even if he is singing "Fly Me to the Moon," a song that was number one on the charts in about 1802. And sing? Christy can really sing! Big bursting notes and proper melodies too!

"He's a bit X-factor-y, isn't he?" murmurs Fleur, doodling on her notebook.

I'm sure if we'd not been sitting beside her, Fleur would have been practicing writing *Mrs. Fleur Sullivan* over and over again in swirly handwriting, or even adding up the letters in both of their names to find the percentage that Christy loved her. Okay, Fleur *alongside* the entire female contingent of the gym, who are all watching Christy with glazed expressions on their faces. In fact, most of them even have their heads rested in their hands, just gazing at Christy like they were gazing at a big basket of fluffy kittens.

"That was great, Christy!" says Claude as he finishes, drawing a big tick on her notebook beside his name. "Er, but one thing. Do you sing any modern stuff? I mean, that's a bit old-fashioned for what we need. No offense, mind."

"Aw, well, none taken, yeah, I know what you mean," says Christy, really blushing now. "I can sing whatever you want, really, ladies. Pop songs, rock songs, er, I've even got some of my own songs that I wrote at home. Me and my brother Seamus in Year Thirteen write our own stuff, you see, he plays the keyboards."

"That's great!" says Claude. "Very promising."

"I didn't know you had a big brother," says Fleur dreamily.

Christy collects his CD and his schoolbag, giving Fleur a little wink as he bids us good-bye. Fleur twinkles her fingers back. As ever, I've become mysteriously invisible in the vicinity of my taller, curvier, blonder pal.

"Thanks for coming, Christy," I add anyway. "We'll be in touch when we've had a good think about things."

As Christy Sullivan leaves the room, fading to a snuggly memory in the hearts of a hundred Blackwell schoolgirls, Fleur turns to us both and says, rather unconvincingly, "He was rubbish, wasn't he?" She winks. "I mean, really bad."

"Atrocious," says Claude with a big grin across her face.

We all fall about in girlie giggles. Christy Sullivan was indeed wondrous. Blackwell Live has its first act!

gotta sing! gotta dance!

And after Christy came the dancing girls.

Sheesh. I didn't realize that so many Blackwell kids took after-school classes at the Anouska Smythe School of Dance, the local dance school. Honestly, I didn't.

I thought most kids just lay about in each other's bedrooms from four P.M. onward, listening to loud music and putting off doing their homework like me, Fleur and Claude do. Well, that was until I sat through four girls, one after another, clad in tight-fitting leotards, chunky leg warmers and sweatbands. Every one pirouetting, leaping and high-kicking to classical music until I felt quite, quite bilious.

They're all so flipping energetic, I think. I bet they don't get lapped by the asthmatic kids when they're doing the 1500 meters, like I do.

"And can I just tell you," gushes one tiny blond girl, "that I'm so excited about this opportunity to perform for you!" The silver ribbons tying up her curly locks match the girl's sparkly ballet pumps exactly. "I mean, I've been singing and dancing around the house since I was, like, two years old or something!"

"Great," the LBD all say.

"And can I just add that everybody in my family, as well as Anouska Smythe herself, says I'm going to be a worldwide superstar!" she says.

"Really?" says Claude.

"Really!" Blondie squeaks before twirling into the distance, a flurry of arms, legs and curls.

"Good," says Claude. "NEXT."

"Did you bring any headache pills?" whispers Claude, touching her scalp. "I think I'm getting a migraine. This is quite stressful, isn't it?"

"Sorry, mate, I've not got any," I say, noticing Matthew Brown, a Year 10 lad, approaching us.

"Hang on, I have," announces Fleur, delving into her rucksack. "Er, but wait a second," she says, furrowing her brow. "Why is Matthew Brown carrying a large teddy bear?"

We all look up at the next audition waiting to do his turn: She's right, he is holding something very bearish. But it's not quite a teddy bear, that's far too cute a word for the disheveled, manky stuffed animal that Matthew is clutching to his chest.

"Errr . . . Matthew?" begins Claude with a puzzled expression.

"Good afternoon, ladies," says the boy. "I am Matthew Brown and this is Mr. Jingles, the amazing talking bear . . ."

"Oh my God, he's a ventriloquist, isn't he?" I shudder. I feel exactly the same about ventriloquists as I do about jugglers. They depress me.

"Let's see if he can do it first." Fleur giggles, waving at the furry freak show. "Hello, Mr. Jingles! How are you today?" she says.

"I'm gelly well, Gleur!" says Mr. Jingles, damn, I mean, says Matthew. I don't know how I'm possibly getting confused. My granny Tish could see Matthew's lips moving from half a mile away, and she's only in possession of one good eye. I've seen ventriloquism before; this is not the dictionary definition.

"Mr. Jingles, what have you been up to today?" continues Matthew to the moth-eaten museum piece.

"Gwell, Maffew," says the bear, "I've bween gwatching twelivision!"

Thankfully, Claude has seen enough.

"Matthew, this is a music festival audition," interrupts Claude quite firmly. Obviously Mr. Jingles has tested her patience. "What's with the ventriloquism?"

"Aha, but we haven't got to the singing, tap-dancing part yet! Have we, Mr. Jingles?" says Matthew, turning to the tufty puppet.

"Gno, we gwhaven't!" says the bear, shaking its head.

"But Matthew, we have got to the end of your allotted time. Sorry," says Claude, tapping her watch and tutting.

This alone seems to annoy Matthew Brown a great deal. In fact, long after he's huffed and puffed out of the gym with Mr. Jingles slung over his shoulder, we can still hear him fuming about "people not recognizing great talent when they see it." He's probably out there now joining forces with the squeaky curly-blond superstar girl, cooking up a plot to storm LBD HQ and batter us to death with his stuffed bear. Could these auditions get any worse?

Claude was looking a little weary by now too, so I prescribed a chocolate muffin to cheer her up. Little C smiles and begins searching in her rucksack. And boy, was Claude going to need cheering in light of the Blackwell Bellringing Society, who have just arrived en masse, proceeding to ding-dong merrily and on high (one of them even stood on the vaulting horse, clanging away) until the LBD begged for sweet mercy.

"Bellringing and migraines DO NOT mix," mumbles Claude, spitting chocolate chips all over her paperwork.

the lost boys

Of course, by this point the very blatant nonappearance of Lost Messiah (and more crucially Jimi Steele) is playing on my mind.

The possibility that I've been blown out began as a tiny seed of insecurity an hour ago, blossoming with each ticking second of the gym clock into a whole forest of self-doubt.

"Lost Messiah coming down to perform a special song for us"? Pah. Yeah, right.

"Jimi wanting to know especially if I was going to be there"? As if. My behavior of late is taking the term "dweeb" to previously unseen depths.

I could give myself a slap for believing the stuff that Fleur comes out with. I mean, it's not that Fleur's a liar, it's just that you have to take a lot of the things she says with a large pinch of salt cos she tends to exaggerate. But when she's saying something that you desperately want to hear more than anything else in the world, it's difficult to stick your fingers in your ears and play the "Can't Hear You" game, isn't it?

I stand up, scanning the line hopefully for Jimi's floppy locks or Naz's spiky shark's-fin haircut. No Aaron, no Danny, no Tyson: no Lost Messiah.

Nothing.

Total blowout.

Never mind, I don't give a hoot anyhow. Not that much. It's not like I made a special effort to look nice today or anything. It's not like I hardly slept a wink last night for going over my imaginary script of what I'd say to Jimi when he showed up.

Suddenly Claude lets out a little gasp, disturbing me from my worries. Another act has arrived; another act that isn't Lost Messiah.

"Liam?" Claude says. "What are you doing here?"

"These are the auditions, aren't they?" says Liam Gelding,

his silver earring glinting in the late-afternoon sun. "Why do you think I'm here?" Liam has an electric guitar strapped around his chest, and he's holding sheets of paper with what looks like song lyrics scrawled all over them.

"We'll just set up quickly, then," Liam says, gesturing to the rest of his, er, band: Benny Stark (plus trademark mad curly hair) and a girl holding a guitar and a snare drum.

I'm truly stunned to see Liam Gelding here at Blackwell Live's auditions. I mean, Liam's in our form, so we see him more than most folk . . . but hang on. Liam Gelding adding weight to a Blackwell after-school activity? This just isn't Liam at all. Liam's exactly the sort of lad who'd call us nerds for even dreaming up Blackwell Live in the first place. I sat with him for an hour today in PSE and he never even spoke, let alone mentioned his band.

Freaky.

"We're called Guttersnipe," mutters Benny to Fleur.

Fleur writes the name down dutifully as Guttersnipe's rather fearsome blond bass player, apparently called Tara, plays a deafening *therwwwwwwwwwang,* checking her amp's working.

It certainly is: The table has just reverberated.

"I'm set to go when you lads are," Tara announces, holding a guitar pick between her teeth.

Wow. Tara really does look fantastic with that guitar. I must remember to ask Mr. Foxton tomorrow exactly why I've wasted three years farting about on a glockenspiel when I could have been mastering bass guitar. By now, I could look exactly like Tara: cool, powerful and totally intimidating. You don't really get that look with two mallets playing "Old MacDonald."

114

As Tara and Benny prepare, Liam hovers center stage, strumming the occasional chord and looking slightly jittery.

"C'mon, Benny, get a move on," Liam starts to nag.

But just what Liam Gelding plans to contribute to Guttersnipe is really puzzling me. You see, I'm pretty sure Liam can't even read or write properly, so I don't suppose mastering lead guitar is high up on his things-to-do list either. I'm not being a bitch here, before you start thinking it, I'm being truthful. I really like Liam, but there's a bit of a story attached to him. He's just a bit "wild," as my mum would say. You see, during Year 8, Liam sort of stopped turning up at Blackwell, preferring to hang around the Westland Shopping Mall instead. Liam Gelding proved to me that if you wanted to "opt out" of school, it could be done. Easily. And even when he did show up, he did stupid things like climbing up on the school roof or swearing at teachers, which meant that Mr. McGraw kicked him out again, *tout de suite*.

"Suits me fine," Liam would snort, heading for the gate.

Claude knows Liam a lot better than I do.

Bless her, she popped around to Liam's flat several times during Year 8 with projects and course work . . . but Liam was hardly ever home. One night, at LBD HQ, Claude got a bit upset and remarked that even when Liam did get suspended from Blackwell, it wasn't like anyone back home cared.

Anyway, I shouldn't gossip.

That's really as much as I know about Liam Gelding. Claude's very tight-lipped about what else she knows. It's cool, however, that Liam is turning up for school a bit more in Year 9. Sheesh, some days he even stays right though till 3:30 P.M. and everything.

• • •

"So, er, we'll just begin then, shall we?" mumbles Liam, fiddling with his hair.

"Yeah, when you're ready," says Claude.

"Okay, cool," says Liam. "Right. A-one, a-two, a-three, four, five . . ."

All at once Guttersnipe strike up a tune, Liam on lead guitar, Benny on a snare drum, Tara on bass. They're a tiny bit shaky and maybe even a touch off-tune, but extremely good nevertheless. Tara's belting out a chunky, quite complex bass line, jutting her hips in time to the notes, while Liam concentrates sternly on his fingers . . . concentrating harder than I've ever seen him in his whole life. Guttersnipe's bitter sound is far more serious than anything we've heard so far today, which is a welcome change after so many happy-go-lucky tunes and "I love you" ballads. And when Liam eventually sings, although it's more of a husky whisper, the hairs on the back of my neck stand up on end.

> *"You believed in me*
> *You didn't believe the hype*
> *And there's no one really like*
> *Really like you*
> *Who*
> *Well, you know what I'm really like . . ."*

This is one of Liam's many verses. It's certainly a good song, and I can't help wondering who the heck Guttersnipe stole it off.

And as Liam sings his heart out, the whole room is transfixed by the blond, pale-green-eyed lad, beguiled for once by his voice and considerable stage presence instead of some idiotic episode he's been part of.

"Er, Claude . . . did you know Liam plays guitar?" I whisper.

"No . . . no, I didn't," says Claude. "He's certainly a man of mystery." Claude chuckles.

"This lot are really good!" announces Fleur. "Whatcha reckon?"

"Yep, I agree," I say, watching Tara's nimble fingers jealously. As Guttersnipe finish their number, the entire gym breaks into applause. Liam's cheeks redden, then he throws back his shoulders as if he was expecting that all along.

"Cheers, er, everyone," he says. "That song was called 'Promise.' "

"It's a track off our new album." Benny sniggers.

"Yeah, our album that'll be released just as soon as we get around to writing another twelve songs," adds Tara dryly.

"Well, cheers for coming," says Claude, clearly still a little stunned by Liam's hidden talent. "Er, Liam." Claude lowers her voice. "When did you begin playing the guitar?"

"Well, don't you always nag me to get a hobby, Claudie?" says Liam.

"Yeah . . . yeah, I do." Claude shrugs. "But when did you ever listen to anything I say?" Claude half-jokes.

"I know. I can't be feeling well," replies Liam, almost back to his cocky self. "I'll have to keep an eye on myself. Got a reputation to keep up an' all that, eh?"

"Benny, we've got your number, we'll be in touch."

"Whatever, man," mutters Benny from underneath his heap of hair.

"Oh, and Liam?" says Claude, extremely quietly now so that only the LBD can really hear her. "I didn't see you in the lunch hall today."

"Nah," he says.

"I've got sandwiches," says Claude, rattling her lunch box. "Can I tempt you?"

Liam's eyes widen.

"Cheers, Claude." Liam smiles. "I'm starving. You're an angel." Liam helps himself to some food before wandering out of the gym with pickle all over his face and a muffin under his arm.

Fleur and I roll our eyes at each other.

"Right!" says Claude rather officiously. "Mr. Gowan's going to be in here playing merry hell soon, he'll be wanting to lock up. Let's get this show moving, shall we? Who have we got now?"

"Lost Messiah," announces Fleur.

"Really!? Are they here?" I say, brightening up, reaching for my lip gloss, straightening my ponytail and craning my neck to spot Jimi, all at the same time.

"No. Not really," says Fleur, sniggering. "They're still not here, but there's some more kids from the Anouska Smythe Dance School next up if you're interested."

"I hate you, Fleur," I say.

"I know," says Fleur, sniggering even louder.

Just when I thought I couldn't face another high kick, a change of pace comes in the form of Frank Gillespie, a huge, six-feet-tall chunk of lad who goes by the Blackwell nickname of Shop (so nicknamed because he spends every breaktime making pilgrimages to the local shop to stock up on sweets and pies. See, I told you Blackwell kids were cruel, didn't I?). Shop's clad in a pair of electric blue brogues boasting turquoise laces, and within seconds he's in full flow, singing . . . you've guessed it . . . "Blue Suede Shoes" by Elvis Presley. Shop has quite obviously practiced his act for many long hours in front of his bedroom mirror, and when his time's up, he can't quite get out of character.

"Cheers, Shop! That was grrrreat!" shouts Fleur. "No, really. It was."

"Huh, thankyouverymuch, little lady," drawls Shop, curling his top lip just like Elvis Presley, the King of Rock 'n' Roll himself, before attempting to walk with dignity out of the gym. No mean feat for a fifteen-stone lad wearing a pair of neon-blue shoes four sizes too large for him.

"Those shoes are enormous!" squeals Claude. "They must belong to Shop's dad, he's the only person in the surrounding area I can think of who's bigger than Shop!"

"Big shoes doth not make a good performer, Claudette," mutters Fleur with a worried expression.

As the LBD begin a small, heated argument about the merits of Shop and his possible involvement in Blackwell Live (me arguing that Shop is cool, funny, and any grown-ups who bought tickets would like him; Fleur arguing that Shop should be arrested for "crimes against music" and she'd rather watch Matthew Brown and Mr. Jingles again than include "that big buffoon"), a growing mumble of excitement begins to creep through the gym. Just as Claude is about to lose patience and bang our heads together, a rather arrogant voice cuts in.

"Ahem. If you're not too busy with your little squabble, children," says the plummy rasp, "we'd like to make a start with things. Thank you."

We all look up at once to see the unmistakable face of Panama Goodyear glowering down at us. Panama's sleek brown chin-length bob is pulled back by her trademark prim scarlet velour headband, her cold hazel eyes look disdainfully at the LBD, almost as if we're maggots she'd found crawling in her lunch box. As ever, Panama is dressed immaculately in perfect black Lycra trousers that taper stylishly to the heel of her incredibly pricey Prada sports shoes, her matching corseted boob tube clinging to every curve of her generous bust and toned torso.

"Or shall we just stand here while you twitter on?" continues Panama, turning to the rest of Catwalk, her band.

"Huh-huh!" sniggers Abigail and Leeza, both equally as chic, clad in designer dance-studio outfits and coordinated sneakers.

"I mean, I don't know about you people," Panama says for the whole gym to hear, "but I'm on the edge of my seat wondering whether these kids will allow us to play at their little concert, aren't you all?"

Fleur rolls her eyes, placing the cap back onto the top of her pen.

"I've tossed and turned all night, haven't you, Abigail darlink?" mocks Panama.

"Oh, totally," says Abigail, flicking around her white-blond dead-straight locks.

"Well, we're ready for you now," says Claude, trying to sound unintimidated.

"Good, good," says Panama sniffily. "Now, we thought we'd do the routine today that we performed for the Wicked FM Roadshow 'Search for a Pop Band' quarterfinals."

Groan. I was wondering how long it would take Panama to bring the Wicked FM competition up. That was under eleven seconds, possibly a world record.

"I mean, *everybody,* even all of the DJs and important record company executives in the audience that day, loved that one, didn't they, Zane?" brags Panama.

"Oh, yeah, loved it. Everyone loved it," bleats Zane, one of the male members of Catwalk. Zane seems to have gone overboard with the fake tan today. Although his neck is quite pale, his head is a strange streaky tangerine color.

I don't dare risk a chuckle.

"Oh, everybody just loves Catwalk. It's a fact," pipes up Derren, Panama's other dismal henchman: a boy with dance trousers so tight, I can see what brand his underwear is.

Sadly, and I hate to say this, Zane and Derren might have a point here about Catwalk being ultrapopular. Everyone in the gym, aside from the LBD, is slavering and fighting for a prime place to watch these local microcelebrities perform.

"And the *Local Daily Mercury,* they adore us too," interjects Leeza all of her own accord, which shocks me, as I'd always had concerns that she was battery-operated and didn't move without Panama on her remote control. "They put us on the front page, didn't they?" Leeza asks nobody in particular. "With the headline *Catwalk Strut Toward Superstardom!"*

"Oh, shut up!! SHUT UP!" . . . is what I want to shout. "You only flipping got through to the quarterfinals of a stupid local dance competition, you annoying little Muppets. And you, Zane Patterson! You can't brag, your head looks like a clementine orange!"

But I don't shout that, of course. I just sit there quietly, waiting for them to stop waffling on.

"As I said, whenever you're ready," repeats Claude, her expressionless face giving away none of her annoyance.

"Fine," says Panama, taking a CD from her Gucci rucksack. She places it into the CD player, gathering her little family around her for a pre-show group hug.

"Good luck, everyone. Break a leg!" Panama shrills pretentiously.

"Or your necks," mutters Fleur under her breath.

And they're off. And from the very first beat of the track, Catwalk spring into all-singing, all-dancing action, with Panama grabbing center stage straightaway with all the most breathtaking dance steps and highest notes. I can't deny it, Catwalk can really dance, exactly like the people you see on MTV, and they can sing too, even if Panama does steal the show a bit, wiggling her bum and letting out the occasional piercing scream.

Unfortunately, I've seen Catwalk performing this track, called "Running to Your Love," many times before. Following Catwalk's success in the Wicked FM competition, Mrs. Guinevere arranged numerous school performances so we could all "share their happiness."

All it did, as far as I was concerned, was make Catwalk's heads even more grotesquely swollen.

"Oooh, baby. I'm floating in the sky!
Like a big love pie!
You make me feel real high!
Oh, my Oh, my
Tra la la la!"

Panama sings as the rest of Catwalk run on the spot and do star jumps behind her.

"You see, I told you Shop was talented," I whisper to Fleur.

Yet, regardless of how the LBD feel about Catwalk, the irrefutable fact was the rest of Blackwell loved them. If you took a quick look around the gym, everybody was clapping along and whistling (including some teachers, who must have been en route to their cars when they heard the opening notes of "Running to Your Love," dropped their briefcases and sprinted back). Everyone was lapping up Catwalk's foot-perfect dance routine and five-part harmonies.

"They're excellent," coos one girl, her eyes alive with joy.

On the closing bars, a rapturous applause explodes, filling the whole gym. Panama looks around at the audience with a meek, ever-so-humble, slightly shocked smile, mouthing to her fans, "Oh, please, please stop it! That's too much. Thank you, everybody!" before taking a deep bow and walking purposefully toward our table. As she draws closer, Panama's expression rapidly changes from a humble smile to a scowl.

"Right, you little morons," Panama says under her breath so that only the LBD hear. "Let me make this very clear: You NEED Catwalk for your sad little concert, so let's not forget that, shall we?"

We all glare back at Panama in utter dumbfoundment.

"And we'll have the top-of-the-bill slot too on Saturday the twelfth. No arguments," Panama continues. "And we don't play sets less than an hour long, so if you need to drop another act to make extra room for us, well, so be it."

"But," begins Claude, quickly shutting up as Panama's face draws closer to her own.

"And just you make sure my name, er, I mean Catwalk's name is printed biggest on all of the posters too, because after all, we'll be the main attraction."

Claude, to give her credit, does try her best to stand up to Panama at this point. No easy task, as Panama Goodyear is quite, quite terrifying. "Look, Panama, we're not desperate," says Claude politely yet firmly. "If we think you're good, you'll be included, that's how the selection process works."

Panama's face flushes with fury, her eyes narrow and her bee-stung lips pucker into an angry, vicious pout.

"Look, Maud, or Fraud, or whatever lame-ass name you're sad enough to be called, let me remind you again." Panama is now jabbing Claude's shoulder with a plum-nail-polished finger. "You NEED Catwalk. You NEEED us desperately. In fact, as desperately as your freaky giraffe mate here needs to stop growing before she ends up in the circus." Panama nods her head cruelly at Fleur, who stares straight ahead, denying Catwalk the pleasure of a reaction.

Panama goes on, "Plus, I've chatted with Mrs. Guinevere and Mr. Foxton. They both agree that without my incredible talent, Blackwell Live will be a total joke." Panama is chuckling now. She knows having Blackwell's teachers on her side is her killer punch. "So don't give me any of your attitude, girls."

"Or what?" says Claude rather bravely.

"You'll see," threatens Panama. "I'll make you all, individually, extremely sorry to have ever met me."

Then Panama withdraws slightly, giving us all a little smile, almost as if she'd just invited us all to her house for a sleepover or something.

Now she's really scaring me.

And I believe Panama's threats, but I don't have time to ponder the dark possibilities of her vengeance, because Panama then spots Mrs. Guinevere, who's popped by the gym for a quick visit. In a millisecond, Panama's face transforms from pure evil to instant sunshine.

"Ooh, Mrs. Guinevere! Yoo-hoo!" Panama shouts, waving her hand. "Good to see you! I'm so glad you could make it down!"

Mrs. Guinevere smiles broadly at Panama, placing her arms around Leeza and Abigail's shoulders, offering them both congratulations on another wonderful performance.

We're doomed, I think to myself.

"Remember what I said," says Panama, turning on her heel and sashaying off.

I look to Claude, trying to stop my bottom lip from wobbling, desperately hoping she might have a sheet in her Blackwell Live folder detailing the perfect murder and dismemberment of a Year 11 bully. Or, at very least, a cunning plan to sweet-talk Panama Goodyear out of taking over Blackwell Live. But I'm not in luck.

And when I turn back around, Fleur has made her excuses and disappeared to the loo . . . where she stays until her eyes stop being puffy.

Chapter 6

an extra-special song

So I suppose I should tell you what happened to "my special song." You know, the one Jimi was meant to be singing for me?

Well, we did get our Lost Messiah performance eventually, but it wasn't quite the life highlight I was bargaining on. It just didn't turn out that way. Life never does, does it?

"Aim low, never be disappointed," that's what one of the great philosophers once said. I forget which one. Oh, hang on now, I think it was Old Bert who told me that. Bert's the bloke who waits outside the Fantastic Voyage's front door every morning for Dad to open up so he can have a pint while he plans his day of betting on horse races. Maybe I shouldn't base my life around Bert's wisdom, he doesn't even remember to put his teeth in some days.

Anyhow, I'll tell you very quickly what happened after Catwalk bummed us all out, but I won't dwell on things, as Claude's keen that we don't. . . .

So Panama sloped off to have a little chat with Mrs. Guinevere, and Fleur returned to her seat, claiming she'd had a bad stomach and hadn't been crying at all. I genuinely don't envy Fleur her looks sometimes. She's always getting it in the neck from some girl or other who thinks Fleur's entrapping her boyfriend. Or that Fleur's being arrogant and conceited when she's actually just walking to lessons. Or wearing a new jacket. Or has just washed her hair, which just so happens to make it more glossy and model-like. Being beautiful is a bit of a pain in the butt, it seems. Girls don't give Fleur a chance. Once, in Year 7, I watched Fleur go through a short stage of walking with her shoulders stooped to try to appear shorter. And when miniskirts came back in fashion last term, Fleur wore a long elegant skirt almost to the floor, almost in protest. "Too much hassle," she muttered, meaning the continuous wolf whistles and black looks Fleur's long, shapely legs drew from Blackwell's inmates. Luckily, Fleur hasn't taken Panama's malice too harshly today. She was soon back at the table, smiling.

Especially as, just then, an angel came in the form of Ainsley Hammond. Despite Ainsley's black clothes, pale face, lilac-streaked hair and predilection for crucifix earrings, Ainsley Hammond from Year 11 really is the loveliest, nonscariest lad you could ever meet.

"Ooh, so we're auditioning right after Catwalk! How exciting!" remarked Ainsley sarcastically as he took to the floor. "If I'd known that beforehand, I'd have brought my autograph book."

Ainsley's band, Death Knell, with their raggedy clothes, uneven lipstick and smudged eyeliner, looked exactly like they'd staggered from the film set of *Attack of the Killer Zombies*.

However, when Claude confided to Ainsley about Panama's demands, quickly the whole band was a united spooky front of support for the LBD.

"Who on Earth does she think she is?" said Candy, a tall hippy girl wearing dangly bat-shaped earrings.

"Ughh, don't worry about it," commiserated another lad, with weird devil spikes at the front of his otherwise short-cropped hair. "You should hear some of the abuse she gives me."

"Now then, let's not give the wicked witch the pleasure of knowing we're discussing her," said Ainsley rather ironically, considering he perpetually looks en route to a Halloween party himself.

"I agree," said Claude.

If only it was that easy to make Panama disappear, I thought.

"What you gonna do for us, then, Ainsley?" asks Fleur.

"Well, it's quite an experimental sound," says Ainsley, absolutely earnestly. "But we're calling it nu-goth speed reggae."

"Right," the LBD all say.

"Okay then," says Claude. "When you're ready."

Death Knell were quickly lost in music, playing a bizarre track called "The Dead Can Dance": a weird assortment of steel drums, crashing electronic noises, bass guitars and melodic flutes.

Freaky-disco, I think to myself.

Death Knell certainly aren't my cup of tea, I'll admit, yet from the way every kid in the surrounding five-mile area who possessed dyed hair, a piercing or a henna tattoo had now appeared in Blackwell's gym, nodding away and punching the air appreciatively, I was obviously in the minority.

"Well, they seem to be popular, don't they?" said Fleur.

"Not half," agreed Claude.

"What do we think so far?" shouted Claude to a Year 7 girl with her hair woven into a hundred minibraids.

"Excellent!" shouted the girl. "Death Knell rrrrrrock! You've got to put them in."

So unofficially it was decided that if we didn't include Death Knell, we'd be lynched, and at this point it was unsaid, but we needed all the friends we could get.

"Right, you lot, you've had your chance," said Mr. Gowan, who had just appeared beside us. He does that a lot, Mr. Gowan, he suddenly appears without warning. He must know a secret Blackwell tunnel system or something.

"It's eight P.M. and it's time to get out. Do you think I've got nowhere else to be but here?" Mr. Gowan grumbles.

The entire gym stared blankly at Mr. Gowan, trying to imagine where exactly else he has to be. I mean, he lives on the premises, for Lord's sake. He spends his summer vacation at a "vacation village" three miles away, it's not like he's a big globetrotter.

"Sorry, Mr. Gowan, can we have five more minutes?" pleaded Claude.

"Well, just make sure it's only five," said Gowan, wilting under Claude's excessively polite demeanor. "But don't you make me have to come back in here and pull the plug on you. Yer hear me, girls?"

"We hear you!" chorused the LBD.

"We hear you too, Mr. Gowan," chorused a group of deeper male voices.

IT WAS LOST MESSIAH. Well, three of them at least: Naz, Aaron and Danny.

Hallelujah!

"Just caught you all, thank God," flustered Naz, trying to find an outlet for his amp. "I'm so sorry, girls, like, a hundred apologies, we've had a bit of, er, trouble, you see."

"Well, you're here now, that's the main thing," said Claude, sounding extremely joyous to see him. Sheesh, if you're a good-looking lad, you can get away with anything, can't you?

But where was Jimi? That was what I was wondering.

"Aren't you missing a lead singer?" asked Fleur.

"Precisely," said Naz. "Our dumb, clumsy lead singer. He's, er, on his way."

And just at that moment the gym doors swung open and in limped Jimi Steele, carrying Bess, his skateboard, under his arm, dragging his left leg behind him like a wounded soldier.

"Jimi!" I shrieked (not at all coolly, now that I think about it). "What's happened to you!?" The knee of Jimi's navy blue combat trousers was ripped and he was holding his right wrist toward his chest.

"Oh, nothing. Nothing, really, I just sort of fell," said Jimi, cocking his head to the side, blushing slightly. "It's, er, like, worse than it looks."

Jimi held up his wrist, showing us a grisly spectacle of blood and gnarled skin.

"*Ugggghhhh!*" chorused the LBD (oh, and every other girl in the gym who had suddenly became interested in Jimi Steele's general well-being).

See what I mean about being good-looking getting you special treatment? Mr. Gowan's entire arm could have fallen off, and just because he looks a bit like a potato, no girl would have turned a hair.

"Yep, Big Brain here has just had an argument with a flight of stairs and a skateboard," continued Naz, shaking his head. "And the stairs won."

Jimi blushed again, then winced as his wrist rubbed against the waistband of his trousers. "It was your fault, Naz," said Jimi. "You shouldn't have told me about the new handrail."

"Ah, I see, this was all my fault, was it?" Naz sniggered. "Sorry about that, Jimi . . ."

From the ensuing Lost Messiah argument, it transpired that the County Council, in their infinite wisdom, had installed a new freestanding handrail to the steps of the Westland Shopping Mall. No big excitement there, you might think. Well, no, except for the fact that Naz had spotted the rail and told Jimi about it. He'd told Jimi that not only was the new installation very steep and newly waxed (ooh, that's like a red rag to a bull for a skater), but then he'd also bet Jimi he couldn't skate right down the thirty-seven steps and land on top of Bess without hitting the oncoming traffic jam.

"Wow!" moaned all the girls in the gym.

"He's soooo sexy," whispered one Year 8 girl to her friend, rather too loudly, her face flushing pure scarlet.

It's a weird fact of life that the more recklessly boys behave, the more attractive they become to us girls. In fact, by risking his life for five minutes of glory, Jimi had the gym agog with adoration.

The girls wanted to snog him, the lads wanted to be him.

"And I nearly had it too," said Jimi. "Well, the first time I did, but the second time I tried I made a real balls-up of it."

"We thought he was worm food," said Naz. "He just lay there not moving for a few minutes after he fell. We were totally freaking out."

"Well done," said Claude rather dryly.

"Are you okay to sing, Jimi?" asked Fleur.

"Yeah, I think so, I'll be okay. I don't know if I can play guitar with my wrist, though," said Jimi. "But I'll give it a go."

Jimi walked over to where Aaron had tuned up Jimi's guitar and attempted to pull the strap over his head. Only he lost balance a bit and stumbled, knocking his damaged knee rather clumsily against an amp.

"*Owwwwwweeeew!*" moaned Jimi. "That hurt!"

Jimi slumped down onto the floor with his head in his hands, he looked really terrible now. A shocked mumble filled the room. I just wanted to run over and give him a big cuddle . . . but I was too late.

"Oh my Lord, are you okay? Do you need to go to the hospital?" came a concerned voice, suddenly taking charge of the situation.

It was Panama Goodyear.

I thought she'd gone home.

"Dunno," said Jimi, looking up at Panama's heaving bosom

and big brown eyes and probably feeling a lot better. "I just felt a bit woozy for a second."

"Well, let's a have a look at you," said Panama, getting down on her haunches to Jimi's level. "Let's see if you've broken anything, eh?"

Silly me, I had no idea Panama had a flipping degree in nursing, but there she was, manhandling MY Jimi Steele, making him bend knees and raise and lower his limbs so she could give her own "diagnosis." I swore to myself, if she asked Jimi to take any articles of clothing off for a proper examination, I was going to go over there and slap her till she was sore too.

"I think you're going to be fine," announced Dr. Goodyear eventually, rubbing Jimi's arm. "You're just a little bit shocked, that's all."

"Shocked? Shocked!" I quietly fumed. "Of course he's shocked! You big strumpet! You practically had his head between your boobs! I hate you, Panama Goodyear!"

"Aw, thanks, Panama, I feel much better now," said Jimi.

"Glad to be of help," simpered Panama, standing up and giving the LBD a little smug smile, as if to say, "Thank heavens for me."

"Panama saves the day," muttered Fleur.

Jimi made a miraculous recovery soon after that; in fact, he was up hopping about with a smile across his chops. Lost Messiah then went on to perform a song they'd written a few nights before called "The Girl with the Golden Mouth," which was all about some troublesome girl who always gave Jimi backtalk and sent him loopy. To be fair, Jimi did sing the song directly to the LBD, and by default a lot of the lines were sung straight to me with him looking me right in the eye . . . but I'm sure he was only being kind.

So maybe it was a special song after all.

But I don't think it was especially for me.

a call to arms

"It'll stick like that, Ronnie, I've warned you before," says Claude, looking up from her notes.

Fleur looks up from her mirror and tweezers.

"What will?" I ask.

"Your face. The wind will change and you'll be left with that frown forever," chides Claude, simply because I've got a furrow on my brow you could put a thong on.

"She could get BOTOX injections if that happens," suggests Fleur helpfully. "My mother had some last year, they iron out frown lines really well."

"Or alternatively, she could just stop frowning," suggests Claude, "which would be cheaper and less painful, wouldn't it?"

"S'pose," I say.

"Come on, then, tell me what's up," says Claude. "We've got a brilliant list of people here to choose from." Claude waves her papers at me. "The trouble will be who to leave out. Why the long face?"

"You know why, Claudette," I say, refusing to play along with Claude's ridiculous optimism. "I'm a bit worried about Panam—"

"Oh, Panama Shmanama!" spits Claude. "Catwalk Shatwalk, we're not letting that walking shop mannequin get in the way of our plans!" Claude is standing up now, blowing herself up to a full five-feet-one-inch of terror. "I mean, what is she going to do to us, anyway?" asks Claude incredulously. "What can she possibly do?!"

"Er . . . beat us up?" suggests Fleur, overtweezing one eyebrow into a permanently surprised arch.

"Yes . . . okay, she may beat us up, but she can't actually maim or kill us. That would be illegal." Claude smirks. "Next?"

"Call us names?" I say.

"Well, yes, that's a possibility," agrees Claude. "But remembering that she's called us names ever since the first day of Year Seven, that doesn't really freak me out. Every single time we see Panama, she says something to one of us . . . I mean, I just feel honored she can be bothered after all these years," says Claude, almost convincingly. "We've obviously not lost that LBD magic, eh?"

Claude is standing with both hands on her hips, waiting for the next reason she can bat into oblivion.

"She could spread lies about us," says Fleur. "She's always doing that sort of thing to people."

"Well, if they're lies, they're lies," argues Claude. "Only stupid people believe rumors without checking out the truth, don't they?"

If only this were true, I think to myself.

We all stare at each other in silence. Finally I raise my deepest fears. "Well . . . what worries me is that Panama could just wreck the festival if she doesn't get her own way," I say. "I'm telling you, Claude, that girl is evil."

That last comment, for Claudette, was a bridge too far.

136

"RIGHT, THAT'S IT!" she shouts, losing all patience. "I have had it up to here with Panama Goodyear!" Claude signifies to an imaginary point in the air above her head. "I'm just not listening to this baloney for one more minute."

Claude's deep brown skin shines quite majestically, illuminated by the swanky spotlights Fleur has on her bedroom ceiling.

Fleur sits up immediately, getting quite a start. I drop my magazine in shock.

"Oh, good. Nice to have your attention." Claude laughs. "Now, listen to what I've got to say, as I'm not in the habit of repeating myself. This has got to stop. It has got to stop right now!"

Claude leaves a long silence.

"What has?" says Fleur eventually.

"All this Panama Goodyear business. I'm not standing for it," says Claude, quickly correcting herself, "I mean we're not standing for it."

"Hmmm," I say.

"What do you mean, *hmmmmm?* I cannot believe you two sometimes!" says Claude. "I mean, do you think I'm scared of what that shower of mono-brain-celled no-hopers Catwalk can do to the LBD and to Blackwell Live? Do you?"

From where I was looking, Claude looked bothered, but in an angry, defiant way, not a meek, defeatist way like me.

"Because I'm flipping well NOT worried at all," continued Claude. "I know the LBD too well."

"Yeah, I know what you're saying, Claude," I say, sounding lame and unconvincing. "I know we're better than them."

137

"Oh, you DO, do you?" says Claude. "Or do you want me to run through exactly why we are the LBD one more time for you?!"

"If you want," I say, beginning to smile. Claude really is hilarious once she gets going.

"Do it anyway!" shouts Fleur. "Go on, do it!!"

We both love Claude's little "why we're the LBD" speech: It's an astute, powerful rant that surfaces every time there's trouble afoot. After three years together, it's become quite a tradition; in fact I don't know where we'd be without it, especially in times such as this.

"The LBD . . . or Les Bambinos Dangereuses," begins Claude, climbing up onto a chair to begin her speech. "Now, I know what you're thinking. You're thinking, Claudette, what is the LBD? What does it stand for exactly?"

"Tell us, sister!" Fleur shouts.

"Oh, I'm going to . . . don't you worry," says Claude, holding her fist to her chest like a Roman emperor. "Well, firstly," begins Claude, "we have the word *Les*, which is a plural article. And I'm not gonna bore you with a grammar lesson here, ladies, but suffice to say, it means there's more than one of us."

"I hear ya!" says Fleur, for some reason now with an American accent.

"And in our case there's three of us," continues Claude. "So whatever you're feeling when you're part of the LBD, you're not alone, as there's three people feeling it. A problem shared is a problem thirded . . . three heads are better than one . . . and all that sorta stuff."

"United we stand?" suggests Fleur, thinking of other clichés. "There's safety in numbers?"

"Misery loves company?" I add.

"Yep, that too," says Claude. "But whatever happens, the LBD don't stay miserable for long. That's just not a Dangerous Bambino thing. We get proactive and we sort things out."

Claude is waving her hands about now; she really loves public speaking, even when the audience is tiny.

"Now: on to *Bambinos*," continues Claude. "Well, *bambino* is a cool, funky, continental type of word for a baby, isn't it? And I think you will find without debate that we are extremely cool, hip young babes with more attitude and charisma in our left bum cheeks than that grinning goon Panama Goodyear has in her entire body. Aren't we, ladies?"

"You're not wrong," agrees Fleur. "Carry on . . . I like this."

"*Dangereuses,*" shouts Claude, almost toppling off the chair, but steadying herself on a nearby door frame. "We are dangerous bambinos for oh, so many reasons. We don't take rubbish from people, specifically not Catwalk. We've always got a trick up our sleeves and we never give up . . . in fact, nobody ever really knows what our next move is going to be, we're cunning like foxes."

"Ha ha ha, we sooo are!" Fleur laughs.

"We're wily like coyotes," shouts Claude, probably annoying Evil Paddy downstairs, who is trying to enjoy a James Bond film in peace.

"We're dangerous like bambinos!" I shout, even louder, which was dangerous in itself if you've ever seen how cross

Paddy gets when interrupted from watching *Goldfinger* for the seventeenth time.

"Dangerous like bambinos!" we all chorus, giggling like crazy.

(You're probably wondering how this all ended up in sort of made-up half-French–half-Italian, "Les Bambinos Dangereuses," but, look, if you'd sat with Fleur, Claude and me for the whole of Year 7 French while Madame Bassett droned on and on about Monsieur Boulanger from La Rochelle, well, believe me, you'd make up stupid names for your gang too. The gods were truly in fine form the day we all ended up sitting in that French class together, because the very millisecond the LBD sussed out that the awesome triumvirate of Veronica Ripperton, Fleur Swan and Claudette Cassiera actually made pluperfect verbs more gigglesome, and the breaktime bullies less fearsome, and the Year 9 lads more lovely to lust over, well, that was the day our clique was born. And okay, on numerous occasions since that day I've wanted to strangle both of them for being exceedingly annoying . . . however, ahem, they're also my life-support system in an otherwise troublesome cosmiverse. Soppy, but true.)

is this some kind of street theater?

I'm feeling a whole lot better now.

Soon the LBD are all sitting on Fleur's bedroom floor, surrounded by paper, having a good hectic debate about who's in, who's out and who had the requisite X factor to appear at

Blackwell Live. Thanks to Claude's amazing pep talk, it's almost like the Catwalk problem never happened, although this isn't the end of today's turmoil. Of course, everyone likes Christy Sullivan, two of us even like Shop . . . but as Claude now fights for Guttersnipe to be included, I'm feeling sorry for Chester Walton and Fleur is playing devil's advocate by suggesting we could open with Mr. Jingles, the amazing crappy talking bear. The debate goes on and on, around in circles, featuring numerous raised voices and long silences, until we're interrupted by a peculiar noise.

Perchang goes what sounds like a stone hitting Fleur's window.

"What was that?" says Fleur.

"Dunno, it's coming from over there," I say.

"It sounded like someone throwing something," says Claude.

Perchang.

"Yep, I think we have a visitor. If it's that pig Dion James, make sure we've got the water pistol loaded," says Fleur, leaping up, with me and Claude following.

As the LBD fights for positions to press their noses against Fleur's window, Fleur lets out a little yelp.

"Eeeep," she says. "There are six strange men outside my window! How good is that? Quick, Claude, open the window."

And she's right, there are.

Outside on Disraeli Road there are six boys aged about fifteen, all gazing up at us. They all look distinctly hip-hop, in baggy jeans, expensive sneakers and gold chains. One of them even has a red bandana around his head like he's just stepped out of South Central L.A. and not come down the high street on a mountain bike, which seems to be more likely.

"Who are you?" shouts Claude.

"And what do you want?" shouts Fleur.

If my nan were here, she'd say something tactful along the lines of "Eeee, it looks like the flipping United Nations down there," as the gang consists of two white kids, a Chinese-looking kid, two black lads of vastly different skin tones, and a Cypriot-looking kid with amazing brown eyes and sharp cheekbones.

"Are you Fleur Swan?" shouts the Cypriot lad.

"I am," says Fleur, arching an eyebrow.

"Good, we're the EZ Life Syndicate," announces the lad, as a few lads behind him do weird gangsta hand gestures. "We wanna be part of your festival."

"Oh?" the LBD say. We're all a bit thrown by this, we've never even set eyes on these lads before, how the heck did they find us?

"Where are you from?" shouts Claude, taking authority.

"We're from Chasterton Secondary, it's on the other side of town," says one of the black lads, who has powerful-looking wide shoulders.

"I know where Chasterton is," says Claude. "Where do yer live?"

"We're all from the Carlyle Estate," the lad says, gesturing at all of the gang, then behind him to two pretty, Hispanic-looking girls sitting on the wall behind them.

"Phhhhhh, 'EZ Life'? 'Course they have an easy life, that estate is well plush compared to around here," says Claude quietly to the LBD.

"Never mind that," says Fleur. "So, what do you do, then?" she shouts down. "Do you rap or what?"

"Well, we're more of a syndicate . . . ," says the Chinese kid. "We rap and, well, y'know, some of us deejay, some of us dance, one of us sings . . . it's a collective thing. It's an EZ Life thing. Yer know what I'm saying?"

More weird hand gestures.

"Er, yeah," the LBD say unconvincingly.

"The guys at the Music Box told us about what you were doing, so we thought we'd track you down," says one of the white lads, who has a ring on every finger and a really high-necked black padded jacket on.

"Well, you've certainly found us," says Claude. "Now what?"

"Well, have you got ten minutes to hear us rhyme?" says the Cypriot boy, placing a CD into a portable ghetto blaster he's holding in one hand.

"Ooh, go on," shouts Fleur, with little regard for the rest of Disraeli Road, who are probably enjoying some light early-evening television.

The neighbors are not going to like this one little bit.

"Nice one!" chorus the EZ Life Syndicate, switching on a bass line and turning the volume up to maximum. Within seconds the street is alive with an eerie, pounding, 132-beat-per-minute rhythm. There's lads throwing back and forth unfathomably fast rhymes, plodding moodily backward and forward, chucking weird shapes, while girls in tight black trousers and midriff-exposing T-shirts shake their booties. One lad is spinning on his back while others just stand around seriously, awaiting their turn to butt in with a line or merely a word of the track. All around them curtains are twitching and faces are appearing at windows.

"Get away from my Volvo!" shouts the bloke from number 42, wrapped only in a bath towel, "or I'm calling the police!"

"Ooh, is this a hidden camera TV show?" shouts the little old lady from number 52 to the two dancing, singing EZ Life girls. "Am I being filmed now? How exciting! I'm going to be on the telly!" she says, waving her hands at the nonexistent cameras in her garden hedge.

If I have to remember one classic moment in the Blackwell Live story, this may possibly be my favorite: the LBD all hanging out of the top window of 39 Disraeli Road, shouting and laughing, the EZ Life Syndicate rapping and dancing their hearts out on the tarmac below . . . and Paddy Swan running around among them, waving his fist, threatening to call the police and the Noise Abatement Society if EZ Life didn't immediately halt that "infernal racket": Paddy's face so angry that his bald head looks exactly like a beetroot.

Priceless.

Thankfully, EZ Life got the message pretty sharpish and started to leave, taking their sound system and their eight-strong crew with them.

"But how will we find you?" shouts Fleur from her bedroom window, thus infuriating Paddy even more.

"What do you want to find them for?" Paddy shouts up at her.

"Text me!" shouts the Cypriot lad, yelling his cell phone number for the whole road to hear. "Drop me a line when you've had a think," he continues.

"But what's your name?" shouts Fleur.

"Killa Blow," shouts the lad, without a hint of embarrassment.

"Oh my good God," says Paddy.

BLACKWELL LIVE UPDATE:

Thanks to everyone who auditioned
for Blackwell Live last Monday.
The following acts have now been confirmed:

* CHRISTY SULLIVAN

* DEATH KNELL

* LOST MESSIAH

* GUTTERSNIPE

* CATWALK

* THE EZ LIFE SYNDICATE

* BLACKWELL BELLRINGING SOCIETY

Please can all acts meet on
Thursday, June 26th at
4:00 P. M. in the drama studio
for a general meeting.

BLACKWELL LIVE TICKETS
ON SALE OUTSIDE DRAMA STUDIO
BREAKS/LUNCH
WEDNESDAY JULY 2ND

—£3—

Chapter 7

another bright idea

It seems, when I was little, I was an extremely joyless child.

According to Ripperton clan folklore, during my formative years I never got enthusiastic about anything, to the huge annoyance of my parents, who expected, nay, demanded their full payback of kiddie wonderment for the stuff they did for me.

Trips to the park? Bags of sweets? Helium-filled balloons? Being allowed to stay up past bedtime to catch the end of a TV show? All these things, and more, were at best met with a non-committal shrug and a blank expression.

"Ronnie," my father once said after I'd single-handedly vetoed a family trip to Chessington World of Adventure, "having your six-year-old daughter force a withering smile for you is an extremely demoralizing experience for a dad."

And I've no doubt it was, especially when accompanied by my curt explanation: "That sounds like fun, Daddy. But maybe it's more yours and Mummy's type of fun. You go instead. I'll stay at home." (Cue much slapping of foreheads and threats to drive me to the nearest orphanage.)

But I wasn't a miserable kid. In fact, far from it.

It was just that I simply wouldn't display the requisite amounts of joy that, say, a long balloon bent into the shape of a sausage dog, or a bowl of jelly and ice cream, was supposed to induce. And, believe me, that freaks parents right out. In truth, the only thing I got truly excited about back then was Christmas Eve, but then the fact that one day a year, an old-age pensioner would break into the house, with my parents' full consent, leaving £200 worth of toys and chocolate . . . well, that would make anyone grin.

But anyway, this isn't some lame trip down memory lane.

I'm telling you this because it seems that now, aged fourteen and a half, I'm in trouble for "being too happy." To my mind, this is conclusive proof that to be a parent, you've got to be vaguely schizophrenic, or at least prone to huge memory lapses and mental delusions.

My parents can't believe how jovial I've been this week, ever since Blackwell Live started coming together. I've been smiling nonstop and chatting everyone's legs off. I've been positive about life and the future. I've not mentioned the possibility of germ warfare once (I get a bit obsessed with stuff I see on the news sometimes). I've even been running out the door to Blackwell early some mornings because the LBD have tons of stuff to sort out. It wasn't a conscious decision on my part to cheer up, but considering the LBD's initial reasoning behind organizing Blackwell Live was to, ahem, perhaps "meet some boys" . . . and here, only weeks later, we seem to have a flood of men all wanting to chat to us and come to our houses, well, yeah, I suppose I am a bit chipper! I mean, we've even met the

EZ Life Syndicate, who are from another school entirely! Yes, we're now *importing* boys from other areas, for crying out loud! And okay, sure, we've had some hard times over the last days with Panama Bogwash and her Goblins, but I've managed to keep my chin up regardless.

"You're on drugs, aren't you?" announces my mother, throwing down a bowl of mush onto the kitchen table before me. I surmise this mess was Frosted Krispies when she poured them for me over an hour ago.

"What?" I say.

"You're taking drugs," she continues. "I can tell. I just can't work out which drug. You won't stop smiling." Mum grabs my face and pulls down one eye bag. "See! Red-rimmed eyes. Drugs," she says.

My mother must have taken the same medical degree as Panama Goodyear.

"Mother, could you at least clean your teeth before you get so close in the morning?" I splutter, shaking her off before she spies a spot she wants to squeeze while she's there.

"I don't believe this," I squeak. "You've spent the last fourteen years badgering me to smile more and look enthusiastic, and now you're giving me jip for smiling too much! You're mad, you are. You're a couple of chicken drumsticks short of a buffet, you are."

"Pah, *you* are," says Mum.

"No, lady. I think you'll find *you are*," I say.

(Since I've become a teenager, me and Mum's arguments have taken a really profound turn.)

"Veronica, don't call your mother mad," shouts my father from another room.

"And he's unhinged too," I say, nodding toward Dad's voice.

"Alas, I can't argue with you there," agrees Mum, wrinkling her nose in the direction of Dad. "You get your defective genes from his side of the family, but let's keep your father out of this."

Dad, knowing what was good for him, decides to stay silent in the living room with his tea and not attempt to argue his defense.

I thought, for about five minutes last night, that Mum and Dad might have ironed out this weird problem they're having. When I got back from school, they were sitting in the kitchen together, talking quite civilly about pub business. Talking *to each other,* no less. Not telling me to say things to the other one. Just like they were friends, almost.

Well, this was until Dad mentioned that next year could be a good year to do the renovations to the Fantastic Voyage's backyard. Dad's had a bit of a dream to convert the back of the pub into a beer garden for about five years now, but it will cost about a squillion quid, according to builders.

"We've got bigger priorities than spending our savings on a stupid beer garden, Lawrence," snarled Mum.

"I'd have thought you'd be in favor, Magda. I could get a tent and live in it. Then you wouldn't have to look at me," shouted Dad.

Thankfully, I was meeting the LBD at Fleur's. We were cooking a big stir-fry and going over Blackwell Live business. It was great to get out of the house and be doing something that didn't involve thinking about them.

When I look up from my Frosted Mush next, Mum is peering at me, waiting for me to confess my rampant drug problem.

"Look, give me a break," I say, shaking my head. "I'm just really really okay at the moment. Everything's going really well with Blackwell Live, it's all just flowing at the moment. . . ."

Mum is still peering.

"I mean, yes, last week I may have been really stressed . . . ," I continue.

"Stressed and depressed," corrects Mum, eating a pickled onion.

"Okay, yeah, stressed and depressed, but now I'm happy and—"

"Happy and ecstatic?" says Mum, raising an eyebrow.

"Yeah!"

"Hmmmm," she says.

"But I'm NOT on drugs. In fact, I wouldn't even know where to get drugs from, so how would I be on drugs?" I say, totally truthfully.

"Well, there's all those drug dealers that wait outside your school every night, peddling their wares," says Mum, who has taken to reading the *Local Daily Mercury* very closely of late.

"Oh, God, Mother, those drug dealers don't even exist!" I moan. "In fact, me and Claude once hung around after school in Year Eight specifically to spy on a real-life drug dealer in action. The only person out there was Mrs. Baggins, the crossing patrol woman!" I say.

"Now, she's *definitely* on drugs," says Mum, beginning to smile in a relieved way.

"Oh, yeah, totally, she's mad as a goat," I agree, happy my

interrogation is over. As ever, though, Mum wants the last word.

"Well, all I'm saying is: I'm watching you, Veronica Ripperton," Mum concedes. "I've got your card marked. And if I see anything I don't like, I'll be down on you like a ton of bricks." Mum's pointing her finger at me now.

"Well, watch away, you mad old crone," I say under my breath as Mum tucks into another pickle. "Cos I'm not on drugs."

"And I bet that Fleur Swan will have something to do with all this," she continues to whoever is listening. "She's at the root of any misdemeanor. Ooh, If I were Patrick Swan, I'd have locked her in the attic long ago."

"Why Fleur?" I say, collecting my schoolbag. "Why not Claude? Maybe she's my drug dealer," I add mischievously.

"Ha ha ha! Oh, don't make me laugh, Ronnie." Mum snorts. "Claude would never get involved with anything like that. She's got far too much sense. She's such a lovely girl, is Claude . . ."

(Let it be noted that if it wasn't for the fact Claudette Cassiera is a completely different color to me, and has Mrs. Cassiera to look after her, my mother would be passing off Claude as her own flesh and blood after abandoning me on a motorway. Mum loves Claudette like the daughter she wishes she'd really had. How does Claude Cassiera do it?)

"Right. Can't hang about," I say breezily. "I'm off to school now to get high on drugs."

Mum looks up from the pickle jar, where she's spooning vinegar into her mouth.

"No, hang on, forget that," I continue. "I'll probably just go to double science and be bored to death, then grab a baked potato for lunch instead."

"Good girl," says Mum.

"See ya later, loonytoons," I say, giving Mum a peck.

"No, you're the mad one," she says, quickly closing the pub door behind me so I can't reply.

My mother is sooo childish.

the meeting

I love the smell of the drama studio.

Mr. Gowan uses this unbelievably great-smelling deep oak polish on the floors to keep the wood all smooth and shiny. It smells amazing. I suppose if I had to sniff any sort of strange substances, in a bid to give my mother the drug-related family crisis she so desperately seeks, I'd probably just sit in the drama studio, inhaling its lovely, rich, varnishy aroma . . . until I got trampled by a load of Year 7 kids pretending to be "sprouting trees" or "soaring birds" to the rhythmic beat of a tambourine.

I didn't believe for one second if we invited all of the chosen Blackwell Live bands to the drama studio for a "General Meeting" (as Claude rather officiously refers to it), they'd all simply show up, no questions asked. Thirty kids? Many of whom don't even like each other? All with different timetables and after-school commitments?

That's a lot of folk to schedule into one place.

You're always going to get one boy who remembers an urgent appointment with his Nintendo GameCube (e.g. Aaron), or one girl who'll need to go and tend to her pony (e.g. Abigail from Catwalk). Yet, with Claude at the helm, sprinting around the cloakrooms between lessons, threatening musicians under pain of death that they MUST be in the drama studio at 4:00 P.M. sharp, everything has come together.

"I told them exactly how it was," said Claude as the LBD were en route to the studio. "No-show means 'no show.' If I can't trust them to turn up tonight, I'm not relying on them for July twelfth."

"Claude, you're a real Scary Mary sometimes," says Fleur.

"Yeah, I know." Claude smiles. "But you're calling me that like it's some kind of bad thing . . . I mean, look, I got them all here, didn't I?"

"Yep, Little C." Fleur chuckles, sticking her head into the studio and spotting a flurry of faces looking back at her. "You certainly did."

All twenty-nine faces, present and correct. What a sight this is to behold!

So we've got Death Knell, all five of Blackwell's nu-goth speed reggae pioneers, sitting directly beside Guttersnipe, Liam's three-piece guitar act. While Liam waits patiently for the meeting to kick off, Tara, Guttersnipe's blond bass player, gossips with the huge heap of hair which is Benny Stark. Benny, as ever, is managing to wear his Blackwell uniform like some sort of ironic fashion statement. I don't know how, he just does. It's something to do with Benny's tie perpetually being a little thinner than other kids' and his shirt collars a little pointier and his

trousers a touch tighter than other lads' (they're always from secondhand shops too, but Panama somehow leaves Benny out of
her bitching). A neat row of badges across Benny's blazer lapel,
heralding New York guitar bands that nobody else has ever
heard of, seals Benny's "Too Cool for School" look. In all hon-
esty, I can't work out whether Benny actually works hard to be
cool or not . . . he's so flipping laid-back, he looks like removing the top from a jar of pickles would fatigue him for an entire
week.

"Yeah . . . well, I heard the Divines' new single," mutters
Benny to Tara, "but the Music Box won't be able to order me
their new CD over from the States till late August, which
sucks."

"Those guys are rubbish down at the Music Box," I hear
Tara sighing above the general studio buzz. "I'm ordering all my
import CDs over the Internet now. It's so much quicker."

Along the raised stage area of the studio perches ten bottoms: one half being Catwalk, the other side, Lost Messiah. The
two bands are joined in the middle by Panama Goodyear and
Jimi Steele, sitting shoulder to shoulder. I can't help but notice
that Panama keeps touching Jimi's knee and flicking her hair
about when she's talking, accompanied by a weird high-pitched
giggle whenever Jimi so much as speaks.

I figure Jimi is either telling Panama a long list of knock-
knock jokes . . . or perhaps Panama really does beat Fleur Swan
in turning into a syrup brain in the company of good-looking
lads.

Catwalk's Abigail and Leeza are calling across to a solitary dark-haired, dark-eyed Christy Sullivan, who's looking completely gorgeous perched on a chair near the door.

"Yoo-hoo! Christy!" squeaks Leeza, patting the space between her and Abigail. "You can come and sit with us, Christy! You've only got a little bum, haven't you?"

"Er, ooh, no, it's okay, girls, really," shouts Christy. "I'm quite comfortable here for the time being. Thanks and all that."

Abigail and Leeza soon brush aside Christy's knock-back and are quickly engrossed in their favorite subject aside from themselves: step aerobics.

But above all the general melee, one voice can be heard above them all: "And I said, 'Daddy, you *can't* buy me the Gucci shoes *and* the bikini for my birthday, that's an obscene amount of money!'" Panama is telling Jimi rather loudly. "But Daddy told me that he's only got one little girl and he can spend his money how he feels. I mean, Jimi, what could I say to that?!"

"Errrr, well, I dunno, really," says Jimi.

"Precisely!" squeaks Panama. "So I let him buy me them both! Hoo hoo ha ha ha ha!" Jimi tries to laugh along, but to be honest, he seems more transfixed by Panama's boobs, which are suspended in some kind of ultra-bra which has "raised and separated" her cleavage somewhere around her ears. (NB: I can hardly fill an egg cup with my knockers, let alone a D-cup. Another reason Panama Goodyear must be destroyed. Preferably in a freak steamroller incident.)

"But anyway, I'm babbling on about me again," says Panama, taking her voice a little quieter now, although I'm still earwigging so I can make out every syllable. "How are you feeling after your accident? It was your arm as well as your leg, wasn't it?" she says, quite caringly. Her hand reaches out and gently rubs Jimi's right hand. "I was worried about you. You silly thing."

"Oh, don't worry about me," says Jimi, blushing slightly. "I'm always getting hurt."

"Well, if you're going to keep on getting hurt, I'm going to have to keep on worrying about you. I'll have no choice," Panama teases, sort of poking him in the belly. "I'll have to keep a very close eye on you from now on."

Jimi pokes Panama's excessively flat stomach back, and they both giggle. Panama's good at this flirting business, I'll give her that.

"Right, everyone!" shouts Claude. "With respect: Shut up! I need to get through a few points, then you can all ask any questions that you want. S'that okay?"

"Yeah," choruses the crowd.

"EZ Life Syndicate, are we all present and correct?" asks Claude.

"We are!" shouts a gaggle of voices at the back of the studio.

"Oh, and cheers, EZ Life, for coming all the way across town, we appreciate that," Claude says, tipping their rather attractive frontman Killa Blow (aka Shaun Jones) a respectful nod.

"No worries," says Killa, "we're all here now, Claude."

And they were, all eight members of the Syndicate, plus two or three other kids who just seemed to be there lending moral support. I don't blame them for bringing reinforcements, it must have been flipping scary coming over from Chasterton to Blackwell. The LBD were sure the EZ Life Syndicate wouldn't show up, especially as both schools have a long history of fighting with each other, but it's flipping marvelous they did.

By the way, in case you're wondering how we convinced Mr. McGraw to let a non-Blackwell band perform at Blackwell Live, well, it's all down to Claudette obviously; she did all the talking.

"So EZ Life are in," said Claude yesterday on her return from McGraw's lair, "but we've had to, er, compromise."

"What sort of compromise?" I asked gingerly.

"Well, you know how much Mr. McGraw digs the Blackwell bellringers?"

"Yessss?" I said with a heavy heart.

"Well"—sigh—"McGraw says we can't have one without the other," Claude continued, huffing and puffing, "so I took them both."

"Ding dong!" I say, beginning to smile.

Claude's depressed expression was so amusing that Fleur and I simply had to laugh. In fact, I'm trying to stop giggling here in the drama studio, as Jemima and George from the Blackwell bellringers perch themselves directly beside Claude, handbells at the ready, waiting to give her a little recital if need be.

Eventually Claude opens up the meeting, battering through some fairly general business: thanking everyone for auditioning and saying "what a hard time we had choosing people," blah blah blah. Obviously, Claude fails to mention that by 10:00 P.M. last Monday night we were so sick of arguing, in particular about the merits of Shop and his blue suede shoes, that I resorted to battering both her and Fleur about the head with a pil-low. We fail to mention also that the Blackwell bellringers were there through sheer bribery, as these were private LBD matters.

Everyone doesn't have to know everything.

"You're probably thinking the festival is months away," con-tinues Claude. "But I'm here to spell it out that it's not. Today's Thursday, the twenty-sixth of June, and we've got to get this whole show together for the twelfth of July: That's just over two weeks."

"What? Two weeks? Oh my God," mumbles the entire crowd.

Jeez, when Claude puts it like that, even I feel queasy.

"So, in brief: We're leaving it up to you guys what you play and how you play it," says Claude. "But the only rule is: Turn up on time and make it good."

Everyone groans, including Panama, who nudges Leeza, then sneers at Claude, muttering, "Good? How could we NOT be good?!"

"Oh, and another thing: Try and keep it clean," continues Claude, "and this isn't our request. I've got a message here from Mr. McGraw saying he won't tolerate 'profanity and lewdness,' that's, er, swearing and 'exposing your underwear to onlookers' in everyday speak."

"Darn," says Killa B, "I was going to show them my—"

"Never mind what you were going to do, Mr. Blow, we'll have none of it," butts in Claude, laughing.

"Oh, and if anyone is in any doubt about which words are and are not appropriate for usage in front of Mr. McGraw," adds

Fleur, "please see me, as I've spent enough time in detention to find out."

Everyone chuckles except the bellringers, who look at each other in abject horror. What kind of debauched nightmare have Jemima and George got themselves tangled up in?

"Is Mr. McGraw even coming on the twelfth?" asks Ainsley from Death Knell.

"Good question," I say. "Last time we spoke to McGraw, he seemed to have suddenly remembered he had relatives from Outer Mongolia visiting that day, so he mightn't be able to make it."

"Errrr . . . Has McGraw got relatives in Outer Mongolia?" asks Ainsley.

"Your guess is as good as ours," I say. "We'll just have to see if he turns up."

With cramps setting into people's bottoms, Claude pushes on quickly: "But to be honest, one of our biggest hurdles with Blackwell Live is funding. We've really got to sell tickets to make it work." Claude delves into her folder and brings out some figures.

"Now, by my reckoning, the least amount we can stage Blackwell Live for is £1000, that will hire us a small outside stage, some speakers, and that's also for a marquee for refreshments and dancing, all that sort of thing," says Claude. "So if we can sell 334 tickets at £3 a pop, we'll be all right."

"And if we sell more, of course, we'll be even better!" adds Fleur.

"But the thing is," I say, "there's one thousand pupils at Blackwell and another one thousand at Chasterton. And obviously, all of these bods have got family and friends who might want to come too. So, what I'm saying is, we really need everyone to start hassling people to buy tickets."

Everyone nods back at me in agreement, which is wonderful, as I'm not much good at public speaking, in fact my hands are shaking as I say this. I hate it when everyone stares at me at once. I'm also a little bit paranoid about my speaking voice, since I heard it sounding so weird and nasal on Fleur's answer machine. Yuck.

"And if we could get some publicity in, say, the *Local Daily Mercury* or on Wicked FM, well, that would be great," says Claude, setting a nifty trap. "Now, does anyone possibly have some contacts there?"

Claude raises a quizzical eyebrow.

At last! This is the very oxygen Panama's ego needs to flourish; immediately she's waving her arms in the air.

"Ooh, me! Me! I mean, us!" she shrieks. "Did I tell you all about the time Catwalk got through to the Wicked FM Roadshow 'Search for a Pop Band' quarterfinals?"

"Yes," groans the crowd.

"Oh. Well, we did, anyway," bleats Panama. "And I know people there and at the *Mercury* and they think that I'm, sorry, I mean *we're* dead brilliant, so I'll give them a ring and see if I can drum up some interest."

"Thank you, Panama," says Claude through extremely gritted teeth. "That would be very helpful."

Panama sits back, letting her large inflated head enjoy the attention it's receiving, before immediately turning to Catwalk's

Derren and Zane, name-dropping loudly, "Oh, Warren will help us out, I'm sure, and Frankie will too . . . ," witters Panama, referring to two famous local radio breakfast DJs by their first names only, just to ensure we all know she's practically their best mate.

"So, that's about it, really," wraps up Claude. "We'll call another meeting when we've got a bit more to discuss—"

"I've got a final question," announces Zane, waving one fake-tan-stained hand in the air.

"Go on, Zane, fire away," says Claude slightly apprehensively.

"Who is top of the bill?" asks Zane.

Damn.

Suddenly all five sets of Catwalk's evil eyes are drilling into Claude, along with every other person in the studio. Claude takes a deep breath, rustling her paperwork to give herself a bit of time, then announces in a slightly faltering voice, "That's still to be confirmed, sorry."

Oh, dear, that's torn it.

In a flash Panama's face transforms to a look of pure venom. I mean, how DARE Claude Cassiera be so insolent after the demands Panama dealt out last Monday? Clearly, this is incomprehensible behavior for Panama, and I wonder to myself, when was the last time the brunette bully didn't get her own way?

If ever, that is.

In truth, it would be easier if Catwalk simply stood up, walked over to the LBD, dragged us outside the drama studio and kicked us up and down the lower-school cloakrooms for a while. At least we could get it over and done with. Instead, they simply stare at us a little longer before muttering something to each other, broad smirks spreading across their collective faces. Then they calmly stand up and leave the drama studio, shouting a fake-friendly "Good-bye, thanks for everything!" as they go.

I think you'll agree, that's far more scary.

I tried to catch Claude's eye to shoot a "we've really done it now" glance at her, but Claude just thinned her lips and pretended to be distracted by her notes. She had her shoulders thrown back and her nose defiantly aloft, but despite her pose, I still knew she was pretending.

home, but not alone

So I'm halfway down Lacy Road on my way home from school, and on this very rare occassion I'm without the LBD.

Claude stayed behind after the meeting tonight chatting with Liam Gelding, while Fleur went home via Gap to return a skirt she's decided she doesn't like. I ducked out of accompanying Fleur, deciding to go home instead. I simply couldn't face another episode of Fleur driving Gap's assistants crazy, demanding a full refund on a skirt she's worn to numerous parties before deciding it's gone out of fashion. I shan't be missed anyway, that Killa Blow offered to accompany her "as he was going that way anyway." Obviously, Fleur was out of the door, reapplying plum lipstick to her ear-to-ear grin as she went, before I even had time to reconsider. Charming.

So I'm ambling home, mulling over the day's events, trying

not to get myself run over on minor-road junctions, when I sense someone gaining ground behind me.

"Er, Ronnie . . . ," a boy's voice says. "Ronnie, is that you? Wait up a sec."

I turn around to find Jimi Steele, aboard Bess, trundling along the pavement toward me.

Oh my God!

Oh my God. This is like the very thing I have fantasizied about happening for as long as I can remember. Happening. Right. Now.

Me and Jimi Steele on a one-on-one! I've got him all to myself: a proper chance to prove exactly why I'm totally the kind of girl he can't live without.

So why do I feel sick? And why does it not feel all lovely and dreamy like it does when I've thought about it for an entire double science? Instead, I'm just feeling clumsy and frumpy and more than a little aware that my deodorant is doing me a disservice.

"Oh, hiya, Jimi," I say. "Why are you following me home? Are you stalking me?" This was meant to sound funny, but it seems to come out a bit snarly.

What is happening to my head?

I feel like just cutting my losses and running off. Luckily, Jimi throws his head back and laughs.

"Yeah, I'm stalking you," Jimi agrees. "I follow you home every night. I usually wear a beard, though."

"Ahhh, I knew that was you," I say, now trying to concentrate on walking casually. I'm holding my stomach in, sticking my meager bosom out and keeping my head tilted toward Jimi

164

so he doesn't see my side profile and notice how enormous my schneck is. On catching sight of myself in a shop window, I realize I look like I've got a trapped fart, so I decide to walk normally instead.

"Okay, I wasn't really stalking you," says Jimi. "But I *was* following you, I wanted to ask you something."

"Oh, what?" I say, praying it's "I wanted to ask you if you fancy being my girlfriend as I'm totally crazy about you."

But of course it's not, it's "I wanted to know if you'd let me into the function room in your pub? I think I left my Quiksilver hooded top in there after last week's practice."

"Yeah, 'course you can," I say, a bit disappointed this wasn't a lead-up to snogging. "Come and have a look now if you want. I've not seen it, though. I'd have thought the cleaner would have handed it in."

"Hell." Jimi grimaces. "I hope it's there, my mum only bought me it last week, she'll go schizoid if I've lost it."

"Don't fret, we'll have a look anyway," I say. "Our cleaner's useless, she's probably missed it," I reassure him, silently thanking God that the cleaner HADN'T found Jimi's top. I don't know how I'd have explained it if we'd reached the pub and found it in my bedroom under my pillow, where I'd have no doubt been cuddling it like the big sap I am.

We carry on walking down Lacy Road in silence, both of us trying to conjure up something to say. Ironically, for a girl who talks and talks most days until she is quite sick of her own voice, someone whose school report every term reads, "A bright girl, but far too talkative"—suddenly I cannot think of a single thing to say.

Why does this happen every time I meet someone I really really fancy? I mean, I'm the daughter of a pub owner, for the love of God! It's in my flesh and bones to talk rubbish with strangers all day! But put someone like Jimi Steele in front of me, with his long eyelashes and aqua eyes and toned upper arms . . . and suddenly all my small talk disappears.

"Warm day today, eh?" I eventually say.

Oh, no. Three minutes of nothing, then I come up with an observation about the weather. I suck.

"Yeah, not half," says Jimi, sounding quite relieved one of us has broken the silence. "It's hotter than yesterday, eh?"

"Yeah, boiling," I say.

"Bit of a change from the rainy weekend, though, eh?" adds Jimi.

"Yeah," I mutter.

Can you understand why I have no boyfriend now?

"So . . . Did you do anything special last weekend, then?" asks Jimi.

"No, I just . . ."

Oh my God, I can't tell him I watched TV in my bedroom with the curtains closed. Damn you, Dad, you were right! If I'd gone out and "made the most of the outdoors," I'd have a good anecdote to share. Quick, Ronnie, make something good up!

"I . . . was planning Blackwell Live. You know, costing the festival out, that sorta thing. We're really busy at the moment."

"Right, I can imagine," says Jimi, flashing me an amazing smile, then sort of touching my elbow as he begins his next sentence. "Actually, I wanted to chat to you about that, you know,

I just, er, wanted to say that I think it's really cool what you're doing. Like, total respect to you for getting around McGraw and sorting out the auditions and all that. . . ."

Jimi looks me straight in the eye as he says this, quite clearly meaning every word.

"Oooh, er, right," I say. "Er, yeah, thanks. I mean, it's mostly Claude really, though, I just sort of help out where I can . . . ," I say, wittering on and on and on . . .

I wish I could take a compliment without pointing out to the person giving me it why it isn't true. It's a really bad habit.

"Well, you *all* seem to be working hard to me, not just Claude," Jimi corrects me, kindly.

"Cheers, Jimi, I suppose we are," I say, with a lovely warm feeling spreading all over my body.

And after this, we chatter nonstop all the way home. In fact, I reckon Jimi Steele has got to be one of the easiest lads to speak to in the entire world. Over the course of the next hour, while we search for Jimi's hoodie, we chat about Blackwell School, and all the folk there that we do and don't like. And before I know it, I'm telling him all about this weird *feud* my mum and dad are having. About the silences interspersed with bickering, that sort of thing, and how it just makes me want to stay around at Fleur's.

It's weird how easy it feels to say this to Jimi. He just seems to understand what I'm saying, even without me giving loads of detail; but then he tells me all about his parents splitting up, twice, then getting back together.

"Both times we all thought it was forever . . . but it wasn't," says Jimi, reassuring me a bit. "I reckon there's always hope. I mean, it takes a lot to really decide to split up forever, doesn't it?" he says.

I just say nothing. I'm not sure anymore.

"Well, I reckon it does," Jimi continues.

At this point, I feel a lump growing in my throat, but I manage to stifle it. If Jimmy did, miraculously, want to snog me at this moment, I'd be a lot happier with a big hug and being told that "everything's gonna be fine." I feel totally poo about all this Mum and Dad stuff.

And I tell him about how being an only child sort of annoys me (Jimi's got three older brothers and they annoy him too) and even about how I hate science (Jimi got thrown out of stream one for maths cos he couldn't do quadratic equations).

"Only weirdos like science and quadratic equations," announces Jimi.

"Totally. I quite fancy a job as a street cleaner, actually," I joke. "Who needs maths or science . . . or any exam passes, for that matter?"

"Not us, thank God," Jimi says.

I even make him laugh, and I mean really laugh from the bottom of his stomach, loads of times too . . . and this is a majorly good sign when attracting the opposite sex, according to *Glamour* magazine.

By the time he leaves with his skateboard and red hoodie under his arm, I feel like I've just taken a crash course in being Jimi Steele's girlfriend. I've studied all the theory, all his little likes and dislikes, I'm now ready to move into the practical stage when he takes me in his arms and gives me a big snog.

But he doesn't.

He just says, "Oh, noooo! Is that the time? I said to my folks I'd eat dinner with them tonight. Gotta go, Ronnie, cheers for helping me find the sweatshirt . . . you're a star. See ya."

And then he's gone.

And although we'd been talking to each other for ages, it was just like we'd been having different conversations all the time.

Chapter 8

a pizza bad news

"So what you're saying to me, essentially, is," begins Fleur Swan, picking the salami off her Americano pizza and shoving it in her mouth, "is that you had Jimi Steele inside your house, all to yourself, for the best part of an hour—"

"Uh-huh," I mumble.

"And you were chatting and laughing and telling each other your deepest, darkest secrets?"

"Mmm, s'pose."

"And NOTHING happened after that? No snog? Not even a phone number swappage!?" Fleur is peering at me, shaking her head from side to side. "You're useless."

Suddenly Fleur is distracted by a rather gorgeous Italian lad brandishing a bowl of Parmesan. "Ooooooh! Yoo-hoo! Gianni! Can I have some more cheese, please!" She giggles, batting her eyelashes.

Fleur always insists the LBD go to Paramount Pizza on the high street for the Saturday lunchtime buffet: not only is it "eat as much as you can for £4"; additionally, the owner, Carlos, employs all his Italian sons and nephews to wait on tables and throw pizza dough about. They do this clad in black silk shirts, tight trousers and lots of pungent aftershave. No wonder we're here today for our little Blackwell Live "business lunch," as Claude keeps calling it.

"This pizza is wonnnnderful, Gianni," says Fleur to the Italian hunk hovering by our table. "Did you make it?"

"Ah, *non*, my *va-ther*, Gianni Senior, is the chef today." Gianni Junior blushes, hopping nervously from one foot to the other.

"Well, it's a really great pizza, make sure you tell your dad I said so," continues Fleur.

"I will. And you make sure you come back again. I'm here next week too. Maybe you will be popping by, er . . . I no know your name?" ventures Gianni Jr. bravely.

"It's Fleur . . . and maybe I will!" she teases.

"Well, I hope you do, Fleuurrr," says Gianni earnestly, turning on his heel to attend another customer.

"Good grief," mutters Claude, staring at Fleur, then back at her untouched pizza. It's practically the first thing she's said since we sat down. "Could you two make it any more obvious you fancy each other? Why don't you have T-shirts made?" she mumbles.

Fleur ignores Claude completely.

"See, THAT'S how it's done, Veronica! You have to make things obvious. Pah. Let's face it, all these meaningful looks and little hints aren't getting you anywhere with Jimi, are they? Are they?"

"Well . . . not really."

"Exactly. Right, I've got Jimi's phone number from the auditions. Let's ring him and get you a date," Fleur announces, pulling her cell phone out of her pocket.

"Don't you dare!!" I yelp, pulling it from her interfering hand. "Claude, tell her!"

But Claude is distracted, gazing at her sheet of figures, biting her lip. A frown creases her forehead.

"Claude! Fleur's going to ring Jimi! Do you think she should?" I say.

"Hmmm, well," says Claude, glancing up at her squabbling pals, "if I thought that you getting a date with Jimi would shut the pair of you up talking about him, well then I'd say yes, but—"

"But what?" Fleur and I chorus.

"But whatever the outcome, you'll probably just blabber on about him even more . . . so I'm saying, both of you, SHUT UP, as I need to tell you something pretty bad about Blackwell Live."

"Fair enough," says Fleur, snapping closed her phone. "Go on, Little C, hit us with your worst."

"What's up?" I say.

This sounds serious.

"I've messed up," says Claude, her voice sounding a little choked. "I sort of assumed something before checking it out properly. And now I've found out the facts, and it's not good . . . I think we might even have to cancel Blackwell Live."

Claude stares back at the sheets of paper again, her bottom lip wobbling.

"Claude, it can't be as bad as that. Tell us the whole story," says Fleur, pushing away her pizza, placing her arm around Claude's tiny shoulders.

"Oh, I've been an idiot. I really have," says Claude, gazing at us both. "You know that I said we needed a thousand pounds to cover our costs for Blackwell Live. Well, I assumed we could pay it later."

"Yeah . . . and we can!" I say. "We'll make that cash back, no bother, won't we? We start selling tickets next Wednesday."

"Well, yeah, but you see, the only company who will hire us all the equipment we need for July twelfth are Castles in the Sky, you know, the folk who usually help Blackwell with the summer fete?"

"The people who owned that bouncy castle that I destroyed with my stiletto heel?" says Fleur, wincing.

"Yep," says Claude, trying not to cry. "But that wasn't the only thing last summer that got us in their bad books. I spoke to the boss, Cyril, this morning. Turns out there was lots of little breakages and spillages last year. Blackwell kids are just clumsy. So anyhow, Cyril won't let me reserve anything without paying the entire one-thousand-pound fee up front."

"All one thousand pounds!!?" I gasp.

"Yes. The full whack," says Claude. "I don't suppose you've got a thousand pounds, have you, Ronnie?"

"No," I say, a little gobsmacked. "I've got £42.50 in my current account. That's not really any help, is it?"

"But we can give him it in a few weeks when the ticket money comes in," argues Fleur. "Did you tell him that?"

"Yeah. I told him that," assures Claude. "He wants it now."

"What a pig," I say, for want of anything positive to add.

"He's just covering his back, I suppose. We're a bit of a risk to get involved with, so he reckons anyway," says Claude, being fair as ever.

"Hang on. I've got a little fund of cash my gran has put aside for me," offers Fleur sweetly. "I'm sure that's more than a thousand pounds . . . ," she says. "But actually I don't think I can have it till I'm aged twenty-one . . . oh, God, that's seven years away, isn't it?"

"No luck, Fleur, we've got until Monday at nine A.M. or he's canceling our order," Claude adds bleakly. "In fact, he's giving our stage and speakers to the Church of Eternal Light, who are holding their annual jamboree that day. They want to book a PA system too."

After this, none of us say anything for a long time.

In fact, not even Gianni Junior pirouetting about in a black silk shirt can cheer us up.

" 'Scuse me a minute, girlies," says Fleur, grabbing her phone and wandering out of the restaurant. Claude and I roll our eyes. This is a fine time for Fleur to choose to go and have a gossip.

"We could ask the bank for a temporary loan?" I suggest, knowing it's a long shot.

"No bank will give three teenage girls a massive loan. Well, not on a Saturday afternoon, anyhow . . . ," whispers Claude. She's already considered that one.

"I thought we could even wash cars to earn the money," says Claude. "But we'd need to find nearly five hundred folk willing to part with more than a couple of quid within the next forty-three hours. It's not going to happen, is it?"

"Er, no," I say.

More silence.

In fact, this time a deafening silence, pierced only by the bill for our pizza plonked down loudly on the table.

More debt. How upsetting.

This is a very big deal for Claude. Her messing up, that is. It just doesn't happen very often. Claude won't, or rather, *can't* let it happen. There's been too much fear of the unknown in Claude's life already; she won't allow it to occur these days without a fight. Not when a "Things to Do" list or a few well-spent hours researching on the Net can make life so organized.

"How can I tell everyone? How can I tell Liam and Ainsley?" mumbles Claude, blowing her nose on a Paramount Pizza napkin. Then she starts sobbing properly, which always takes me by surprise.

"Oh, come on, Claude, we won't have to," I say, knowing full well we might have to. Fleur is outside the restaurant window, walking up and down, yapping on her phone, waving her hands about in the air as she speaks. Suddenly she snaps the phone shut and comes back indoors.

"Well, I'll have to tell them soon," says Claude. "They're all practicing their hearts out. What will I say?"

Claude hates letting people down. If you say you'll do something, in C's books, you have to do it. Or else you have to give them about nine years' cancellation notice.

"RIGHT!" says Fleur. "I've been thinking . . . ooh, hang on, the bill . . . actually, I'll buy this as my little LBD treat."

Fleur gets out her charge card and throws it down.

"Ta, Fleur," we both say, trying to smile. Fleur's a star like that sometimes.

"What we need is a sponsor, isn't it?" continues Fleur, flicking her blond hair from her face. "Someone who could give us a little helping hand until we get on our feet?"

"Yes, please," says Claude.

"Someone who's sympathetic to the LBD and their work. You know, a person who knows us and knows that we're cool bambinos who can pull this whole Blackwell Live thing off?"

"That's exactly what we need," I say, raising an eyebrow.

"Well, come on, then. I've got us an appointment with a potential investor in twenty minutes," Fleur announces, signing her name, *Fleur Gabrielle Swan,* in big, swirly, proud letters at the bottom of her charge card receipt.

our hero, sort of

"So what you're saying to me, essentially, is," begins Paddy Swan, reclining in his plush black leather study chair, "that you want me to offer you an instant, high-risk, unsecured monetary loan? And you're asking for a thousand pounds?"

Fleur rolls her eyes. Claude and I grin nervously, realizing now how preposterous it sounds.

"You *know* that's what we want, Dad. We've been through this twice," says Fleur.

"Okay, okay. I know that's what you want," admits Mr. Swan. "I just like saying it, as it's by far the most amusing thing I've heard all week."

"Ho, and indeed, ho," groans Fleur.

Behind Mr. Swan's bald head, a large framed certificate upon his study wall reads:

There's even framed pics of Paddy cuddling James Bond castmembers at the last Bond convention he attended.

And *he* thinks *we're* amusing?

"But let me get this straight," Paddy continues. "Because maybe my senile dementia is taking hold more rapidly than I bargained. You actually intend to spend the money on village idiots like that 'Killa Blow,' oh, and that buffoon who lurks around the high street wearing his mother's makeup?"

"Ainsley Hammond," says Fleur.

"Ainsley Hammond! That's him!" Paddy scoffs. "Oh, and that prize numbskull who got up on the school roof last year and had to be escorted down by police."

"Liam Gelding," sighs Claude patiently.

"Hoo hoo! That's him!" Paddy chuckles, grabbing a man-size tissue and dabbing his eyes rather theatrically. "So you're asking me for money to put on a rock festival where they can play their music. Oh, my giddy aunt! You girls just get worse!"

This is not sounding good.

"Look, Dad, stop being like this," says Fleur rather firmly. "You sounded really impressed when I told you on the phone half an hour ago. You said you couldn't believe how mature and responsible we were being by organizing Blackwell Live."

"*Pggghh,*" Paddy splutters. "That was before I knew you

wanted the shirt off my back. Lordy me, that's all the Swan family see me as, isn't it? The Royal Bank of Paddy?"

"We'll give you it back," persists Fleur.

"When?" demands Paddy.

"Sunday, the thirteenth of July," chirps up Claude confidently.

"Hmmm," says Paddy, reaching for his chunky desk calculator.

"So let me see," he says, beginning to push buttons with his thick fingers. "One thousand pounds. Loaned on a short-term basis using Royal Bank of Paddy rates of nine percent . . ."

Claude gulps; she'd not even thought of paying back interest on a loan.

"Well, that's £1090 you'd owe me on the thirteenth," announces Paddy. "A bargain, I think you'll agree, ladies. And I'm not even charging you an administration fee . . . BUT I think we should look at the loan's terms in the event you hit upon problems."

"We won't," says Fleur.

"You might," argues Paddy. "It might be a tragic failure. And in that eventuality you'll be seeking a long-term loan, paying the cash back slowly at whatever your pocket money can cover."

We all stare at him blankly. Paddy is enjoying himself now.

"Now, let's take my delightful daughter Fleur here as the named loan holder," Paddy continues, punching numbers in furiously. "Fleur Swan . . . with her twenty-pound-per-month allowance, wants an unsecured loan of one thousand pounds at my long-term loan interest rate of twenty-seven percent."

We all groan now.

"Now, bearing in mind Ms. Swan already owes the Royal Bank of Paddy £347 for her last British Telecom bill," says Paddy, "and £421 for the Year Eight school ski trip she vowed to pay me back . . ."

Crunch, bash, ker-chunk go the buttons on Paddy's calculator.

A roll of paper spews out of the machine, covered in figures.

"And taking into account that Fleur spends every penny of her allowance every month and begs me for more, I reckon she could afford to pay me back around two pounds per month. Which means it would take . . ."

Paddy presses a final button and inspects the half-meter of calculator roll curled before him.

"Ninety-three years and five months to give me my money back."

We all look at Paddy mournfully.

"And between you and me, girls, I'm dearly hoping to be dead by then and not still bickering with my daughter about allowances and clowns called Killa Blow!"

Paddy is grinning, but then he notices how sad we all look and his expression changes to something a little more thoughtful.

I don't want to appear too desperate, so I concentrate on staring at Paddy's collection of framed family pictures, cluttering the far wall of his study. There's one of Paddy and Fleur, looking bronzed and athletic, playing tennis in France. And one of Fleur, aged about four, fixed up as a rabbit at a fancy-dress party wearing two shoe Odor-Eaters for bunny ears. (Oh, Lordy, how I'd love a copy of that picture to show to the EZ Life Syndicate.)

There's also a dead nice photo of Paddy on a beach somewhere, looking much younger (and, dare I say it, quite handsome) clutching three tiny, sandy kids to his chest. He's wearing a big grin, like he's won a gold medal or something.

"Look, kiddywinks, get out of my office and go and enjoy the day, eh? I'll get back to you on this one," he says. "I've got important things to do, you're cluttering up my heavy schedule."

Even though Paddy is making shooing motions with his hands, no one moves. We're not being insolent. I just don't think anyone knows where to go from here. If this means Blackwell Live's over, I don't feel much like going outdoors and playing swingball in Fleur's garden.

Suddenly Claude's phone lets out a little bleep indicating she has a voice mail; she checks the number.

"It's Wicked FM," she announces to nobody in particular in a voice so weary, it's obvious that the local radio station calling her is just adding to her worries.

"What do they want?" asks Fleur.

"Well, they've been interested about Blackwell Live. They want to interview some of us . . . so do the *Local Daily Mercury*," says Claude quietly.

"You're going to be on the radio and in the newspaper?" says Paddy.

"*Were* going to be," corrects Claude. "And I spoke to someone yesterday at *Look Live,* the local TV news program too. They sounded interested too."

"Hmmm," says Paddy again, clearly mulling this over.

"See, Dad, there would be lots of good publicity for you if

you got involved, eh?" says Fleur. "I can see the headlines: 'Local entrepreneur Patrick Swan supports good cause.' That sorta thing."

"Local entrepreneur?" Paddy repeats, clearly liking the sound of that.

"You could introduce some of the bands too!" says Claude, buttering him up further. "We need someone confident with a good speaking voice. You know, someone with a real air of authority."

"Authority . . . ," repeats Paddy, straightening his tie.

"Yeah, we totally need a grown-up who can appear on TV and radio talking about why Blackwell Live's such a brilliant idea," adds Fleur, knowing full well that Paddy would love, love, looooove to be a mini-celebrity.

"I could do that, couldn't I?" says Paddy, beaming. "I could be your official sponsor . . . ah, I can see it now . . . 'Blackwell Live, brought to you in association with Patrick Swan.' That's got a certain ring to it. . . ."

"You'd be a bit like a dark, mysterious, powerful character who everyone is in awe of," Fleur tells her dad. "You know, Patrick Swan to the rescue! Patrick Swan, the tall, handsome hero who saves the day for the damsels in distress. A bit like—"

"A bit like James Bond," announces Paddy Swan without a hint of irony.

"A LOT like James Bond," choruses the LBD, nodding madly.

Paddy seems quite giddy with delight, but then regains his composure.

Shaking his head as if he can't quite believe what he's doing, Mr. Swan slowly opens the top drawer of his desk, pulling out a leather-bound checkbook.

"Don't make me regret this, ladies," he warns, picking up his silver fountain pen, then pausing only to look up at three sets of teeth gleaming in his direction.

"Okay," he says. "Who shall I make this out to?"

a totally wicckkkked morning

Things I didn't know about the Wicked FM "Wake Up with Warren and Frankie" 6–9:00 A.M. Breakfast Bonanza until I visited the studio:

1) "Wacky Warren" Hart and "Fun Time Frankie" Foster are not half as sexy as they look in those photos Wicked FM send when you win a phone-in competition. They're both at least forty. And they wear old tracksuits to work and smoke Regal King Size cigarettes between records.

2) The "Wake-Up Crew" are not, in actual fact, a big gang of their laughing, hooting krrazy mates crammed into the studio, like I imagined. It's just a tape recording of people cheering. Warren just presses PLAY every time he sees fit. I'm not saying Frankie and Warren haven't got any real mates. This is just a practicality, as . . .

3) . . . the Wicked FM studio is the size of my bedroom. Tiny. In fact, the LBD, Ainsley Hammond, Liam Gelding, Jimi, Christy Sullivan, Panama and Killa Blow have to loiter in the drafty corridor until it's our time to go on air plugging the festival. Panama is being extra-annoying at this stage, warming up her singing voice just in case she gets asked to perform. "Doh-Ray-Mi-Fah-So-La-Tee-Doooooooh!" she warbles, as well as batting her eyelashes at anything in trousers and begging for some warm honey and lemon to "soothe her esophagus." Grrrr. Jimi, the numbskull, slopes off to find her a cup of tea.

4) Frankie and Warren really DO know Panama; she wasn't making it up. And they think she's fantastic.

"Annnnd we're back! Good morning! It's Wednesday, the second of July! And hey, listeners, it really is fabulous to have the Blackwell Live kids with us this morning on the Wicked 86.4 Wake Up with Warren and Frankie Breakfast Bonanza!" says Warren. "Isn't it, Frankie?"

"It's grrrreat!" says Frankie, pressing PLAY on the Wake-Up Crew Tape.

"Woooo-hooo!!!" goes "the crew."

On the recording, a party-popper explodes and someone honks a kazoo merrily. This all sounds faintly ridiculous now that I'm standing beside it.

"Yup, it's seven forty-seven A.M. and we're over the moon to have these amazing kids with us live in the studio," continues Warren. "They're putting on a krrrazy-cool live music event to rival Astlebury or Reading Rock Festival on July twelfth in the school grounds, and they wanna spread the word. Don't you, kids?"

"Yeah," we all murmur, fully aware we're Live On Air and the entire town is listening. Jimi is hiding at the back of the group with Liam, whose face is bright red. Ainsley is just peering at "Fun Time Frankie" as if he's an alien.

Fleur and I aren't much use either, we're just grinning.

"Thanks for having us! We're so glad to be here!" pipes up Panama.

"Yeah, really happy," butts in Claude.

"So, Panama Goodyear, we've seen a lot of you in the past year along with your very talented group, Catwalk. Blackwell Live must be an exciting opportunity for you guys to perform," asks Warren.

"Oh, amazing, yeah!" purrs Panama. "I mean, after we won the Wicked FM Star Search quarterfinals, we all remarked on how there's just not enough live music in our community."

"Totally," agrees Warren.

"So that's where we came up with the idea for Blackwell Live . . . ," says Panama.

This is the most shockingly blatant lie I've heard since Fleur claimed her last lovebite was an allergic rash.

"Splagh pghhhh!" grunts Claude, trying to think of a polite way to call Panama a sniveling little liar on live radio.

"Grrrreat!" shrieks Frankie, slightly pointlessly, while also picking a lump of sleep out of his eye.

"But there's something for everyone at Blackwell Live too," announces Claude. "I mean, as well at Catwalk, we've got five other brilliant local bands. Like Lost Messiah and Death Knell."

"Yes, I see you've got quite a lineup. Have you all been practicing, then, kids?"

"*Murrr, mmm,* yeah," mumbles our gang, our shyness simply giving Panama Motor-Mouth more chance to warble on and on.

"Catwalk practice every single day!" shrills Panama. "We're absolute perfectionists when it comes to *our art.*"

"Oh, *purlease,*" mutters Ainsley, finally finding his tongue.

"Well, good to hear that, Panama," says Frankie. "And we've got to go to a record now, so we'll get back to the Blackwell Live gang later."

"Woo-hoo! Yeah!! Part-eeeeee!!" cheer the imaginary posse.

"But just one quick question," cheeps Warren. "I'm assuming that Catwalk, being the local celebs they are, will be the head-lining act on the twelfth?"

Warren grins at the Blackwell gang, not understanding the gravity of his question.

After four seconds of silence—which is a very long time indeed when you're Live On Air—both Panama and Claude speak at exactly the same time.

"Yeah, of course!" squeaks Panama, shaking her glossy brown hair behind her.

"No, not necessarily," contradicts Claude. "We've got so much talent to choose from, it's really undecided at the moment."

Claude and Panama turn to each other, scowling.

Ouch.

"Ooooh, listeners! A little bit of controversy there to go with your cornflakes. We seem to have a disagreement!"

"There's no disagreement," says Panama. "Claudette is just a bit confused. Catwalk WILL be the headline act, no one needs to worry about that—"

"Well, actually," begins Claude, "I think you'll find—"

"Oh, don't make me have to come over there and slap you," snarls Panama.

"Don't threaten me, you bully," snaps Claude back.

"Oh, that's great, kids, but there's no more time!" butts in Warren, sensing a fight about to break out. "Now, on 86.4, here's the grrrreat sound of the Happy Clappers with 'La La La Love!'"

And then we're off air.

Along with the entire town, I think I just witnessed Claudette Cassiera very nearly lose her cool.

Big time.

It's an exceedingly long, quiet journey back to Blackwell School.

Warren and Frankie never did "get back to us" after the Happy Clappers. In fact, we were ushered rapidly out of the studio by a Wicked FM researcher.

In a bid to "make it obvious" to Jimi I think he's hot, I planned to nab a seat in the minibus beside him; however, Panama's tiny bottom was already perched in place. For once she wasn't speaking. She was simply staring at her reflection in the minibus window, reapplying glistening pink lip gloss to her luscious, full lips. And sort of smiling at herself.

Bizarrely enough, at Blackwell's school gates, a gaggle of

Year 7 kids have gathered to wave and cheer as we pass by. Panama perks up when she sees some fans and waves graciously. In the middle of the throng stand two unlikely Catwalk devotees: Benny Stark and Tara from Guttersnipe lurking on the curb, smiling from ear to ear.

"Nice one, girls!" says Tara, clapping me on the shoulder as I tumble out of the bus.

Claude sighs.

"Everyone is talking about Wicked FM this morning, man," begins Benny.

"Yeah, that was really funny. I almost peed my pants!" chips in Tara.

"Hmmm, maybe," mutters Claude, "I think we let ourselves down a bit."

"Nah . . . you didn't," argues Benny, beckoning us to follow him in the direction of the drama studio. "That's what we came to tell you. Come and see what's happening . . . it's brilliant."

We all look at him with perplexed expressions.

"Those two Bellringing dudes," mumbles Benny, "the ones you left in charge of selling Blackwell Live tickets this morning . . . they're a bit, er, stressed-out. Mrs. Guinevere has been making them cups of sweet tea and trying to instill a bit of order down there—"

"What do you mean?" Fleur asks.

"Well, have you ever heard that saying 'All publicity is good publicity'?" asks Tara, cocking her head to the side rather coolly.

"Uh-huh."

"Well, since your little spat with Panama this morning, they've already sold 487 Blackwell Live tickets—"

"Four hundred and eighty-seven!" mouths Claude.

"It's all gone a bit freaky-disco," sniggers Benny, his ringlets shaking as he chuckles.

"What?" we all gasp, spying queues of kids reaching right out of the drama studio and past the gym.

And when I look back around, Liam is twirling Claude round and round shrieking, and Fleur . . . well, Fleur is glued to the spot, for the first time fully realizing the sheer gravity of what the LBD have created.

hold the front page

How the *Look Live* TV crew condensed an entire day of filming around Blackwell School into *three and a half measly minutes* was astounding. And they also sandwiched our story between a clip about local otters and the pollen forecast!

This was not how I'd envisioned my TV debut.

I thought we were going to at least be a news headline. Serves me right for spending the entire day clutching a clipboard, trying to look professional, aiming to get my schneck into every shot. For all my dramatic efforts, the *Look Live* crew eventually reduced the whole Blackwell Live scoop down to some footage of Catwalk's Leeza and Abigail shimmying in tight-fitting fuchsia leotards, a bit of Death Knell's Ainsley Hammond and Candy wailing and hitting steel drums with wooden spoons, plus two seconds of Claude saying: "Er, please buy a ticket. It'll probably be quite good, honest!"

"I didn't say it like that!" moaned Claude. "That was me messing about. I said it another ten times after that in a really sensible way. Ooh, I can't belieeeve they used that take . . ."

Thank Jehovah Paddy Swan wedged his face into the report. We never heard the last of it after we totally forgot to mention him on Wicked FM. "The ink's not even dry on that check, and already I'm yesterday's news!" he'd grumbled.

Luckily Paddy's face filled the screen for almost twelve seconds at the end of the *Look Live* report (yes, he did count them). He was billed as "a local entrepreneur and music fanatic," and was shown harping on about giving something back to the community that had given so much to him.

Ha ha ha. "Music fanatic"? This is the man who actually *cut the plug off* Fleur's stereo when she refused to study for the Year 8 exams.

"I look fantastic, don't I?" announced Paddy to Mrs. Swan, rewinding the video to make us all watch him for the tenth time.

"Yes, darling. You look outrageously handsome," Saskia Swan concurred.

"Shall we watch it again?"

"Oh, yes, let's!" gushed Mrs. Swan.

Feigning homework, the LBD managed to escape.

Then, later this week, a *Daily Mercury* reporter and photographer showed up to snap the LBD for a Blackwell Live preview article. Very exciting, huh!? And, this time, with only three faces in the picture, it was a breeze stealing a more starring role . . . even though the very moment the newspaper plopped on the doormat of the Fantastic Voyage this evening, with the LBD plastered all over the front cover, I immediately regretted it.

I'd been quite nervous, you see, about looking good in the local paper. So nervous, in fact, that I'd spent my entire lunch hour preening my hair into something more fluffy . . . then changing my mind and combing it flat again. Then trying to work in a hip side parting. Then spraying ultrafine hair serum all over it to make it a bit more orderly . . . then eventually trying to breathe a bit of life and movement into it again. By this stage my hair was lying flat and rock hard against my skull like a fifty-year-old businessman's hairdo. It was at this point Fleur Swan, who once partook of a Fashion Modeling Course (which cost Paddy stacks of money and promised to make her a supermodel the second she finishes school) stepped in with some great advice.

"Never mind your hair," she said. "When you're being photographed, the trick is to follow the golden rules of modeling if you want to look amazing."

"Which are?" I said, trying to remove a comb tangled in the back of my head.

"Okay, well, number one, point your chin slightly down so you can't see any double chinnage."

"Okay," I said, trying to remember this.

"Then, two, swivel your hips to the side with your hands on your waist. This makes you look sleeker and also emphasizes your curves," Fleur said, demonstrating the pose.

"Wow," I gasped. Fleur looked like a real fox when she did that.

"Three: Hold your upper arms slightly away from your body," advises Fleur. "This avoids chunky corned beef upper arms problem."

"But I don't have—" I began.

"Oh, you will if you don't do this, believe me," Fleur announced. "And try to look confident and enthusiastic, not so flaky. You really wind me up when you do that."

"I'm *not* flaky! There's that word again! 'Flaky.' Stop calling me fl—"

"Then, most importantly," continued Fleur, "place your tongue gently behind your top teeth, open your mouth ever so slightly and SMILE!!!"

It seemed an awful load of trouble to go to for one photograph, but I was willing to give it a go. Especially as Jimi would no doubt see it.

Of course, when the *Daily Mercury* came out this evening, Fleur and Claude were standing completely normally, while I was standing like some sort of contorted, deeply disturbed circus sideshow escapee with a backward wig on.

"I'm going to keep this beside the cash register. It'll scare people from robbing my takings," remarked my dad before giving me a big hug.

I really really hate Fleur sometimes.

a small oversight

But somewhere this week, between schmoozing reporters and TV crews, amongst the band practices and the battles with Panama, between flirting with Jimi and arguing about the worst-case scenario with Mr. McGraw, as well as stinging Paddy for a grand and fantasizing a whole lot about July twelfth . . . I seem to have overlooked something quite obvious.

I've not set eyes on my mother for four days.

In fact, it's only this moment, as I walked though the pub doors and noticed Muriel, our sous-chef, gazing at me pitifully before offering to make my a couple of nice poached eggs for my dinner, that I realize something is wrong.

"Where's my mother, Muriel?" I ask.

"Oh . . . well, I'm not too sure, darling," lies Muriel. "Maybe you should ask your dad."

"Well, why don't you tell me?" I say.

"Cos I don't know, honeypie. Now, those eggs . . ." Muriel turns her head and pretends to look for a saucepan.

"MURIEL!"

"Okay! Okay!! She's at your nan's house. She's moved out. Er, I think. I'm not sure, though. Oh, Veronica, go and ask your father, I shouldn't be telling you this, it's not my place," Muriel says kindly but firmly.

"Where is he? Has he moved out too!? What does that make me? An orphan?" I say in a high-pitched tone.

"No, he's upstairs. Go and talk to him, Veronica, he needs you to be sweet to him. He's upset."

"*He's* upset? What about me? I'm the one missing a mother!!" I storm upstairs, bypassing the den, where I can hear some excessively sad blues music flooding from the stereo.

This is a fine time to be lying about, listening to records, I think. Then I remember that last week, when Jimi didn't ask me out after collecting his hooded top, I was so depressed that I listened to track four, "Merry Go Round," which is the saddest song on the Spike Saunders CD, thirty-two times in a row.

Maybe Dad really is upset after all.

I storm into my bedroom, snapping the door firmly shut

and flinging myself on the bed, where I lie for almost twenty minutes brainstorming reasons my parents might have for splitting up.

I can't really think of anything valid.

I mean, they bicker quite a lot. But that's not really surprising, what with both of them being fairly irritating.

I suppose Mum does have that running niggle that Dad's family are all of a far lower social class than hers, and that lots of them are "career criminals," while Dad always bitches about Mum's family having "delusions of grandeur" and are actually descended from Gypsies. But that can't be it, can it?

That's mostly a joke, isn't it? Well, so I thought.

And they argue about money a lot. Like when Dad forgets to pay bills and we get our meat supply canceled. Or when Mum goes out to buy a new dress and comes home with a new state-of-the-art trunk freezer worth over two thousand pounds. Yep, that argument was a doozy.

But they always get it together again.

Don't they?

I put on Spike again to drown out the sounds from the den.

Maybe one of them is seeing another person?

Oh, God, that can't be possible.

No, that would mean someone has literally spied either my mum or my dad and thought, "Oooh, hang on. That is one hottie over there! Be still, my beating heart. Blah blah blah . . ." before setting about wrecking my happy family home.

(Funny how you don't realize what you had until it's gone, eh? It was quite a happy home.)

But that doesn't make sense.

I mean, if I, Ronnie Ripperton, in the prime of my life, trying my damnedest to look gorgeous, can't get a single soul to fancy me, how the heck can a psychotic chef with bizarre eating habits or a man who perpetually smells of stale beer and ashtrays attract the opposite sex?

How?!

And then suddenly I start feeling very cold and alone in my little room. Because maybe this was all *my* fault.

I mean, I'm not much of a daughter, am I? And I'm always pulling stunts that annoy one of them. And then whoever I have the fight with bawls me out . . . leading the other one to start defending me. Then they both have a big row with each other.

This has definitely got much worse lately.

Mum's always on my back about something petty, and Dad usually tries to smooth things over by saying: "Oh, come on, Magda, leave her, she's only a little girl!" which drives my mother totally stark raving bonkers, as she knows full well that I'm fourteen and not a little girl at all. I'm completely capable of cleaning my own bedroom or remembering to lock the back door when I come home at night. Or all those other stupid, thoughtless things I do.

So maybe this is all my fault.

I really don't feel so clever now.

"Mum?"

"Oh, hello, darling," she says. "Oh, so you've eventually called me. Have you run out of clean knickers or something?"

Touché.

"I didn't realize you'd gone."

"Exactly," says Mum.

"Is that why you've gone?" I say, deciding to skip straight to the point of the phone call, sparing formalities. "Because I'm thoughtless and you have to wash my underwear and do loads of stuff for me?"

My voice is all wobbly now.

"Oh! Oh, God, no, Ronnie. No, not at all," Mum says, realizing that I'm putting two and two together and coming up with 157. "I didn't mean that last bit. I know you're really busy at the moment. I'm not really annoyed you didn't notice I'd gone."

"When are you coming home, Mum? And why are you there? And what's going on?" I say, mumbling all my key questions at once.

"It's okay, Ronnie, chill out," says Mum.

"Chill out!? What are you doing at Nan's house?" I say, beginning to raise my voice.

Long pause.

"I'm having some time to think."

"About what?"

"About what I want."

"What, about whether you want to live here anymore!? What's wrong with living with me and Dad?" I say.

My mother has quite clearly gone mad.

"No, I need to think about the future," says Mum.

"But you can do that here!" I snap back.

"I can't," says Mum firmly. "Me and your dad . . . we want different things."

"Like what?"

"Well, right now he wants me to live at the Fantastic Voyage. And I, well, I want to live at your nan's," Mum says. Then she starts softly chuckling.

I am in no mood for her hilarity.

"Mother, have you been drinking?"

"I wish I had," she sighs.

"Mum, I'm really getting freaked about all this now," I say, even though freaked isn't really how I feel. I can't explain how I feel. A bit numb really. A bit like life as I know it has just unceremoniously crashed and burned, and I'm too stupid to even work out why.

"Just tell me what's going on," I eventually say. And this time, by asking the obvious question, I seem to gain a smattering of information.

"Okay. Okay," Mum sighs. "I know I'm being unfair, that *we're* being unfair. I just didn't see the point in dragging you into things. Look, shall we just say that something important has happened. And me and your dad have got different opinions on how to handle, er, it."

"What, has a big bill arrived? Something like that? Or do you want to fire someone and he doesn't?"

"Er, no. Not like that. It's bigger than that. Look, don't worry about it—"

"Oh, all right, I won't worry about it then," I snap at her.

And then we both don't say anything for ages. I can hear Nan's cuckoo clock ticking away in the background.

"Look, Ronnie, I'm really riled by what your dad said last

night. I don't want to look at him at the moment," she says. "I just need a few days—"

"Days?" I repeat.

"Or weeks. Months. I can't tell. You'll be fine whatever we decide to do. You're dead important to us, Ronnie," says Mum. "I've gotta go. I need the toilet, Ronnie. I'll call you."

And then she hung up.

I really don't know how to feel about all of this. So I opt for "angry." And in strict alignment with the universal rule of bad moods, I decide to bum out the day of the very next person I come across. This just so happens to be my dad.

"Hmmph," I say, flouncing into the den, throwing the door back so heavily, it hits a nearby freestanding wall cabinet with a huge smash. I've only been told not to do this about seven zillion times before.

"Hello, sweet pea," says my dad rather glumly. He's surrounded by mountains of old vinyl LPs, coffee cups and overflowing ashtrays. It's almost as if he's forgotten that it's Friday evening and hundreds of beer addicts are heading toward the Fantastic Voyage for fun and lager-fueled frivolity. Oh, no, that's not a priority. He's too busy listening to old blues records.

"Why is Mum living at Nan's house? What have you done?" I begin, as subtly as a tornado.

"I've not DONE anything," says Dad, looking deeply wounded. "Well, not much. Your mum's decided to move out. For a bit. Er, well, I hope for a bit anyhow. There's more space for her to think at your nan's."

"Space to think!?" I splutter. "Why is everyone talking in rid-dles?"

"Hmmm," says Dad, staring into the middle distance. "Actually, that's quite a good point, Ronno. I'm not sure what that means either."

"Wonderful," I say sarcastically.

"She'll be back, though," announces Dad meekly, picking a bit of dried chicken tikka masala sauce off his shirt. He hasn't shaved for days either. "If she knows what's good for her."

He doesn't look too much like a "Welcome Home" treat to me.

"You're really angry at me, aren't you?" he asks, perceptively noticing my eyes drilling into him and my nostrils flaring.

"Well, yeah. I am! I mean, it just makes me mad that no one tells me anything around here—"

"You hear about most things—"

"And I mean, there's only THREE of us in this house, so it's not too much to ask that I be informed of the latest departures and arrivals—"

"Actually, I wouldn't speak too soon on that one," Dad mut-ters.

"But somehow," I say, ignoring Dad's mutterings, "SOME-HOW I still get treated like a BABY!! And I'm not a BABY. I won't be treated like one anymore!!" I announce, pointing my finger at him.

"That's a good job, really, because . . . ," Dad begins, but then he stops whatever it was he was going to say as tears begin to drizzle down my cheeks.

"Ronnie, you've got loads on your plate at the moment. It's your school festival in like seven days, isn't it?"

"Sheven daysh from tomorrowsh," I say, snorting tears and snot back up my nose.

"Listen, I've been thinking about that. You know what you were saying on Wednesday? About more people buying tickets than you ever imagined? And about Claude having hassles with hiring equipment and all that sort of thing?"

"Yeah. We're all right now, though. Fleur's dad lent us a grand. I told you that too, didn't I?"

Dad went slightly white when I said that.

"Oh. No, no, I didn't know that. You can pay it back, can't you?" he asks, to which I just roll my eyes at him and thin my lips.

An adequate answer in my opinion.

"Well, anyhow, it was just that I was thinking. Well, you know that I used to dabble in the music industry before you were born and that I still know a load of the old faces who work touring with rock bands on the road?"

"Uh-huh," I say. Of course I do. He's always going on about it.

"Well, seeing as this whole Blackwell Live thing is getting so big . . . well, how's about me calling some of my old mates up and seeing if they can lend a hand?" he says, grinning at me like this is the best idea in the world.

I stare at my father incredulously, without blinking, for about half a minute.

"Well, what do you reckon?" he says, clearly glad to be

thinking about something other than my missing mum for five minutes. "Good idea?"

I stand up and walk toward the door, carefully preparing my exit speech. Dad has really done it this time.

"That is just typical! Really typical!!" I begin in a rather raised voice.

"What is?!" shouts Dad.

"YOU! You think I'm some sort of stupid kid with stupid mates and we can't do anything by ourselves. Like I need you and some other crinkly old duffers to sort out our mess? I don't believe it!" I shriek.

"Ronnie. Don't be daft. I didn't mean it like that, I just thought that—"

"Yeah, that's right, call me daft! I am daft. I'm really stupid, aren't I? I'm so stupid that you and Mum are splitting up and no one even tells me why."

"Ronnie, calm down. Where are you going?!"

"I'm going out. Nobody cares where I'm going, anyway!" I yell. And by this point I'm pretty much just saying the first things that come into my head without really knowing why, just because shouting is making me feel better. Which does, by no means, excuse the following gems that drip from my lips.

"And because I hate you. I hate both of you. I hate being alive. I wish you'd never had me . . . in fact, I know that you two wish you'd never had me either!! Good-bye!!"

SLLLLLLAAAM!

I've said so many shocking things in that last sentence that as I crunched shut the den door, my final view of my father's face was pure "rabbit caught in the headlights."

So I throw back the gate of the Fantastic Voyage, I kick a nearby pile of refuse bags, I hiss at the neighbor's cat, who seems to be mocking me from atop an adjacent garage, then I begin stomping up the high street toward Fleur's gaff.

I feel amazingly angry, and by default I actually feel quite amazing.

Huh, I really told him, didn't I?! I think, recalling every second of my outburst. *He knows where he stands now, doesn't he! Huh?*

And on I plod . . . except that now with every shop I pass, and every few meters I travel, I'm becoming a little more creepingly aware of what a total idiot I've been.

As the seconds tick past and I'm almost halfway to Fleur's, I'm beginning to realize just how hurt Dad looked and how nasty I was to him when he was probably just trying to be kind. And how much I just want to run back home, if my pride would let me, and tell him that I'm not mad at him. It's just that the thought of Mum leaving us makes me want to hurl with fear, and I'm stressed about the festival, and I don't really know why I said all that stuff.

And I'm dead sorry.

But I don't. As that seems a difficult thing to do, as opposed to just going to Fleur's house, bitching about him for a while, then watching a video. So I keep on walking.

And that's when I see them.

Jimi Steele and Panama Goodyear.

In the window of Paramount Pizza. Jimi's arm draped

around Panama's shoulder, while Panama feeds him a tempting spoon of tiramisu. Within a millisecond Panama spots me and is waving, nudging Jimi, who looks up, attempting a smile that just looks extremely sheepish. Panama is distracted by this point, gently kissing the apple of Jimi's cheek.

And I want to scream out. But by this point all my adrenaline had trickled away, leaving me standing in the street all alone, with a knotted stomach and a heart shriveled to the size of a piece of old chewing gum.

Chapter 10

a special visit

I didn't get out of bed yesterday.

Instead, I hid beneath my duvet with the curtains drawn for the entire Saturday, reading a novel I stole from Mum entitled *A Certain Taboo*. It's rubbish. No wonder my mother always drinks too many margaritas, then falls asleep on the beach with a book on her face, if this is the sort of drivel she reads.

I didn't get dressed yesterday either.

I wore my underwear all day, simply pulling on a sweater for bathroom trips. There didn't seem to be any point.

In getting up and getting dressed, that is.

Or living.

I'd texted Claude and Fleur first thing and lied that I was at Nan's, then I bolted my bedroom door with my Do Not Disturb sign hanging from the handle. Every time Dad knocked, I faked snoring until I heard him padding away down the landing, sighing. I was feeling highly antisocial. There was, and still is, nothing that any individual can possibly say to make me feel any better. Especially as my mum has still not come home. Or even called me back on my cell phone like she said she would. Okay, I could have called her, but that's not the point, is it? I mean, I'm her daughter. It should be her motherly instinct to call and check if I've had my breakfast or have got enough spends for the day, instead of just lazing about at my nan's house "having time to think." My social worker, when I get one, will be hearing about this, mark my words. About the day my mum abandoned me as she "needed time to think," and I spent a day alone, in my underwear, starving.

And "think" about what, exactly? You don't have to think about whether you want to live with your husband and your daughter, do you? Huh? No, you "need time" to think about stuff like whether you want to buy that top you've tried on in blue *or* in black. Or "time" to think about what you fancy off a restaurant menu. You don't have to stop and think about living with your family, do you?

Mum should come back straightaway, Dad should make her.

I feel like I'm going mad.

I really just want everything to be back to normal. It's not nice thinking we can't all live here together anymore. And, er, I realize now that I really love them both too.

There, I've said it.

I love them both.

But I'm not saying that to them, as I'm not speaking to either of the miserable, irritating gits.

I cried my eyes out on Friday night after I saw Jimi and Panama. I sat in the little swing park behind the shops all by myself and cried till my eyes swelled up and my sleeves were covered in snot. In the end a tramp sidled over to me to ask me if I was okay, offering me some of his White Wizard cider. (I refused, but it was still a kind thing to do, now I come to think. I mean, he needed the cider more than me.)

But now that I've had time to think about it, I can see exactly why Jimi's going out with her. She's really pretty. Like, drop-dead gorgeous. And she's got gigantic boobs she's not scared to put on show. Not like me, I've got bigger boobs on my back, well, so some kind lad pointed out in physical ed last year. And she's always doing really cool stuff, like popping to London for the weekend to see her cousins. Or having parties. Or going on holiday to dead exotic places where she has jet lag when she gets home.

And yes, I know she's a horrible, soulless, vicious school bully. But boys can never see that, can they? They just *don't* see it. I can think of tons of times in class when the LBD have been gossiping away about some really heinous, gutter-level, wicked thing Panama has said or done. The lads in our class will earwig intently, devouring every gruesome detail of Panama's wrongdoing, then at the end, one of them will always pipe up: "Who? Are you talking about Panama Goodyear? That bird in Year Eleven with the long brown hair and the big scones?! She's fit as anything, she is!" Then they'll dissolve into a loud and heartfelt *"Phwoaaaaarrrrr!"*

I was a total dweeb for thinking Jimi was any different. Or thinking that someone as amazing and X-factor as he is could have maybe had the hots for me. Me, with my combination skin, my pear-shaped bottom and my loonytoons family.

But anyway, as I said, I cried for ages the other night. But now I just don't want to think about them. I hope they're really happy together. In fact, I hope he plummets between the gap in her monstrous cleavage and has to be retrieved by a passing mountain rescue crew.

I'm just really happy here, all alone, in my underwear, with my book.

Even if it is poo.

So it's now 10:00 A.M. Sunday morning and I'm still in bed, reading a totally riveting part of *A Certain Taboo,* when I'm disturbed from bad-book land by a noise from downstairs: the unmistakable sound of several guitars being tuned up.

Oh, no.

Oh, please, no.

It's Sunday, isn't it? It's Lost Messiah's day for practicing at the Fantastic Voyage. They're downstairs now. Jimi Steele is on the premises and I'm in underwear and I haven't washed my hair or cleaned my teeth for two days! I smell like a WWE wrestler's jockstrap. Damn. I better get up really quickly and choose an outfit and get a shower and . . .

Hang on a minute! He goes out with Panama now, doesn't he? What I look like is now superfluous to the plot. Game over. Right, I'm not moving a muscle. I'm just going to languish here in my pit, reading my book, looking like a swamp donkey. Which I manage, just about, for the next half hour despite drumming, singing, guitar riffs and amp feedback reverberating through my bedroom. Occasionally, as I overhear yet another voice join the merry throng downstairs, I emit a little *"Hmmmph"* of disapproval. But I certainly don't leap out of bed and start attempting to beautify myself.

How strong am I!

But then I hear Dad's voice, shouting up the stairs, "Ronnie! Ronnie, I know you're up there. Come here."

I freeze and pull the duvet over my head.

Not on your life, chum.

"Ronnie, your pals are here to see you," he finally shouts.

In the background I can hear some girlish giggles. Aha, it's Fleur and Claude! I knew they'd come and find me before long.

"I'll just send them up," he shouts. "Go on up, ladies, she's just hibernating."

I leap out of bed and fling open the door, wearing only my big pair of outsized lilac knickers accompanied by an old gray vest with tomato sauce stains down the front.

"Welcome to my world," I mutter mournfully, by way of explaining why I look so skanky.

But instead of Fleur or Claude, all I hear is two high-pitched screeches and someone muttering: "Ugggh, how revolting."

When I look up, to my utter horror, it's Panama Goodyear, Leeza and Abigail standing on my landing outside my bedroom door, sneering at me, my knickers and my house.

Joy.

"Mmm, gorgeous decor," quips Leeza, grimacing at our flock wallpaper, which to be fair is the sort that only mums think is smart. "It's very lived-in, isn't it?"

"Yeah, I must look out for this hovel in *Beautiful Homes Magazine*," simpers Abigail.

"Wah?" I grunt, trying to hide my entire body behind the door.

"We were just passing by," begins Panama. "Well, y'know, I was just popping in to see my boyfriend, who's practicing downstairs. Jimi Steele. I go out with him now. Oh, but you know that, though, don't you?" Panama smiles smugly. "We saw you on Friday when we were having pizza. Your face was a real picture!"

"Mmmm," I say, lost for words.

"Jimi mentioned that you and him are quite good friends," continues Panama. "And I was saying, hee hee, I bet Ronnie fancies you and she'll be gutted that we're an item now, but Jimi seems to think not. Hee hee, isn't that funny?"

"Hilarious," I say through very thin lips. "Look, what can I do for you exactly? Shouldn't you be practicing or something? Blackwell Live is this week, you know—"

"Ooh, we know!" Leeza giggles.

"We're *very* excited!" says Abigail.

"Zane and Derren and us girls have been practicing our five-part harmonies all week," says Panama. "We sound incredible."

"I've no doubt," I say sarcastically.

"But, you see, that was what we were stopping by to talk about. Blackwell Live," says Panama. "I just wanted to talk to you about this whole 'who's the headline act' saga. It's getting a little tiresome, isn't it?"

"You don't say," I sigh.

"We need to iron it out once and for all," shrills Abigail.

"Exactly," says Panama. "I mean, to be honest, it's not the fact that we want to perform top of the bill that's the biggest problem. Not as much as the fact that a trio of insolent, common, ugly little mutants such as you are actually disobeying us. It really is unbelievable and quite, quite unacceptable." Panama's voice is a snarl now. "And I won't tolerate it."

Panama draws her face up to mine, but then smells my rather fuggy breath and quickly withdraws.

"So, what are you going to do, Panama, beat me up?" I say bravely. Not even Panama would have the nerve to pulverize me with my dad downstairs. Would she?

"Of course we're not going to beat you up. What kind of amateur operation do you think I'm running here?" Panama sneers, adjusting her scarlet velour headband. "No, we've got better ideas than that."

"Much better!" confirms Leeza.

"Firstly, we've been contemplating canceling our Blackwell Live slot altogether," says Abigail. "Obviously we'd tell Mr. McGraw, Mrs. Guinevere and Mr. Foxton that it was down to your unprofessional and childish way of handling things. That won't be very nice, will it? Ticket refunds? Teachers shouting at you? Feelings of failure and hopelessness? That sort of thing?"

I just stare at them blankly. Yes, that would be hideous.

"But better still, we'll tell people at school all about the little problems you've been having with your mummy and daddy. Poor Ronnie, huh? Awww, such a sad tale, eh? Jimi told me all about it . . ."

What? I cannot believe that Jimi has told Panama Goodyear how sad I am about my mum and dad. I cannot believe it. I feel like someone just kicked me in the stomach.

"But of course, that will be a really boring story, so I'm going to spice it up and say your mum's an alcoholic and your dad used to hit her."

"You can't do that!" I begin to shout, realizing instantly that I'm playing straight into their hands, as their faces all light up at once.

"No one will believe you, Panama," I say more quietly. "Anyhow, no one cares what you say," I mumble, knowing that at least some people will and that'll be enough.

"Ahem, I think you'll find they will. It'll be the best rumor ever!" snaps Panama. "Especially when they hear about you and the boys from EZ Life Syndicate. What's all this about you snogging three of them already?! How perfectly . . . grubby?!" She sneers.

"Panama, I have NEVER even touched a single member of EZ Life. Who told you that?!!" I yell, eventually losing my temper.

"No one!" screeches Leeza. "We just made it up. Brilliant, aren't we?!"

"And the best bit is, we just made those rumors up on the way here. Imagine what we'll conjure up about your other two freaky friends once we've had time to think?" Abigail laughs.

"Exactly," says Panama. "So, sort it out, Ronnie. It'll be a lot easier for you all, believe me," she says, disappearing down the stairs.

"*Ciao, ciao!*" Abigail and Leeza giggle, waving and blowing me kisses.

And then they were gone, leaving me all alone, totally gobsmacked, trying to work out why adults bring up kids to believe total hogwash like "Sticks and stones will break my bones but names will never hurt me." Because when it comes to Panama Goodyear, I'd rather take a physical pummeling with a big stick anytime.

with a little help (Prom my Priends)

It's Sunday at 7 P.M. You'll be pleased to know that I've abandoned my self-imposed house arrest and have made it, fully clothed, to LBD headquarters. The instant Fleur heard my very snot-fueled *"Gnnnnn splgh snnnniiiiiff"* emitting down the phone, she prized every terrible detail of Panama Goodyear's royal visit from me.

"I hate her, Fleur," I sobbed. I actually had a sore head from crying by this point.

"Well, that's okay, cupcake," said Fleur. "I hate her too. Look, Ronnie, get yourself around here right now, I'm ringing Claude. I think a rendezvous is in order."

Sure, I was tempted to stride down the high street clad only in lilac undies and a stained vest, just to stress the point to passersby that my world had collapsed, but I decided against it. Of course, naked may have been preferable. That magic basket in the corner of my bedroom that I put laundry into, then it appears magically clean and fresh again in a pile on my bed . . . well, it seems to have stopped working ever since Mum left. So I had to wear crumpled, dirty stuff instead.

"I'm not telling you," announces Fleur, shaking her head.

"Tell me," I say.

"I'm not telling you. Look, why do you want to know, anyway?"

"Oh, just tell her," announces Claude. "It'll give her, er, closure."

"Are you sure? Well, okay, but this is only the gossip I heard . . . ," begins Fleur. "It was on Thursday night, apparently the girls from Catwalk and Jimi, Aaron and Naz from Lost Messiah were all messing about rehearsing in the drama studio."

"And?" I say, my bottom lip wobbling.

"And what? Oh, God, Ronnie! Do you really wanna know? Okay, he walked her home and they had a big snog on Panama's garden path, apparently her mum and dad were at the supermarket, so there was no one in. So she invited him into her kitchen for a drink and they had an even bigger snog there and—"

"I DON'T WANT TO KNOW THIS!" I shout, throwing my face down in Fleur's duvet.

"Precisely," Fleur says, rubbing my arm. "Besides, Ron, I was looking closely at Jimi the other day, and I was thinking, have you ever noticed that stupid face he pulls when he's skateboarding? He's borderline circus freak, if you ask me. And he's got weird floppy lips. He's probably a really slobbery kisser."

I sit up, placing my finger to her mouth.

"Fleur. Don't say too much. Cos me and Jimi *are* going to get together someday and I don't want there to be bad feelings between me and you."

I'm only half-joking.

Claude and Fleur gaze at me pitifully, dressed in my disheveled clothes.

"Okay," agrees Fleur, but as I reach down to change the CD, I can see her swirling her finger around her ear, mouthing to Claude, "She's gone mad! Mad, I tell you!!"

"Actually," pipes up Ainsley Hammond, who's been listening silently to all of this from his seat on Fleur's futon, "I wouldn't rule that out either."

"Really?" I say. Ainsley can certainly attend more LBD meetings if he's going to speak such complete sense. Plus, he wears better makeup than any of us girls.

"Pah, I give them a week together. Two weeks, max," continues our pale and interesting friend. "Jimi will *never* put up with Panama. He's a cool lad, Jimi. Y'know, really funny? And really sharp too. He'll soon wake up to the fact he's with Blackwell's biggest airhead."

"Cheers, Ainsley," I say. Who'd have guessed that someone dressed like the Grim Reaper would bring me the weekend's first slice of happiness?

"Anyway, Mr. Hammond," says Claude. "You promised you had something cool to tell us. Come on, spill it . . ."

"Oh, of course. I nearly forgot," tuts Ainsley, delving into his black rubber rucksack, which is covered in crucifixes drawn in correction fluid and silver studs, pulling out a cassette tape. "This is hilarious," he says.

"What is it?" the LBD chorus.

"Well, ladies, I had the pleasure of being in the vicinity of the drama studio on Saturday when Catwalk were rehearsing. What a joy that was."

"They were perfecting their five-part harmony," I say glumly, recalling Panama's visit.

"Er . . . no, they weren't." Ainsley smirks. "That's what I wanted to tell you. I think they've given up on that."

Ainsley pops the tape into Fleur's stereo and presses PLAY. Immediately the room fills with a curious wailing noise.

"Runnnnning to your looooooove . . . ," screeches what appears to be several voices, clashing and straining horribly in vastly different keys. This has to be the worst singing in the world ever. It sounds like a fire at a zoo.

"Turn it down!" says Claude, wincing.

"Hey! These people sound in pain. Who is that?!" says Fleur, covering her ears.

"Love! Love loooooove!" groans a voice on the tape, breaking into a coughing fit. Another female voice tries to hit a high C, merely dissolving into a morbid off-key caterwaul.

Ainsley presses STOP.

"It's Catwalk," he says, beaming.

"What? I don't understand." Claude frowns. "They're really good singers."

"No, Claude, they're really good *mimers*. As far as I can gather, for the last year Catwalk've just been lip-synching to a tape of their voices put through one of those voice-enhancing machines. This tape is of them singing 'Running to Your Love,' er, live." Ainsley is as smug as smug can be now. "And I took the liberty of taping them in their raw, natural form."

"So Catwalk can't actually sing at all?" I repeat, beginning to really chuckle.

"Mmmm, well," says Ainsley, pressing PLAY, "let's have another listen, shall we?"

"LOOOOOOOOOVE, running to your lurrrrrve!!!" groans

what sounds like Derren from Catwalk with one of his vital organs trapped in a combine harvester.

"Er, no," confirms Ainsley. "They just open and shut their mouths in time to a tape. Catwalk are a big bunch of frauds. How funny is that?"

Claude and Fleur are grinning like maniacs as we rewind the tape time and time again for yet another play, relishing every second of Catwalk's awfulness. And at this point it's unsaid between us girls, but we know that if we ever got the chance, we could have a lot of fun with this piece of information.

A lot of fun indeed.

"Hey, anyway," says Claude eventually, drying her eyes, "I better bring you up to speed about my Friday meeting with McGraw, Guinevere and Foxton."

"Oh, sorry, Claude, I forgot to ask. How is McGraw?" I say.

"He's sort of . . . depressed," answers Claude, a corner of her mouth slightly turning up. "He's got his *concerns,* shall we say, about Blackwell Live."

"Ahh," I say. "What specifically?"

"Specifically," says Claude, picking up a sheet of paper and putting on her reading glasses. "Specifically: Well, did you know Christy Sullivan keeps getting mobbed by Year Seven girls every time he attempts to move between lessons? They keep trying to rip his clothes and kiss him. Poor Christy is having to hide in the library at breaktimes now just for safety. So McGraw reckons we need some sort of security on the day—"

"Security?" I gasp. "We can't afford that!"

"Mmm. But we might have to find the money. Especially as

McGraw is now positive that Killa Blow and the EZ Life Syndicate are some sort of urban street gang who carry guns and shoot people."

"But they're not!" I argue. "They're really sweet."

"Don't tell *me* that. He also reckons that Ainsley's band, Death Knell, are a cult of Satan worshipers who need to be *closely monitored.*"

"He's the one that needs his brain examined," mutters Ainsley.

"That may be," sighs Claude. "But sadly he's the headmaster and he's in charge of Blackwell School. Oh, and don't even ask what he thinks about Liam Gelding being involved."

"Not a happy man?" I venture.

"No, in fact, he started clutching his forehead and saying un- kind stuff about 'the lunatics taking over the asylum' before an- nouncing that we definitely needed security to stop 'that prize chump' trying to get up on the school roof again."

"He only did it once," moans Fleur. "When is McGraw going to forget about that?!"

"Never," says Claude. "Mrs. Guinevere even snapped at him to shut up at this point."

Thank heavens for Mrs. Guinevere, she has been like a guardian angel to Blackwell Live over the last week. She's been only too ready to drive us to places, or fight in our corner when- ever McGraw or the caretaker, Mr. Gowan, start moaning about us. She even gave up her lunch hour loads of times to sell tick- ets, which is more than can be said for almost every other teacher. What a woman!

Saying that, Mr. Foxton has been more than a little useful to have around too. It turns out he actually played in rock bands when he was at teacher-training college. No one famous, of course. But he knows quite a lot about sorting out gigs and instruments and how much rehearsal musicians need to do, all that sort of thing. He's quite cool for a grown-up, really.

"So does McGraw actually like any of the Blackwell Live bands?" I ask.

"Hmmm," replies Claude. "Take an educated guess."

"Catwalk?" I say, rolling my eyes.

"And the Blackwell bellringers, don't forget." Fleur sniggers. "He lurrrrrrves the Blackwell bellringers."

"How did you guess?" Claude laughs. "Oh, yeah, and McGraw's other concern is that we've sold too many tickets. Apparently 1,220 is far too many already, and a riot is bound to break out."

"It does seem a lot." I gulp.

"Mmm, I know . . . he could have a point," Claude concedes. "But, Ronnie, people keep buying them! They just keep wanting more and more every single breaktime. We can't say no, can we?"

Claude looks to my lips, hoping for a pearl of wisdom.

I don't know what to say. It seems to me that our only problem is Blackwell Live is *too popular*. It's grown bigger than we even fantasized, and then some. It's becoming a pretty scary responsibility. But doesn't my mum always say that anything that's worth doing always involves taking a bit of a risk, and risks are scary, aren't they? So that's what I tell Claude.

"I think the LBD can either be frightened of Blackwell Live and how it's turning out . . . or we can move with it and expand," I say, sounding a lot more confident than I am. I'm more than a little bit freaked out by what awaits us in under six days' time, even if I am proud of our "problem."

It's 10:30 P.M. as I slip sheepishly through the main doors of the Fantastic Voyage. Dad is behind the bar, polishing a pint glass, staring into space, while Old Bert, the toothless regular, pours forth his tedious opinion on the state of the British monarchy.

"Dad," I begin.

"Hello, Ronnie!" Dad smiles, running his hand over my hair. "Are you okay, pet lamb? I've been trying to speak to you since Friday—"

"I know, I'm really sorry, Dad—"

"It's okay. Don't worry. We're all a bit mixed up at the minute," Dad says kindly. And in an instant we're friends again.

"I know, Dad. I'm just a bit . . . well, you know . . . ," I say.

I love the way that with your family, sometimes you don't have to say anything, they just understand what you mean.

"But anyway, I've been thinking, Dad. About what you said the other night . . . y'know, about your music industry mates?"

Dad's face brightens up.

"I'd really like you to help me, Dad, er, I mean if you still want to, that is? Will you help, Dad?!" I ask.

Dad's sandy sideburns bristle with delight. He puts a pint glass under the lager pump and then begins pouring me a celebratory Diet Coke.

"Of course I will, Veronica. In fact, it would be an honor," he says, plonking our drinks before us and pulling a pen from behind his ear.

"Now, brains, where shall we start?"

a week's (not) a long time, in rock and roll

It felt pretty good having Dad back on my side.

Isn't it weird the way that, when you're not speaking to your parents, it just hangs over your head like a drizzly gray cloud? How can silence be so negative? Even when you're laughing and messing about with your friends, there's always something in the back of your mind about life that's not quite right. And even when you reckon you don't give a hoot what they think about something, well, you do really. Even hardened parent tormentors like Fleur Swan, who spends most of her life either sulking with her folks or being blanked by them . . . well, deep down even Fleur quite likes Paddy being proud of her.

"This is absolutely one of the most impressive things I've ever seen a group of kids set their minds to," enthused Paddy on Monday night as the LBD perched around Fleur's dining table. Our mobile phones were bleeping constantly with discussions of this coming Saturday's plans. We also had to chat about all the fab suggestions that my dad had made about "running orders" and how to arrange the festival site.

"Cheers, Father." Fleur smiled, blushing a touch as her mum, Saskia, ruffled the top of her daughter's honey-blond hair. "Get off, Mum!"

"No, honestly," continued Paddy, who in fairness had been just picked up by Saskia from his golf club, where he had been "socializing in the bar" since 4:00 P.M. "I mean, when you told me that you wanted to spend my cash on a day of hippy-hoppy-hip music and all that *bang bang bang* stuff you play upstairs, well, okay, ladies, I'll admit, I thought you had a screw loose, but now—"

"Don't spoil it, darling." Saskia grimaced. "You were on a roll there."

"It's hip-hop music, Dad." Fleur giggled, quite clearly bristling with pride that Paddy had publicly cracked, admitting she was a brilliant daughter. "Thank you anyway, we'll take that as a compliment."

"But it *was* a compliment," persisted Paddy as his wife led him to the den as a damage-limitation strategy.

"I love you girls!" shouted Paddy as he went. "You're a wonderful exshample of today's youth."

"Now that *is* a first." Fleur chuckled. "His special brain pills must have kicked in."

"That's all my work, you know!" we could hear Paddy announcing proudly. "That dynamic, maverick, business-brained young lady . . . she takes after me!" Paddy was slurring.

"Yes, dear, she's a carbon copy of you," agreed Saskia, slightly dryly. "In so many ways."

But when I looked back at the LBD, I noticed that Claude looked a little sad. Even though every sheet of paper on the table indicated that things were going marvelously to plan.

"What's up, Claude?" I said.

"Yeah, C. What's up?" asked Fleur.

"Oh, nothing," she said. "It's nothing. Well, nothing really. It's just that I was thinking about how proud your dads are of you . . . and I was just sort of thinking, well, y'know, well, I was just being a bit stupid . . ." Her voice trailed off.

"You're not being stupid," I said, reaching out and sort of grabbing her wrist.

"Yeah, I am. And there's no time to be daft now, anyhow," said Claude, regaining her composure instantly, doing that enviable thing Claude can do when she just "switches off and gets on with things."

"Well, I think," announced Fleur, who is fantastic at situations like this, "if your dad was here today, he'd be totally proud of you, Claude. Cos you're the reason all this is happening really, you know?"

"Mmmm," said Claude, and then a little tear escaped down her face, which she vamooshed with her sleeve, and then smiled.

"No, really, Claude. We're all really proud of you," said Fleur.

"Thanks, girls, I'm okay, really."

"And anyway, if you really feel left out," I said, "I know a lovely, albeit slightly depressed, man who adores you and would love you to be his daughter."

Claude smiled, then rolled her eyes.

"Are we perhaps talking about a certain Samuel McGraw here?" Fleur giggles, raising an eyebrow.

"Mr. McGraw!" repeated Claude, chuckling and shaking her head. "I could live with him and Myrtle, couldn't I? We could sing songs from *Happy Voices, Happy Lives* around the piano and eat homemade scones! That would be fantastic."

"And when you did something wrong, like snogged a boy or wore too much makeup, McGraw would come into your room and say . . ."

Fleur then broke into a near-perfect mimic of Mr. McGraw in all his gray-faced glory:

"I find it very difficult to believe you were involved in this, Claudette Cassiera. You're a credit to this household!"

"A credit!" the LBD chorused together, falling about laughing.

Of course, the week wasn't destined to go without problems.

By Tuesday the LBD were duly rounded up by Edith and marched to the administration corridor for an "emergency meeting" with Mr. McGraw over ticket sales. It emerged that during Tuesday morning's break, on one of McGraw's rare excursions outside of his office, he'd overheard a Year 7 kid squeaking that Blackwell Live ticket sales had reached over 2,000. (We'd actually sold 2,221.) He also heard that kids from schools other than Blackwell and Chasterton had been buying them. Lymewell Academy and Cary Hill girls had begun eagerly pitching up at breaks with their pocket money.

"Right! That's it!" shouted McGraw, raising one hairy hand at us like a traffic policeman. The tension was broken here slightly by the fact that McGraw's hand had *Remember to pay gas bill* scrawled upon it in green felt-tip pen. "This has *got* to stop."

"What has, sir?" asked Claudette, straightening her glasses. I love it when Claude says "sir." She can totally pull it off and sound respectful. I just sound like I'm in a BBC period drama.

"The tickets. You have to stop selling tickets! That's enough now."

"But the school field is massive, Mr. McGraw," chirped up

Fleur, breaking our cardinal rule: Always let Claude do any talking to McGraw. "We can fit in loads more people than two thousand," Fleur argued.

"Ha! Well, that is *exactly* the sort of careless devil-may-care response I'd expect from you, Fleur Swan," snapped McGraw, who was actually quite rattled by events this time, not just depressed, as I'd predicted. "Let's have a riot, shall we? That's what you want, isn't it? The school razed to the ground? Looting? Chaos?"

"Errrr." We all stared blankly. He was beginning to scare us a bit, as his eyes were bulging.

"And I suppose you'll be carrying the can when the worst-case scenario happens and somebody loses a foot in a stampede, will you?" shouts McGraw.

"*Can?* What *can?* And how will someone lose a foot?" muttered Fleur, genuinely flummoxed.

"Okay, shall we stop selling tickets then, Mr. McGraw?" said Claude. "Like, right now?"

"Hallelujah," whispered Samuel McGraw. "Thank you, Claudette Cassiera. I knew you'd take my point."

"*Pghhh,*" said Fleur, who obviously couldn't keep her displeasure under wraps a second longer.

"Right, you can go now. Off you trot," said McGraw as we filed out. "But believe me, if I see one more ticket on sale, well, you girls will see a dark side to my countenance."

"Mmmm," we all murmured.

"I mean, let's get something straight here, ladies," McGraw shouted after us as we slumped away down the corridor. "Nobody likes a good time as much as myself. And I mean *no-*

body. But there have to be limitations and boundaries to the fun. Do you hear me?"

"Gnnnnn," we all moaned, walking faster.

"We can't all just have fun willy-nilly, you know? That's not how life works, is it?" he yelled. Thankfully we were too far away to care.

Naturally, the second we told people that tickets were sold out, they became the most very desirable piece of paper a kid could have. Things just went berserk.

I have never been so popular.

My cell phone began to buzz at all times of the day and night with people I'd not spoken to for months. Like people I once sat beside on a school trip in Year 7 who'd suddenly remembered what "really good mates we were after all." Oh, and by the way, could they have two tickets for themselves and their cousin Hubert? It was really tough saying no to people, but we were determined McGraw wouldn't catch us out.

By Thursday, demand was at fever pitch. McGraw himself was patrolling the school confines, rounding up enterprising black-market ticketsellers and making them enact humiliating punishments like litter-picking and chewing-gum removal. Sadly, this just gave the illegal market for tickets a more dangerous, glamorous edge; tickets began to change hands for £20 a time, which I'd have been happy about if we'd been seeing a penny of this profit. In fact, the LBD were so busy trying to distance themselves from these nefarious activities and trying to appear disgusted whenever McGraw goose-stepped past us, as well as sorting out squillions of other things, lordy me, I was quite exhausted. I wasn't too busy, however, to notice Panama and Jimi, who seemed to be going everywhere together by this point.

It was vile.

"I don't understand boys," mulled Claude aloud on Thursday afternoon as we wandered home, totally shattered, from school. "They make absolutely not an iota of sense at all. I mean, what do they actually want from a girlfriend? Why would Jimi Steele bother with Panama?"

"Thank you," I sighed. I'd been saying that every day since last Sunday, at least twenty-seven times a day, on repeat play.

"Well, I've got an idea, Claudey." Fleur smiled. "Why don't you ask Liam Gelding about what goes on in a lad's mind? You'll be seeing him later, won't you?"

"Might be," murmured Claude.

"Oooooooh hooooooh!" Fleur and I singsonged, extremely childishly.

"It's not like *that*," Claude snapped back. "He just keeps turning up to help me with Blackwell Live stuff . . . and then he, er, well, ahem, he stays for his tea."

Fleur shot a knowing glance across at me. I winked back. There was something old tight-lips wasn't quite telling us here.

Claude carried on walking like this was a totally normal thing to admit.

"What, like, you have romantic dinners together?" said Fleur, grasping at straws.

"No, Fleur," says Claude. "It's more like, well, you know how my mum really loves cooking? Like stews and curries and cakes?"

"Yeah," we say.

"I think she's trying to feed him to death," Claude said solemnly.

"What a way to go," gasped Fleur.

When I got home to the Fantastic Voyage that Thursday night, I found my dad huddled in one of the back alcoves with a posse of rather hairy strangers. Large steaming plates of Cumberland sausage and mashed potatoes with oodles of onion gravy cluttered the table, along with many pints of lager. Everyone was eating, drinking or smoking merrily. Immediately, I spotted my uncle Charlie among them!

Oh my God, I'd not seen this man for about five years! And he hadn't changed a bit. (Charlie's not my real uncle, by the way. He's just a mate of Dad's who has turned up every few years since I was a baby to rattle on with Dad for *entire weekends* about guitars. I truly hope Mum doesn't come back at this moment. She'd probably just turn around and walk out again.)

"Miss Veronica Ripperton!" shouted Uncle Charlie, putting down his half-rolled cigarette and attempting to bear-hug me into his stinky leather jacket.

"*Mghgh*UncleCharlie!" I said.

"Now, boys," shouted my dad. "And here we have my Blackwell Live Festival–organizing daughter, Ronnie. This will be your boss for the next few days, so watch yourselves. She takes no prisoners."

"Like her mother," said Uncle Charlie.

"Very much so," whispered my dad.

"Dad. Who are all these people?" I said, removing bits of rolling tobacco from my hairline.

"Now, don't be too shocked here, but I've got you some proper help, in the shape of this road crew for Blackwell Live," said Dad rather proudly. "I mean, come on, Ronnie, don't we always say that if you're going to do something, you may as well do it properly?"

"Yes!" I laughed.

"Well, now we're really doing it properly!" he said. "Another lager, anyone?"

Everyone cheered.

blackwell (really) live

"Dad! I think I can see that bloke's, er . . . bum."

"What? Where? Oh, *him* . . . oh, that's fine. That's normal."

I'm transfixed by a staggeringly hairy bottom, rising like a hirsute moon over the back of a pair of grubby denims. The bum's owner, Vinny, is bent double, wiring up a microphone in the center of Blackwell Live's rather impressive stage.

"He's a roadie," announces Dad, biting into a veggie burger. Not Dad's usual breakfast fare, but the lady setting up the burger van, one of the many culinary delicacies selling at Blackwell Live, offered him a free sample.

"What do you mean, 'a roadie'?" I ask.

"That's what Vinny is. He works on the road with rock bands, you see, setting their gear up and dismantling it all again and—"

"Wearing jeans that show his bum crack?" I giggle.

"Unfortunately, yes, it goes with the territory." Dad smiles. "Hey, but don't knock them. These lads your uncle Charlie brought with him are like gold dust, Ronnie. Best in the business."

I can see that.

They've never stopped slaving away since the second they arrived on the Blackwell Live festival site. True to his word last Sunday, Dad called in a few favors from my uncle Charlie, who works with rock and pop bands; and, lured by an offer of free pub grub and limitless lager, Charlie rounded up a small team of rather jaded, equally hairy guys who could lend us a hand for Blackwell Live.

"Dad, what does Uncle Charlie actually *do* for a living?" I ask, squinting in the morning sun.

"He's a tour manager; on the road with rock bands," Dad explains, as if that makes things any clearer. Dad sees my bemused look. "Okay, well, when a band goes on tour, Charlie's the bloke who makes sure they get to where they're meant to be, and sorts out their money . . . and makes sure they're in bed in time to look pretty the next day. All that important stuff that no one wants to do." Dad nods at Charlie, who's in deep conversation with Claudette.

"So, he's like the band's dad?!"

"Yeah, I suppose he is." Dad chuckles. "But I bet they give him less trouble."

"Cheers, Dad," I groan.

"Hey, Ronno, it's a bit of luck, though, eh? That these lads had a few days going spare? They're on their way down south to another gig, y'know? I told 'em your gig was for charity. A kiddies' charity. That's it, isn't it?" says Dad, wiping onions and ketchup off his face.

"Yeah, sort of," I reply.

Charlie's arrival was more than "a bit of luck," it was a godsend: Blackwell Live's road crew comprised of three roadies, Vinny, Blu and Pip, as well as three enormous, burly, bald-headed security guys with awesomely wide necks and biceps the size of my thighs. One of our security blokes, who boasted an eagle tattoo on his neck, went by the nickname of Masher. I didn't press Charlie for a reason why. It was just great knowing that McGraw now had to quit his yakking about Blackwell Live getting out of hand.

"Anyway, Charlie owes me," concludes Dad, watching as a multicolored Blackwell Live banner is hoisted above the stage by two Year 7 girls. "I've bailed that rogue out of trouble enough times over the years." Dad adds, burping majestically, "Hey, fantastic burger, by the way, Ron! You wanna try one?"

Tempting, but I couldn't eat a thing.

Today is the big day! It's July twelfth! Today is Blackwell Live!

I don't know whether to laugh, cry or vomit.

It's 10:00 A.M. Surreally enough, in under three hours our opening act, Christy Sullivan, will take to the stage. The lovely Christy is backstage already, pacing back and forth in an expensive Italian silk shirt in navy, snakeskin jeans and dark sunglasses; he's chatting nervously to his, in my opinion, even better-looking older brother, Seamus.

"Er, are you sure you need me today, Ronnie?" Christy says, his voice faltering. "I mean, I'm not bothered if you wanna cancel me. I know I'm not much of a singer and all that . . ." Christy's face is as white as chalk.

"Oi! You're not getting out of this that easy, Christy

Sullivan." I smile reassuringly. "Besides, then there *would* be a riot."

Christy attempts a smile, but a worried frown battles through. Seamus rolls his eyes at me.

I make a mental note to have Masher keep a close eye on him—we can't have our opening act absconding over the back fence. Saying that, I'm not much calmer. I barely slept a wink last night and I certainly can't face breakfast. I must be functioning right now on pure nervous energy.

The LBD were here on Blackwell's playing fields until almost 10:00 P.M. last night, taking delivery of one rather magnificent all-weather stage, two huge powerful speakers, and a modest refreshments marquee and dance tent. That was very exciting!

All paid for in full too!

Ha, stick that in your pipe and smoke it, so-called Cyril from Castles in the Sky.

It took hours of hammering, carrying and hoisting by the Castles crew, but as darkness fell, we had a proper festival site with a real PA system, just like you see on MTV!

"Pah, who needs Astlebury? This is much better!" announced Fleur, which made the roadies laugh out loud.

"Hey, you're not wrong, kiddo," chirped up Uncle Charlie. "Small music festivals are always better, there's a better vibe," he drawled.

That made us all smile.

Well, for a short while anyhow. Charlie then continued to tell the LBD an exceedingly long-winded story about his first Astlebury Festival experience back in 1978. "Back when the festival was only fifty people and a few goats" and "it was all about the music then" and "not the big corporate event that rock festivals are these days blah blah blah. . . ." But by this time the LBD's minds were on other matters at hand, such as getting back to Fleur's to make backstage passes. Yes, you heard that right. Backstage passes! Apparently we needed them.

"Look, girls, there's no point having a backstage VIP area and Masher and the lads guarding it if we don't know who's meant to be inside or outside of it!" Uncle Charlie had warned us. "Especially if you're expecting trouble with that . . . wossisname? Christy Sullivan? That's 'im. Christy Sullivan's fans. Oooh, they're the worst offenders at festivals, those young teenage girls. They'll spend their whole day either screaming their lungs out, giving me a migraine, or plotting to get backstage and manhandle the talent. Bane of my life . . . ," Charlie moaned.

So with that peril in mind, the LBD were up till well after 1:00 A.M. last night, cutting and pasting Access All Area passes for bandmembers, friends and crew; and with their glittery, laminated finish and candy-striped ties, very chic they are too! Poor Fleur has been delegated the task of dishing the passes out, a job I do not envy. Every Blackwell kid wants to go backstage and rub shoulders with the bands, and every band had a posse of mates they want to take backstage with them. It's a nightmare working out who to say no to! Fleur's phone never stopped buzzing on Friday, the worst offenders being the EZ Life Syndicate, who by 11:00 P.M. last night had demanded THIRTY AAA passes for "the Syndicate" and "their entourage"! Bless Christy Sullivan, he only wanted three passes: for his mum, dad and granny. Awww. He's so sweet, you could eat him, isn't he?

Of course, even with the AAA passes made, I still had my hair to dye from dark brown to "Auburn Gloss," my nails to French manicure and my festival outfit to choose! Every combination of every garment I own was tried, assessed and discarded, creating a towering clothes mountain of skirts, denims and tops, then eventually, at 4:00 A.M. this morning, I settled for the outfit I'm wearing now: my hippest deep-indigo-colored hipster jeans, a minxish midriff-exposing baby-pink T-shirt and . . . wait for it . . . a hot-pink lacy thong that Fleur bought me last Christmas, arranged so you can see a glimpse of it from the back of my jeans! Obviously, I've spent the whole morning turned away from Dad so he doesn't see the thong and burst a main artery.

"Sure I can't get you anything to eat, Ronnie?" asks my dad, placing his arm around my shoulder as Ainsley and Candy from Death Knell stagger past backstage, carrying flutes, synths, steel drums and bags of costumes. "You've not had a bite yet," Dad worries.

"I'll have a large coffee, please, Dad," I say. "As strong as you like."

It's going to be a long day.

By 11:00 A.M., backstage is really hotting up: Fleur Swan is flitting about with an armful of Access All Area passes, her tiny pert posterior clad in perilously miniscule black velvet hot pants. Obviously, Fleur looks a zillion dollars and certainly has the eye of Killa Blow from the EZ Life Syndicate, who never misses a chance to cup her waist with his arm or direct a joke in her direction, making her dissolve into fits of giggles.

"You're terrible, Killa! Leave me alone," squeals Fleur unconvincingly until they spot our compere Paddy Swan, clad in a pinstripe suit, looking ever so slightly like a simmering psychopath.

"Errr, morning, Mr. Swan, lovely to see you." Killa winces, removing his hands from Paddy's daughter, then continues to beg Fleur for more Access All Area passes so more of his "crew" can "show him some love" backstage. And as each face arrives, Claudette Cassiera, looking blithe and beautiful in close-fitting black jeans and an aqua-blue crop top with *Top Bird* across the front, plus funky handlebar bunches in her hair, ticks them off on her bright red clipboard, warning everybody to listen out for an important announcement at 11:30 A.M.

"If you want to know what time you're going on stage and in what order, do yourself a favor and be here," Claude warns, turning to me with a quizzical look. "Ronnie," she whispers as Guttersnipe's Benny and Tara report in for duty, "have you any idea which band your uncle Charlie's roadies and security usually work for?"

"Funny you should ask," I reply, helping pin a rose into Tara's crimped white-blond hair. "They're very tight-lipped about it, aren't they? I can't get a straight answer. That roadie Pip keeps changing the subject, and as for Vinny—"

"Vinny says he can't remember!" Claude adds.

"And Uncle Charlie just said 'no comment' when I asked." I laugh. "Hey, it must be someone reeeeally embarrassing, eh? They're too ashamed to admit it."

"Must be," agrees Claude. "But never mind, they're being absolute stars anyway. Masher is doing a brilliant job on the main entrance gate. There's hundreds of kids here already waiting for us to open and not one of them has got past him!"

"Er, that might be something to do with the fact he looks like a bulldozer in a bomber jacket," I venture. "He's got SATAN SLAVE tattooed on his left hand, have you seen that?"

"Exactly," Claude chirps. "He's the perfect security guard."

She has a very hard streak, that girl.

As Claude prepares to speak to the group, I scan the backstage area: There's the whole extended EZ Life Syndicate, Killa Blow with his breathtaking defined cheekbones wearing an ostentatious bright white padded jacket-trousers combo and more gold than Queen Elizabeth II on a state occasion. Killa is flanked by pretty Chasterton chicks with high ponytails and large silver hoop earrings and lads wearing designer sportswear, Burberry caps and expensive shoes. Close by, Aaron, Naz and Danny from Lost Messiah are messing about, dressed in ripped combats and sleeveless vests emblazoned with gold dragons and prints of ninja warriors. Very sexy. Naz is plastering liquid hand soap into his hair, trying to form a perfect Mohawk, while beside him, Catwalk's Abigail and Leeza are making a big display of brushing their toned bodies with strawberry-scented talcum powder.

"Our outfits are so tight, we have to use talc to slide them on easier!" shrills Abigail, showing off her black rubber catsuit. It appears the whole of Catwalk will be coordinated today in identical ultra-close-fitting Lycra and rubber items. Derren and Zane (who are both extra orange-skinned today) are pouring their

236

taut limbs into rubber trousers and ripped black Lycra vests. If you ask me, they look like some sort of lame intergalactic fighting force.

"Remember, Leeza, I'm wearing the most expensive suit!" pipes up the irritating tones of Panama Goodyear, who is drawing a perfect plum lip line around her pouting mouth. "So don't even think about putting it on," she snaps.

Leeza looks embarrassed, then mutters: "Okay, Panama," opting for a less impressive catsuit.

And I should have guessed what was coming next. I mean, you can't have one without the other, can you?

"Yoo-hoo, Jimi!" squeals Panama as Lost Messiah's lead singer eventually makes his appearance, winking at Claudette and nodding a nervous hello to me while Panama crawls all over him like the Ebola virus.

"I was worried about you, darling!" she simpers, trying to kiss his face.

"Oh, give it a rest, Panama," says Jimi, gently trying to push her off with more than a flicker of discomfort.

"Oh, don't be silly." Panama giggles. "I just want to kiss my boyfriend, is that so wrong?" she asks, groping his chest and slobbering on his face.

"Gerroffff," Jimi says, pushing her makeup-laden face away from his pristine white T-shirt.

Sigh.

I wish with all my soul that Jimi wasn't so unbelievably hot: It wouldn't feel like someone was kicking me up the bum with a pointy shoe every time I see him with that evil witch.

"Ooh, things don't look too rosy over in Camp Panama and

Jimi, do they?" whispers Fleur, arching an eyebrow. "What was that Ainsley said about giving them a week?"

But I know she's just being kind.

"Don't," I groan.

"So, hello, everyone!" shouts Claudette, climbing up onto a chair to be seen. "Can I have a bit of order now?! Yes, that means you too, Lost Messiah, shut up!"

"Sorry, Claude," shouts Naz, his hair now jutting skyward like a bass-playing cockatiel.

"Okay now, I've gathered you all here to tell you today's running order and . . . er, hang on a second. Liam, are you okay?"

Claude breaks off, spying Liam Gelding copiously vomiting into a nearby bin.

"Stage fright." Benny Stark winks, patting Liam's back.

"Well, can he hurl quietly, please? I'm trying to speak here," continues Claude. "Now, our gates open in under thirty minutes' time, at noon. As you all have probably seen, we've got the bell-ringers positioned at the front gate, so that's one act safely accounted for. Now, I want the first stage act, which we all know is Christy Sullivan, ready to go on at one o'clock. Christy, are you with us?"

"Sort of," says Christy regretfully.

"Good. Then, at quarter to two, I need Guttersnipe ready to rock. Tara, Benny, Liam, are you fine with that?"

"No bother, man." Benny nods.

Splagghhhhhh goes the sound of Liam's breakfast splattering on the side of the bin.

"Has he got hollow legs?" asks Claude. "That's a lot of vomit."

"He'll be okay," assures Tara. "Once he gets it all up."

Panama wrinkles her nose in Guttersnipe's direction. "Uggh, how vile," she mutters.

"So that takes us up to two-thirty, when I want Death Knell on stage. Then, after that, at three-fifteen, I need EZ Life Syndicate ready to rumble. Now, EZ Life, there's only room for twelve of you on the stage, so decide now who's performing and who's gonna be left at the side holding the coats. If all thirty of you—or however many of you there are now—jump up and down on stage together, I have it on good authority from Pip and Vinny, our roadies, that the stage could collapse like a souf-flé. We do not, repeat, do NOT want that, do we?"

"No, Claude," mutters EZ Life as a huge debate explodes about who is and isn't performing today.

"But I wrote that first song!" moans one lad with a red bandana wrapped around his head. "I should go on for verse two at least."

"You only joined EZ Life two days ago!" one girl is yelling across to a tall black lad, apparently called Dane, with intricate mini-dreadlocks all over his head.

"Yeah, but I drove the van here!" Dane argues back. "And if I don't get to rap, I'm driving it home again without you lot in it!"

"He's got a point there," announces Killa, clearly imagining the entire EZ Life Syndicate on the Number Thirty-nine bus back home to the Carlyle Estate.

239

"Okay, that's decided, then: Dane is rapping on *all* the songs," announces Killa, causing much uproar.

"Oh, and EZ Life, remember, I need you off stage, no ifs, no buts, by four P.M.," says Claude. "Because next up is Lost Messiah. If there's any problems at all with either band, just shout up now. Oh, and good luck!"

Of course, sadly, we all know what that means.

I know. Fleur knows. Claude obviously knows.

And Panama Goodyear and her goblins certainly know too, if their expressions of boundless glee are any indication.

I hate to even say it, but it's the irrefutable truth: Catwalk is Blackwell Live's starring act.

Panama didn't meet our gaze or even murmur a word; however, we all know Catwalk are certain victory is theirs. Bullying and nastiness has won the day. It's simply *less hassle* to just give Catwalk their own way. And what is more, it's what the crowd really really wants.

That sucks.

"And after this," Claude continues, unfazed, "the refreshments tent will keep serving drinks until nine-thirty P.M., where Johnny Martlew from Year Thirteen will be spinning, er . . ." Claude reads from a piece of paper, "An eclectic mix of rare grooves and party anthems."

"So, anything he feels like, then?" shouts Tara.

"Er, yeah." Claude laughs. "And I'll be there too, so buy me a drink!"

As Claude leaps down from her chair, Fleur and I whisk her aside for a private chat.

"Claude, are you sure we've done the right thing here?" I say, feeling more than a little sad.

"Yeah, Claude. It just doesn't feel right," whispers Fleur. "I always thought that we'd have the last laugh with Catwalk, but we've made them the stars of our show! Okay, I know we had no choice, but still . . ."

"I know," says Claude. "But let's face it, the whole of Blackwell School have bought tickets to see an unforgettable show, haven't they?"

"S'pose," we both mumble.

"And they all want to see Catwalk, don't they?" Claude asks.

"Yeah, s'pose," Fleur admits begrudgingly.

"Well, let's be gracious about it, then. We have to give the ticket buyers what they want, haven't we?" Claude says calmly. "And to be frank, we've got bigger priorities to deal with now anyhow. It's time to open the gates!"

liftoff

"Mayday! Mayday! Operation Eagle Has Landed is GO!!!!" shouts Masher into his walkie-talkie as Blackwell's gates fling open and the first ticket holders pour in. I sneak onto the stage to watch the first arrivals.

"Chrrrrrrrrrrrrisssssssstttttyyy Sullivan, I love you!" squeals one girl, accompanied by two dozen or so assorted Year 8 lovelies, clutching roses and teddies, running as fast as their legs will carry them toward the main stage. Predictably, the first hundred bodies all seem to be Christy's loyal fans. *WE LUV U CHRISTY*

XXX reads one banner, already being waved aloft proudly by a blond girl. *SHOW US YOUR BUM, CHRISTY! YOU MAJOR HOT-TIE!!! XXX* invites another.

"Told ya," says Uncle Charlie, who has appeared beside me. "That's where the trouble lies. Teenage girls . . . mark my words, I'd rather supervise football hooligans, far less scary," he remarks, observing Gonzo, one of our security men, splitting up a squabble involving a gaggle of girls who are trying to climb over the front barrier, closest to the stage.

"But I've been in line since eight o'clock this morning! I should get the best view!" squeals one girl, elbowing another young lassie who for some mysterious reason has felt-tipped *CHR* and *ISTY* on her right and left cheeks. (Yeah, like that's going to improve her chances of snogging him.)

Meanwhile, up at the front gates, I watch as a steady flow of girls and boys hand their tickets to Masher and flood into the field: kids with facial piercings, shaved heads and gothic jewelry, kids with chic designer labels on show and patterns shaved into their eyebrows, kids with jeans worn so baggy, the bum section droops by the back of their knees. I can barely recognize some familiar faces without their school uniforms; in their "civilian clothes," people take on whole new guises. It's especially fantastic to see audition rejects like Chester Walton, Shop and Constance Harvey have swallowed their pride and bought tickets; I can even see Matthew Brown, happily without Mr. Jingles, his talking bear, standing in the ever-growing queue for hot dogs and burgers. And in the middle of the thousand or so festival-goers already present, meandering gingerly through the crowd, observing the field like a social experiment, is Mr. McGraw, our headmaster, and his laugh-a-minute wife, Myrtle.

"Having a good time, Mr. McGraw?" shouts one lad.

"Hmm, we'll see, shall we?" replies McGraw glumly, spotting a group of Year 9 girls who are already stripped down to bikini tops in the glorious lunchtime sunshine. "This place is like a nudist colony," he mutters to his wife. Nearby, enterprising Year 13 girls are doing hot business selling aromatherapy massages and henna tattoos, while at a little stall adjacent to them, Blackwell's resident psychic, Candice from Year 9, is selling "Spiritual Readings from the Other Side" for £5 a time.

"This is tantamount to witchcraft!" mutters Myrtle McGraw. "I'm not sure the Reverend Peacock would approve."

"Don't worry, dear," assures McGraw. "Here are the Blackwell bellringers ready to give their recital, now this is more like it."

And he's sort of correct, I suppose. Indeed it is George, Jemima, et al, from the bellringing team; Claude has placed them nearest the main gate, figuring the atrocious noise will hurry people through the gates toward the main stage more efficiently; however, I feel McGraw is going to be less than pleased with the selection of pop music we've convinced George's team to learn and play.

"Saints preserve us! What's wrong with 'All Things Bright and Beautiful'?!" moans Myrtle as the bellringers clang and ding-dong through a selection of R-and-B and nu-metal classics.

"What about 'Land of Hope and Glory'?" shouts McGraw, as if his entire world is collapsing.

I could people-watch all day, just taking in the developing scene proudly as seas of faces, kids from both Blackwell and Chasterton, plus a generous sprinkling of mums and dads, fill the festival site.

Not my mum, though.

I left a few messages with her and even asked Dad to call her, but she never gave a proper yes or no whether she'd come.

"It might be a bit difficult," Mum said, whatever that means. But I've not got time to think about that now, Claude and Fleur have appeared by my side, and Vinny is giving us the thumbs-up. The equipment is sound-checked and ready to go.

"Come on, Dad!" Fleur yells to Paddy, who seems to be giving Christy Sullivan a stern pep talk by the side of the stage. "It's time for you to kick things off!"

"Pull yourself together, boy," Paddy is saying to Christy. "They love you out there . . . and you haven't even sung a note yet!" Paddy assures. Then he marches onto the stage to a rapturous applause from the first ten rows of near-hysterical girls.

"Hello, Blackwell Live!" begins Paddy. "Welcome! And I'd like to start today by thanking you all for—"

"CHRRRRIIISSSTTTTTY!!!!! AAAAAGGGGH!" erupts the front row.

"Er, for coming along and supporting today. We've got a lot of great—"

SCREEEEEEEEEEAM! goes the crowd.

"Ahem, great music in store for you today, so I hope that—"

"I LOVE YOU, CHRISTY! MARRY ME!!" pleads one girl, drowning Paddy out completely. "GET YOUR PECS OUT FOR THE GIRLS!!"

All the front row begin cackling like drains.

"Oh, forget it," grunts Paddy, admitting defeat. "Here, without any further ado, is Christy Sullivan!"

"HURRRAY! WOOOO-HOOOO!!!"

Well, from where I'm standing it doesn't look like Christy is going anywhere. He's rooted to the ground, opening and closing his mouth, shaking like a trifle on top of a tumble dryer. Eventually, as Christy's brother Seamus, playing the synthesizer, is forced to play the opening bars of the track for a second time, Claude and I grab Christy by the collar of his navy silk shirt and literally hurl him onto the stage!

YYYYYYYEEEEESSS!! leaps the hearts of a hundred Christy Sullivan fanatics. One tiny girl who has had a picture of Christy made into a T-shirt promptly begins to sob gently. Bizarre.

"Er, hello," begins Christy meekly, picking up his microphone. "It's great to see you all today, and this is my first song that I wrote myself, called 'Back to Square One.' "

Initially Christy's voice is shaky, but within a few verses, he loosens up and begins to enjoy himself, especially when he realizes that nobody can hear a note he's singing anyhow. The screaming is drowning him out. In fact, as long as our man Sullivan wiggles his bum in the right places and occasionally pops open another button on his shirt, revealing a further inch of his sumptuous chest, Christy's fans are happy as happy can be. At one point during Christy's second track, Vinny and Pip run on stage and hand Christy another microphone.

"That mike's broken!" Vinny shouts. "It's been dead for the last three verses! Did you not realize?!"

"No!" Christy blushes. "I can't hear anything for those girls!"

"Pah. And he's not even *that* good-looking," tuts Uncle Charlie, watching the drama, which is quite ironic, as Charlie himself has a face like a dropped pie. In fact, when Dad used to say Charlie "lived on the road," I always took it to mean he literally lived in the gutter, as he almost looks like a tramp. "I can't understand it me'self," Charlie says, shaking his head.

I retreat backstage, where there's now well over two hundred people crowded together, all with much-coveted AAA passes tied around their necks. Frankie and Warren from Wicked FM are interviewing Claude while Fleur is doing her best to appear in all the *Look Live* TV footage of the gig by dancing suggestively near the cameraman in hot pants the size of a tea bag.

Suddenly Mrs. Guinevere appears from nowhere with a huge smile on her face. "Excellent! This is just excellent. I'm so pleased with you girls," she says. "It's just like I imagined it would be!" Then she gives me a big warm hug, which feels surprisingly unweird, considering she's a teacher.

"Oi, Ronnie!" shout Naz and Aaron, who are standing close by. "Nice one!"

"Cheers." I blush.

"Better go and meet your fans." Mrs. Guinevere giggles.

"You did it. It's unbelievable!" Aaron smiles, wrapping his arms around my waist, planting a big kiss on my forehead. Then Naz grabs me and does the same, sort of swinging me around by my hips as he smooches the top of my hair. I could get quite used to this.

"Hello, Ron," says Jimi, appearing beside them. "It's going really well, isn't it?" he begins.

"Yeah, it is. Thank you," I say, trying to sound normal. In

fact, "normal" at this moment would be a great look to pull off. Because if I've only imagined that Jimi had fancied me, then I can't really have a problem with him having another girlfriend, can I? In fact, I must be imagining now that Jimi is acting a bit weird and awkward around me again. Because there was never anything between us in the first place, was there? So why would he be? I mean, why?

God, I wish I could turn my head off sometimes. I wish the back of my neck had a Jimi Steele ON/OFF switch I could flick off when he's around so I wouldn't act like a crazed loon. I'd be using it right now.

"Looking forward to your turn?" I ask.

"Bit scared," says Jimi. "Don't tell the boys, though." He nods toward Aaron and Naz, who are chatting up two of the EZ Life girls. "If one of us starts freaking out, we all will."

We both giggle, then we just look at each other.

There's a little silence.

"Well, good luck," I say.

"Cheers, Ronnie," Jimi says a little sadly, looking at the floor, his long eyelashes batting against sun-burnished cheeks. "I'll come and have a chat with you later at the disco, eh?"

"Yeah," I say, "sure thing!" And then I wander off to find Fleur.

Of course Panama will never allow that, and he didn't mean it anyway; but it was a kind thing to say.

As Christy crashes off stage, sweaty and exhausted, and is immediately wrapped in a blanket and given a cup of hot sweet tea by his mum and granny, Claudette is rounding up Guttersnipe to replace him on stage.

"We're already running late," shouts Claude. "It's two o'clock! Christy played fifteen minutes more than he was meant to!"

Christy tries to apologize, but Mrs. Sullivan butts in: "Well, it's not my son's fault if he had to do four encores, is it?" she announces proudly. "The crowd wouldn't stop screaming!"

"Don't worry, I'm sure we'll shut them up," remarks Tara, pulling her black bass guitar's strap over her neck and strutting toward the stage as confidently as her tight black pencil skirt will allow, Benny Stark tagging behind her.

"Come on, Liam," Claudette is whispering. "You can do this. You know you can. You're a really good guitarist. Just do it."

"But people don't think that, do they?" Liam is whispering back, clearly in the grips of extreme last-minute nerves. "People will just laugh. They just think I'm some kind of joke. I am a joke," he adds quietly.

"Well, I don't think you are," says Claude, grabbing his hand. "You're not a joke to me, Liam." Claude notices me standing close by. "Er, or to Ronnie. Or to Fleur. We take you very seriously."

"Thanks, Claude," says Liam.

And then he's gone, up the little set of stairs onto the stage, where Christy Sullivan's fans have since dispersed in search of drinks to soothe their raw throats, leaving a less screechy, music-appreciative crowd.

"This one's called 'Promise,' " begins Liam, picking up his guitar, earning a small cheer from the audience. Claude watches him proudly, singing along with the first verse quietly to herself.

• • •

"Excellent, I've found you," begins Dad, brandishing a carton of Singapore noodles and a yellow plastic fork. "And now, my child, it is time for Veronica's lunch."

"Dad, I can't eat a—" I begin to resist.

"Woman cannot live on music alone," interrupts Dad. "That's the old proverb, isn't it?"

"Hmmm, not really," I say as Dad wafts the tempting carton under my nostrils.

"Well, I've not seen you eat a morsel now for twenty-four hours. So I'm putting my foot down," Dad argues, being as stern as he possibly gets.

"Oh, I suppose I could try a forkful." I smile, grabbing the noodles with both hands, as admittedly they do smell fantastic, then flouncing off to the rear of the backstage area to grab a well-needed seat for ten minutes.

"My fatherly work is done," announces my satisfied dad, heading back toward the beer tent.

So I'm sitting slurping my noodles, watching Death Knell change into their stage costumes with mild amusement. Not only are Ainsley Hammond and all the Death Knell boys wearing white laboratory coats smeared with (I hope) fake blood plus doctor's stethoscopes, Candy and the rest of the girls are clad in tasteless secondhand white wedding dresses with lashings of black lipstick. Yessirree, Death Knell really are going overboard on the freaky look today. They look outrageously mad. Behind Death Knell, Leeza and Derren from Catwalk are having a last-minute rehearsal.

"And a one, two, three, four, spin! Turn! Flutter your hands! Sashay!" shrieks Derren as Leeza prances around, pouting and spinning.

"Perfect, darling!" announces Derren. "Just perfect!"

Schluuuurrrrrrp I go loudly, my face drenched in soy sauce, pausing to pick a chunk of chicken from my back teeth.

"Mmm, what fetching table manners." Derren winces, throwing a snotty look in my direction. For some strange reason, I see this and just . . . well, I flip out, somewhat.

"Oh, bite me, tangerine face!" I yell to Derren, standing up and taking my noodles elsewhere.

Oh, how I wish I'd got a picture of that moment.

Derren is uniquely lost for words, while Leeza, well, she almost collapses with shock that someone has answered them back. It feels great! Even if, bravely, I'm running away as rapidly as my hooves can carry me, I feel utterly jubilant; I'm barely looking where I'm going as I dart through the backstage crowd, half-expecting to be lynched by the evil Lycra-clad duo.

And that's when I spot a face weaving through the VIP area I find strangely familiar. Like a long-lost friend, but not quite, standing directly before me, seeming vaguely adrift and vulnerable. I stare for about a minute at the boy, who's aged around nineteen or twenty, wearing a bottle-green baseball cap pulled right down, displaying only the smallest tuft of his sandy hair.

Is it one of Fleur's brother's mates? No, that's not it.

Does he drink in the Fantastic Voyage? Nuh-huh.

I'm too scared to say hello now, as I don't want one of those embarrassing moments when I have to 'fess up I've forgotten his name, so I end up just staring even more, checking out his gray

T-shirt and slightly flared pale-blue jeans, his strong jawline and perfect white teeth. I even recognize the distinctive way he walks. This is freaky. I feel like I've met him at least a thousand times before. But not here. Definitely in a different place. This makes no sense. Eventually he catches me staring and makes tracks toward me.

"Hey, I'm, er, looking for Charlie. Have you seen him?" says the familiar voice.

"Uncle Charlie?" I begin, my cheeks slightly flushing. "Er, I mean Charlie, yeah, he's about. Somewhere . . ."

"Uncle Charlie?" repeats the lad, smiling. "That's too funny. I suppose he's my uncle too, really. He certainly acts like it . . ." He chuckles. "So, you've seen him around here lately? I sorta need to tell him I've showed up. He'll be, shall we say, surprised."

"Look, do I know you from somewhere?" I begin, deciding to come clean.

But at that moment, Uncle Charlie appears like a furry tornado, whispering as loudly as a man can without actually shouting, dragging both me and the mystery guest into a corner for a private discussion.

"OH, FOR HEAVEN'S SAKE?!" Charlie exclaims, poking the lad's chest. "What are YOU doing here? We agreed you'd lay low for the day."

"*Pggghhhh,* but I was soooo bored," moans the lad. "I've been in the hotel for two days. I'd watched all the movies and ate all the room service toasted sandwiches I could face. . . . I want to meet some real people, Charlie!"

"Well, that's a good job, Mr. Saunders. Because there's

nearly two thousand of them out there. Is that real enough for you?" Charlie snaps, pulling his walkie-talkie from his pocket and barking into it. "Masher. MASHER! Gonzo! Calling all security!" bellows Charlie into his walkie-talkie. "Do you read me? We have an incident in the backstage area. Repeat: an incident. Spike has decided to make a little impromptu appearance. Repeat: Spike Saunders is in the area! Are you receiving this? Over."

Every milliliter of blood seems to drain from my body. I feel like I'm going to faint. The mystery guest just gazes at his shoes, clearly quite ashamed of the fuss.

"Sorry if I'm causing a fuss, er, Ronnie, is it?" the boy begins, rearranging his baseball cap.

"WHAT??? ARE YOU!? Er, I MEAN . . . ARE YOU HIM!!! Like, really him?! REALLY SPIKE SAUNDERS!! THE REAL ONE!! OH MY GOD! I can't believe it??!! You're Spike Saunders!" I splutter and pant, gazing at a face I see every day in magazines and on TV.

" 'Fraid so," says Spike, then he grins.

I have GOT to pull myself together: It's either that, or simply die of shock directly here on the spot. And that's not cool.

"But, er, how? And why? Yes, why? Why would this happen? And why are you . . .? And, can I just tell you, Spike, that I loovved your last CD and I play it all the time. Especially when my mum left last week . . . I played 'Merry Go Round' continuously for about an hour," I begin to twitter, realizing that this is now so far away from cool that cool is actually in a distant galaxy.

So I shut up.

"Cheers," says Spike. "That's nice to hear."

"Right!" announces Charlie, scratching his head. "Ronnie, I'm dead sorry, lovey, I should have been straight with you, but this one 'ere always causes a bleeding all-out riot, so we kept *schtum*." Charlie takes a deep breath. "For my sins, Ronnie: I am Spike Saunders' tour manager."

"SPIKE SAUNDERS!!!" I shriek. Charlie quickly shoves his hand over my mouth.

"Shhhhh," Charlie says. "Likewise, Vinny, Pip and Masher, et cetera, are Spike's road crew. We're on our way down to Astlebury, where Spike's playing next weekend."

"I know! I know! You're headlining the main stage next Saturday night!" I say. "My dad won't let me go . . ."

Okay, I have now officially hit rock bottom on the cool stakes. It might be time to show him my period-knickers. It can only improve things.

"Anyway, we had a few days off before some warm-up gigs next week," Charlie continues. "So us lads decided to help you girls out."

"But I wasn't allowed to leave the hotel," moans Spike, who is a lot smaller and thinner than he is on TV but totally gorgeous nevertheless.

"No, you weren't, bozo, because it's not safe for you. Too many teenage girls wanting to rip your trousers off. You, my sunshine, are too expensive an asset for me to get damaged."

"Well, I'm here now," says Spike, slightly sulkily.

"Indeed you are," replies Charlie, even more sulkily.

"Can't I stay? Please?" pleads Spike. "I'll keep a low profile. No one will know. I just wanna watch a few bands. I'll stay with my mate Ronnie 'ere, I'll say I'm her long-lost cousin from down south."

"Oh, go on, Uncle Charlie," I say. "Let him stay!"

"Go on, Uncle Charlie!" giggles the one, the only, the legendary number-one pop superstar Spike Saunders, who just—did you notice that?—called me HIS MATE!

"You kill me, Spike Saunders. You'll have me in an early grave," moans Charlie, delving into his pocket and pulling out a pair of extra-dark sunglasses.

"Okay, you can stay till after the last act. But put these glasses on, and keep 'em on! And if anyone asks either of you, it's not Spike Saunders, it just looks like Spike Saunders. Got it?"

"Hurray!" we both cheer.

"And while you're here. . . . How did you get into the VIP past Masher with no AAA pass?" quizzes Charlie.

"Easy." Spike shrugs, not realizing what he's starting. "Through that gap in the fence over there. Loads of people are doing it!"

Charlie pulls out the walkie-talkie again.

"MASHER, get your bum around here this minute!"

Cross my heart, I do, for about twenty seconds, intend to keep Spike Saunders' appearance at Blackwell Live a secret. But precisely then, Fleur, Claude and Masher appear, desperate to find out what the emergency is. Of course, they find "the emergency" standing beside me, grinning his famous devilish grin.

And to give Spike ultimate credit, he handles meeting the LBD extremely well. Even when Fleur gives him a really tight bear hug and gently sobs onto his shoulder: "Spike! I really love you. No, really. Okay, I bet lots of other girls say that, but I really feel like I know you. And I do love you! I think we've got so much in common! I've got all your CDs and I've got a Wall of Spike in my bedroom. I'm not weird, though. You think I'm weird, don't you?" Then she asked him to sign the T-bar in the back of her thong.

Yes, Fleur lost her mind. Big time.

I'm soooo relieved. Fleur has managed to make me look, by comparison, virtually normal.

"Spike, will you go on stage and sing a song from the *To Hell and Back* CD?" Claude chances, her eyes as wide as tablespoons.

"No, he won't," snaps Charlie. "In fact, he's going back to the hotel right now if we don't all stick with the original plan. Remember: Spike Saunders is NOT here. This is on a strictly need-to-know basis, no one else *needs to know* but you."

Spike puts on his extra-dark glasses and pulls down his baseball cap. "Am I allowed to watch some bands now?" he says as we slip incognito out of the VIP tent and into the festival crowd, just as the EZ Life Syndicate are bringing the house down, making two thousand people wave their arms in the air from left to right, cheering "Wooo-hoo" at exactly the same time.

"EZ LIFE SYNDICATE. MAKE SUM NOIZZZE!" shouts Killa Blow as the crowd goes berserk.

"Pretty impressive stuff, girls!" says Spike as we weave our way unnoticed through the festival mayhem. "I used to mess about at school all the time and cause trouble when I was your age. Not do stuff like this." He chuckles, clearly a little nonplussed.

"So do we . . . er, usually," claims Fleur, realizing how totally unfeasible that sounds like now. "Honestly!"

Spike laughs out loud.

"Well, we caused some trouble earlier on today, anyway," illustrates Fleur. "You both missed what happened when Death Knell performed! Myrtle McGraw, the headmaster's missus, had a bit of an *episode.*"

"What happened?" I gasp.

"Oh, you tell the tale, Fleur," says Claude.

"Well, it all began when Ainsley came on stage with that fake blood on his laboratory coat, which, fair enough, was total grimness, but you know what Death Knell are like—"

"It was fake blood, though," I persist, "from a joke shop. I saw the bottle."

"Hmm, I'm sure you did. I did too. But Myrtle didn't. So they were halfway through that track of theirs called, er, whatsitcalled? 'The Coffin Song,' that's it, and all hell broke loose. Pardon the pun."

"Tell us more," says Spike, riveted by Fleur, who always tells a good yarn.

"Well, Death Knell brought on this box with a sheet pulled over it. And Ainsley pulls off the sheet during the chorus and it was . . . it was actually a coffin!"

"A real coffin? How?" I splutter.

"Don't ask me how. They've kept it hidden from all of us all day. I had no idea they had it, Claude didn't either. Well, when Myrtle McGraw saw it and realized Ainsley was going to get in the coffin and lie down, she went bananas. Ooh, you could have sold her for ninety pence a kilo, she went ballistic!"

"Did she try to stop the gig?"

"Well, she did her best. *'SATAN IS AMONGST US!'* That's what she was shouting! 'Stop this Satanic show!' She was causing a right scene. I mean, come on, it was only flipping Ainsley Hammond with some joke-shop blood and a coffin loaned from the local amateur dramatics society's production of *Dracula*. Lighten up, for Pete's sake."

Spike is laughing so hard, tears are streaming down his face.

"I'm so glad I came today. You lot have cheered me right up." He chuckles.

"So, is she still here?" I ask, looking around.

"Oh, no, their son Marmaduke had to come in his car and pick her up. She was still grumbling about Satan as they stuffed her into the backseat."

"I can't believe I missed it," I complain.

"Well, kiddo, them's the breaks," says Fleur, still jealous that I had Spike all to myself for well over half an hour.

"So, who's on next?" Spike asks as we wander nearer the front of the stage, where hundreds of skatey boys and baggy-jeaned girls with messy hooded tops and scuffed trainers are gathered. I can't believe no one has so much as double-checked who our new friend is. I'm hoping people might think it's my new boyfriend and it gets back to Jimi. Before I can answer Spike, I can hear the unmistakable voice of Paddy and the not-so-soft lilt of Mrs. Guinevere breaking over on the loudspeaker.

"Give me that microphone. I'm the announcer. Yes, me. I announce the bands. No one said we were taking turns!" argues Paddy, sounding very annoyed.

"Oh, grow up, I'm doing this one, give me that thing here,"

Mrs. Guinevere insists. With a deft pull, she commandeers the mike.

"Hello, Blackwell Live!" she begins. "It gives me wonderful pride to announce another very talented band. This is Lost Messiah!" But before Guinevere even finishes announcing their name, an explosion of sound rips through the humid summer air, and Aaron, Naz, Danny and Jimi are belting out "Golden Gob" as loud as our PA system will tolerate before melting.

"Yeeeeeeeeeeeeeeeeeeeeeeahhhhhh!" is Jimi's opening line.

"Wahhhhhoooooooooo" is his next.

He's not big on lyrics, really, is Jimi Steele. Still, something about him beguiles you to watch him every second he's before you.

"Excellent frontman," says Spike, nudging me. "He's a talented guitarist too. Should go far, these lads. Well, the lead singer will, anyway."

"Jimi Steele," I sigh.

"Good name for a rock star," says Spike Saunders. "Not as good as mine, though." My expression must speak volumes, because Spike is quickly poking my shoulder.

"Ooh, hello, I think someone is a bit hot for Lost Messiah's lead singer. You fancy him, you do." Spike sniggers as my face goes crimson.

"She does, but I don't," butts in Fleur, clearly thinking she's in with a chance. Oh, dear. "And I'm single too!"

"This one's called 'Stupid Things,'" says Jimi before the Lost Messiah crash into another teeth-shakingly loud number. "And believe me, I've done a few of them in my time." He must be talking about one of his many skateboard accidents, although it seems like a weird thing to write a song about. At the front of the stage Gonzo is trying to dissuade some Year 8 lads from crowd-surfing.

"Right, I've got to go and check on our extra-special head-lining act," announces Claude, vanishing into the cheering crowd. Spike raises an eyebrow.

"Catwalk," I explain, exhaling deeply. "Flipping Catwalk."

"Catwalk," sighs Fleur, and then we both stand in mournful silence.

"I can't wait! I'm having a great time," says Spike genuinely.

"Neither can we," we lie.

leaving the best till last

After what seems like an overly long time since our last act, a thick cloud of dry ice pumps onto the Blackwell Live stage, filling the late-afternoon air with billowing, atmospheric white clouds. The stage is filled with fluffy whiteness, like rolling mist. Catwalk's rather lame intro music is building momentum: A drum machine flutters on top of repetitive synth chords.

"It's time for a Catwalk Nation," repeats a voice pretentiously again and again. Unmistakably, it is Panama's. The entire crowd leaps to attention expectantly, pushing forward to enjoy the headline act, some kids climbing onto each other's shoulders, cheering and beating the sky with their hands in time with the drums. And as the smoke begins to clear and more cymbals crash, I can just detect five silhouettes posing moodily together center stage. Clad in black Lycra tops, rubber catsuits and trousers, each with a silver microphone headset clipped around

their faces and far too much makeup, Catwalk stand dead still with their arms and legs held in strange robotic poses, waiting for their cue to begin. The crowd are actually going berserk as the snare drum grows more frantic, then suddenly a loud crash rips through the speakers.

And they're off!

Leeza and Abigail first, cartwheeling down the center of the stage and then back again, followed by Derren and Zane walking on their hands, then launching into perfect backflips. Finally Panama steals center stage, pirouetting a hundred times perfectly, smiling like an android from ear to ear.

"Hello, Blackwell Live," she shrills. "Thanks for coming to see me! This is your favorite and mine, it's 'Running to Your Love'!!!"

"Woo-hoo!" screams the crowd.

"Oooh, baby!" mimes Panama.
"I'm floating in the sky!
Like a big love pie!
You make me feel real high!
Oh, my Oh, my
Tra la la la!"

Leeza and Abigail sashay past her as she sings. Derren and Zane are doing some bizarre tap dance, whirling their arms around as Panama reaches the chorus.

"Oooh, baby, baby—I'm running to your love!
Wanna give my heart a big shove!

You fit me like a glove.
Cos I'm running to your love!"

"I had no idea Panama was such an intellectual," remarks Fleur sarcastically. "That chorus is really quite profound."

Spike is giggling and cheering, clearly having the time of his life. "Are these, like, your mates?" he asks.

"No," we both reply, in stereo.

And I'm about to explain to Spike Saunders the entire sorry tale, about how Catwalk menaced us into headlining Blackwell Live, and all about their nasty threats, and about Panama ensnaring Jimi and life being totally unfair . . . but then, as Panama begins her second chorus, something very very wonderful occurs.

"I'm ru-ru-ru-ru-ru-ru-ru-" stutters Panama, waving her hands frantically at Vinny, the roadie.

Oh my God! Catwalk's backing tape seems to have jammed!

"Love lo-lo-lo-lo-looooove," stutters the tape, before correcting itself and running normally once more.

Perhaps the crowd hasn't noticed? Catwalk's dance routine has certainly been thrown well out of sync, but they seem to catch themselves up.

"Did you hear that?" One girl chuckles. "Panama's voice was totally out of time with her lips."

"It's just a tape! They're miming!" I hear people whispering as Catwalk try to shimmy on regardlessly.

"Wanna gi-gi-gi-gi-gi-gi-gi-gi!" stutters Panama's voice. The tape is stuck again. This time for much longer! Panama's face is beginning to turn violet.

"Gi-gi-gi-gi-gi!" it stutters as Vinny bangs the side of the sound deck, trying to rectify the problem. Brilliantly, this just stops the tape altogether with a loud screech. Then it winds backward!

"Evollllll ruoy ot gninnur!" garbles the tape before grinding again to a halt.

"You're miming!" screams one lad. "It's just a backing tape!"

"Sing us a proper song!" shouts another.

Vinny is frantically pushing buttons and fiddling with wires. The tape bursts to life again.

"Running to your love!!" sings Panama's taped voice.

"Keep going! Just keep dancing. The show must go on," Panama snarls at the rest of Catwalk. But by this point Abigail has legged it off stage and Derren is frozen to the spot with his head in his hands; Zane attempts to save the show with one nifty double front somersault, but nerves get the better of him and he lands on his bum with a mighty crash.

Ther-dunch! is the sound of his bum colliding with the floor.

And then the backing tape stops again, this time for good. Not even lovely Mr. Ball, our science teacher, who helpfully runs forward with a Swiss penknife, offering to work some boffinlike magic on the fuses, can help Catwalk now. Vinny is just sitting with his head in his hands, trying to suppress fits of giggles.

I'd like to say here that sidesplitting laughter and jeers immediately rip through the field, but instead there's a deathly stunned silence. Complete dumbfoundment. Everybody is simply staring forward at the emptying stage, mouths ajar. A crisp bag blows by. In the distance a church bell tolls. Still, no one speaks. Eventually, after what seemed like an age, a singular clap is heard at the very back of the field.

"Thank you very much," shouts Panama, sadly realizing it was the woman from the burger van slapping the last dregs of tomato ketchup from one of her bottles. On this note Panama makes a bid for escape too, running past what is most definitely Claudette Cassiera, smiling serenely on the side of the stage. It's almost, just almost, as if Claude has had something to do with this whole catastrophe.

"I find it very difficult to imagine you'd be involved in any-thing like this, Claudette Cassiera," I can imagine McGraw's voice saying. *"Very difficult indeed."*

Throughout the festival site, people are now openly hooting and jeering.

"Encore!" kids are yelling. "More!"

"Put the tape back on! Mime us another song!" chants one particularly rowdy section of the crowd.

"Oh, that's just too bad," Spike says sympathetically. "The poor things. They started so well too," he adds. "I've died on stage before. It's no fun at all."

Okay, yeah, we could correct Spike and tell him why this is the most wonderful end to Blackwell Live ever, but instead Fleur spies a golden opportunity.

"Well, er, you could smooth things over by singing a few songs, couldn't you?" Fleur suggests.

Spike looks at her, then raises an eyebrow. He's clearly think-ing about it. "Well, I suppose it wouldn't hurt, would it?" Spike says, removing his sunglasses, exposing his beautiful, instantly recognizable face to the crowd. A few girls standing right beside us gasp, nudging each other frantically.

"Spike Saunders. Spike Saunders! Oh my God!" they shout, informing everyone in earshot. The whisper beings to spread rapidly, growing louder and louder until everyone within fifty meters is pointing and shouting, "Spike! It's Spike Saunders! Look, over there!"

One girl simply faints, right there on the spot before us.

"I mean, seeing as I'm here, eh?" says Spike. "If nobody minds, that is."

From where I'm standing, I can see Uncle Charlie clutching his brow and shouting hoarsely into a walkie-talkie at the side of the stage. His face is practically burgundy, the poor bloke.

As a non-negotiable riot erupts around us, Spike runs as fast as he can through the crowd, mounting Blackwell Live's main stage and grabbing a nearby acoustic guitar.

"Hello, Blackwell," he begins. "I'm Spike Saunders."

"Wooooo-hoo!" screams the bewildered crowd en masse.

"Er, thanks for letting me hijack the festival," Spike says, strumming the guitar a little. "You know, I don't like to turn up uninvited to places, but hey, you seemed like a friendly bunch."

"*AAAAARGH!!*" screeches a thousand girls.

"Sing us a song!" screams one young lass.

"Er, okay," says Spike. I think he might actually be a bit nervous. He looks at the crowd in a puzzled way. "You know, it's been a long time since it's been just me and a guitar, I'm kind of not sure what to play for you," he teases.

" 'Merry Go Round'!" screams some rather noisy fans near the front barrier. "We want 'Merry Go Round'!"

"Ah, 'Merry Go Round,' no problem at all!" Spike shouts, and the audience erupts as he plays the very familiar opening bars.

"Ooh, hang on," Spike says just before he begins the first verse. "This one is for my mate Ronnie. She likes this one, she does."

And as I turned around to grab Fleur's hand and yell, "That's me! He means me!" I saw something very wonderful indeed.

Making her way through the crowds, brandishing a large veggie burger smothered in onions and ketchup in one hand, stepped the one and only Mrs. Magda Ripperton.

My mum had shown up!

And at that very second, I was so happy, I thought my head was going to explode.

Chapter 12

So, in conclusion

So many unforgettably fantastic things happened during Blackwell Live, it's all the LBD have talked about for the last week, from dawn to dusk and sometimes even in our dreams.

We must be quite, quite intolerable. Thank heavens we have each other to natter with. Okay, thank heavens we have each other, full stop.

Like, there was that excellent finale, where Spike Saunders sang "Cold Heart" (an excellent track from the *To Hell and Back* CD) with the entire crowd joining in with the choruses.

That made me cry for some curious reason.

I don't know why nice things make you cry sometimes, they just do.

And the police weren't even that angry about what happened. Well, not really, considering. Once Chief Superintendent Johnson heard the LBD had collected over a thousand pounds for charity, he turned a blind eye to the riot van and police reinforcements he'd had to deploy.

Whoops. Next time we "invite an international superstar to

our garden party" (his words), we've promised we'll tip him off.

Thank heavens for Mrs. Guinevere, who dealt with the police with outstanding diplomacy; and later on, when she returned from informing Mr. McGraw of the goings-on, well, she wasn't even the slightest bit ruffled. She was actually still quite jubilant.

"But did McGraw miss out on Spike Saunders?" Fleur asked.

"Oh, well, he barricaded himself into his office hours ago." Mrs. Guinevere smiled. "I believe he'd seen quite enough once Death Knell began jumping out of coffins covered in blood. It was a lot of visual stimulation for him to take in."

"But what's he doing in there?" asked Claude.

"Well, to be exact, he's listening to a recital of Barber's *Adagio for Strings* on Radio 4 with the blinds firmly pulled down . . . oh, and doing the *Guardian* crossword." Mrs. Guinevere chuckled. "His parting comment as I left was 'Alas, even Emperor Nero fiddled while Rome burned.' "

"Well, at least he's happy, then," concluded Claude. "Well, er, sort of."

no need to shout

By the time the dance tent kicked off and Johnny Martlew was spinning his "rare groove classics," the floor was jumping; I was delirious with exhaustion, but determined to stay. Through the crowded dance floor, where Mrs. Guinevere and Mr. Foxton were dancing like kids and laughing like drains, I remember spying Jimi thoughtfully enjoying a drink. Apparently Panama and him had fought monumentally after Catwalk bombed on stage; then Panama stormed home expecting to be chased. But Jimi didn't, he stayed for the disco instead.

Ha ha. Too funny.

Oh, and I do remember a lot of snogging.

Not me, of course. But there was certainly a whole lotta snoggage going down, it was tongue central. Fleur was canoodling behind the DJ booth with Killa Blow; in fact, they've been on two dates since then and Fleur is still not even bored with him.

It must be a true love thing going on.

Oh, and beside the bar, just before closing time, I even spotted Tara from Guttersnipe with her face stuck passionately into a large pile of black, curly hair, beneath which lurked one Benjamin Stark.

"We're just friends, really!" Tara blushed when I tackled her en route to the ladies' loo.

What a fibber!

Her face was covered in her own smeared red lipstick!

Of course, Aaron and Naz took their pick from the EZ Life Syndicate ladies, they're such lads, and let's face it, everyone else was bumping faces, so why shouldn't they?

But the best part of all was seeing my dad walking gingerly around the side of the dance floor, carrying two drinks in each hand, a lager and a Coke, accompanied by my extremely healthy-looking mum wearing loose black trousers and a cropped T-shirt. The smallest hint of belly pushing over her waistband.

Too many puddings at Nan's house, I thought.

I'd hugged, kissed and clambered all over my poor mum when she first appeared during Spike's set (not very cool, now that I think about it, but hell, I love my mum, so shoot me!) but I knew that there wasn't the time to have the "big talk" with her about her disappearance. And I had *plenty* to say, believe me.

Of course, now that I had Mum and Dad back together in front of me—in perfect position for me to rant and rave at them, and scream about how badly treated I'd been—I completely forgot what I was furious about. It was just so absolutely lovely to see Mum and Dad together, having a laugh, that nothing else in the entire world at this precise moment seemed to matter aside from getting closer to them.

"Mum! Muuuuuuum!!!" I shouted, running over and hugging her, breathing in her familiar Mumish smell.

"Ronnie! Hello, darling! We've both been looking for you." Mum looked fresh-skinned and joyous, even if she did seem pretty emotional.

"Look, I'm really sorry, Ronnie, I've got a whole load of things to explain—"

"It's okay, Mum," I began to garble, noticing Dad's misty eyes. "You don't have to bother explaining—"

"No, I really have to," Mum said. "I think we'd better go outside for a second." Mum grabbed my hand. "I need to tell you the real deal here. You know I wouldn't have not given you an answer about coming today, or left you alone without a dead good reason, don't you?"

"Don't, Mum. It doesn't matter," I said, tears starting to drizzle down my cheeks like a big baby. "I'm just dead glad you're back. You are back for good now, aren't you?"

Mum nodded.

"Well, you don't need to explain, then," I said.

"No, Ronnie, let her tell you," said Dad, smirking. "It's a corker. This is the best excuse anyone has ever given you in the whole world."

And it turned out it was.

In fact, I've officially decided to let Loz and Magda both off the hook now for acting like absolute maniacs for the last four weeks.

I mean, it's not every day you find out you're going to officially be a big sister, is it?

Me! Ha ha! A big sister? That sounds great, doesn't it?

And now that I think about it, I suppose I'd have behaved a little insanely and needed "time to think" if I'd discovered a real actual person growing inside me too. Especially as it seems now that Dad then started being an even bigger prize durrbrain by saying weird stuff like they were "too old to have another little baby in the house."

That was not what Mum wanted to hear at all. Apparently she was furious, so she went off to Nan's to think about some serious life stuff.

"But what were you thinking about when you were there?" I asked her.

"Well, strangling your father, mostly," Mum sighed. "That . . . and pickle and banana sandwiches, really," she admitted.

"Here we go again," Dad said, wrapping his arms preciously around my mum and her bump.

He doesn't look very much like a man who doesn't want another baby anymore. He actually looks highly pleased with his lot.

I mean, how much trouble are kids anyway?

All we ever do is spread joy.

My mum perched both her hands on her extended belly, like she still wasn't quite used to the idea of the baby herself. Then she looked out at the disco-dancing throng.

"I'm really sorry for missing today, Ronnie," she whispered. "I was feeling wretched. But when your dad called me from here tonight and we had a really long talk about how we both felt, well, I just got straight in a taxi. I just wanted us all to be together."

"Eh? And you can't blame her, really, can you?" Dad chuckled. "I mean, we're a damn fine family, aren't we, us Rippertons?!"

We're not bad.

So here I am, in the rehearsal room of the Fantastic Voyage, playing my new shiny bass guitar.

Okay, attempting to play.

I've been plugging away in front of *Teach Yourself Bass Guitar in Five Days* for *well over* five days now. All I've got is sore fingers, broken nails and a stiff neck.

It's amazing what you can get out of your parents when they're feeling guilty, isn't it? I dragged my pregnant mum out shopping last week after her three-month maternity scan, and before I could mutter the words "severe psychological damage," I had a bass guitar to make up for the last month's fruit-loop behavior. Ha, it almost makes it worth them arguing if I get cool stuff like this. In fact, I need a guitar and drum kit now for Fleur and Claude, so I'll be keeping a close eye on them. Joking.

Dum dum dum dum dum. Perchang. Ouch.

I am useless on this bass guitar. It's going to end up in my bedroom as a clothes horse, I can see it now. I have no natural rhythm.

"No, don't give up, you're getting there. Just hold the chord more firmly, you're holding it like a girl."

I look up with a start to see the delightful vision of Jimi Steele dressed in baggy blue jeans and his red Quiksilver top. He's shaved all his hair off too!

Mmmmm. I love shaved heads!

His split with Panama has done him a world of good.

"Have you joined the Marines?" I say dryly.

"No. Why?" He smirks.

"You've had a haircut."

"Have I? HAVE I?" Jimi starts grabbing his head furiously. "When? Who would do such a thing without my permission? Ronnie, call the cops!"

"Very funny," I say, trying not to smile.

"*I* thought so."

I continue picking at the bass, pretending it's the most normal thing in the world for Jimi Steele to pop over and see me during summer vacation. I am *too* cool.

"So, can I help you at all, or is this just a social visit?" I eventually say.

"Er, um, murrr . . . well, yeah, I actually came to bring back this . . . ," Jimi mutters, delving into his bag. "I took it by mistake when we last practiced here." Jimi pulls out an old bit of cloth.

"A beer towel?" I say, fixing him with one of my best bemused gazes.

"Uh-huh."

"You came around here to give back an old beer towel?" I repeat. "Of which we have thousands?"

"Yeah." Jimi shuffles.

"Really?" I say.

Long silence.

"Uh . . . well, okay, no," he admits.

"So, er, why are you really here?" I say, placing the bass on the floor and sitting down on a seat beside where he is fidgeting nervously.

"Well, I just, you see . . . well, it was just something I've been thinking. And I keep on thinking it. So I thought I'd come over and say it right to your face."

"You're annoyed about Panama's backing tape jamming, aren't you?" I tut. "That was nothing to do with me, I'm afraid. I know zilch."

Not exactly true.

"NO! Not Panama's tape. Actually, that was the funniest thing I've seen for a long time. No, I wanted to talk to you about . . . look, can I be frank here?"

"You're not Frank, you're Jimi—" I begin, using one of Loz's jokes.

"Ronnie, be serious! I'm being really serious."

"Okay," I mumble.

273

"Right, I don't know how to say this." Jimi blushes. "Cos, well, I've been a real complete idiot over the last month. A total idiot. I should never have snogged Panama, I don't know what I saw in her—"

"Huge bazonkas?" I suggest.

Jimi wrinkles his nose at me.

"But look, Ronnie, tell me if I'm wrong here, cos I might be wrong, and if I am wrong, I'm going to go straightaway and then we'll just have to ignore each other at school from now on as I'll be so totally embarrassed . . . but I think that me and you have got a sort of connection."

I just stare at him. At his pale blue eyes and stupendous full mouth.

He carries on, "And if I fancy you, which I, erm, do. By the way. There, I've said it, *I fancy you.* And you fancy me, which, okay, I'm not that sure about. Well, maybe, if you agree to it, that is, we should try and maybe give things a go."

I'm mesmerized now. Has Jimi lost his mind or does he mean this?

"So, er, that was what I wanted to say."

"Uh, okay."

We both stare straight ahead for about a minute.

"Well, aren't you going to say something?" Jimi eventually says.

"Well, I s'pose I sort of fancy you too," I mumble. I am absolutely gobsmacked.

"That's a start!" says Jimi, relief spreading over his face. "So, er. Well, right . . . that's dead good! Er, thank you! So, where do you want to take it from here?"

Jimi moves closer, taking my face in both of his hands and then sort of staring at me, before running his hands down my hair, blushing even more. My heart is bashing a hole through my chest. I can see every bristle on Jimi's newly shaven head.

"I don't know," I whisper. "What do you think a possible next step would be?"

"Mmmm, well," he begins, slightly nervously. "I don't suppose a small snog is out of the question, is it? You know, just to seal the deal that we like each other."

Jimi moves his lips toward mine, shutting his eyes and wrapping my entire torso in his strong arms. And . . .

. . . Oh, well, come on, what would you do?

Where did **grace dent** get the idea for *LBD: It's a Girl Thing?* "Tradition stands that a first novel should be 'about what you know.' Although I didn't know any goblins or talking mice, I did know intricately about being a troublesome teenage girl, back when the world was my oyster . . . or at least would have been if I didn't have a ten P.M. curfew! I love Ronnie, Claude, and Fleur and the whole extended LBD clan more passionately with each paragraph I write. I wish they'd gone to my school—I might have attended a tad more willingly."

When she isn't dreaming up new adventures for the LBD, Grace is a regular contributor to British teen magazines and newspapers such as *CosmoGIRL!* and *The Mirror*. She is also a columnist for the *Guardian* and *More!* magazine. She lives in Putney, Southwest London.